'Come now, Miss [...] better than this if we [...] I must ask you, no [...] it, to put your arms [...]

He held her trembling body firmly, but the abject dread which engulfed her filled her consciousness to the exclusion of all other emotion—even distaste. Straining her ears for sounds of the redcoats' stealthy approach, she heard a branch rustle, and instantly a cold sweat broke out on her brow and palms. A taut cord of tension in her throat seemed to stretch and stretch, and had almost reached snapping-point when Colin murmured in a whisper which she barely caught,

'Are you aware, my love, that you have the most delectable little hollow just behind the lobe of your ear? Assuredly I must kiss you there the minute you give me permission.'

Isobel's teeth came together with an audible click. Fear was forgotten in a hot surge of contempt and dislike. 'Beast,' she mouthed at him. 'How can you think of such things at a time like this?'

'I confess, I can think of little else,' he said huskily . . .

Joyce Holms was born and educated in Glasgow but has had eleven homes in the last twenty-three years ranging from a hotel on the island of Arran to an apartment in Andalucia. Writing is her one abiding passion and she has been writing articles and short stories for magazines and broadcasting for almost twenty years. She is a self-confessed 'health nut' and starts the day with a brisk three-mile circuit of the 'Meadows' in Edinburgh where she now lives with her husband and two teenage daughters.

Miss MacIntosh's Rebel is her first Masquerade Romance.

MISS MACINTOSH'S REBEL

JOYCE HOLMS

MILLS & BOON LIMITED
15–16 BROOK'S MEWS
LONDON W1A 1DR

First published in Great Britain 1985 by Mills & Boon Limited

© Joyce Holms 1985

Australian copyright 1985 Philippine copyright 1985 This edition 1985

ISBN 0 263 75106 6

Set in 10 on 11½pt. Linotron Times 04–0785–64,600

Photoset by Rowland Phototypesetting Ltd Bury St Edmunds, Suffolk Made and printed in Great Britain by Cox & Wyman Ltd, Reading

CHAPTER
ONE

'BONNETS! DRESSES! Dancing lessons! Parties!' James MacIntosh roared, accompanying each word with a thump on his desk that made his inkstand rattle. 'Two seasons in London that cost enough to beggar a duke, and what thanks do I get for it, pray? Not a word! Do you ever consider the amount of hard cash it takes to introduce a daughter into polite society, eh?'

Isobel threw him a glance from beneath her lashes, but knew better than to make reply.

'And here's Fiona rising eighteen and expecting me to do the same for her! The pair of you think I'm made of money. Well, it's going to stop, do you hear? If I had been firmer with you earlier you might have been married years ago instead of taking it into your head that you are too good for every man that offers for you!'

At this Isobel was forced to protest, but he cut her off with an impatient gesture. 'Young Fergusson was too fat for your taste. Beresford's son had bad breath. Captain Armstrong was too old. Dammit! Am I to have you on my hands for ever? In my young days it was never heard of for a chit of a girl to tell her father whom she'd have and whom she'd not have! If I decide that a man is good enough for you, that should be the end of it!'

Isobel dropped her eyes and did her best to appear browbeaten. They each had their parts to play in this charade: he the strict and inflexible parent, she the suitably chastened daughter. But, in fact, James MacIntosh was putty in his daughter's hands, and both of them knew it.

He was now leaning back in his chair and breathing loudly in the forlorn hope that this might be taken as evidence of terrible wrath. 'Well, miss! And what about this one I'm to be annoyed by this morning, eh? I cannot for the life of me see what you can have against him.'

Isobel could understand that very well. To a man like James MacIntosh, any young man with a considerable fortune and all his faculties was worth cultivating, and if he also happened to be the son of a close friend—why, that was the end of the matter. Unfortunately, Colin Frazer, who filled all her father's requirements, did not come up to Isobel's standards.

'Well, come on, lassie!' James barked, evidently expecting an answer to his last remark. 'You can't turn down a good-looking young fellow with a fortune like his just because you are not in the mood. Dammit all, are you hanging out for a prince of the blood, or what? I'll have no more of your nonsense! You are nearly twenty-one and should be a mother twice over by this time, as your own mother was before you!'

Flinging himself out of his chair, he began striding up and down the room, waving his arms about and muttering under his breath. Isobel watched him warily.

Finally he halted in the window bay, staring out at the wind-tossed trees, and when he spoke there was, in his voice, a real effort towards calm rationality.

'All right. I don't blame you for not jumping at Beresford's son. And yes, Captain Armstrong was mebbe a wee thing long in the tooth for you. And to tell you the truth, for all he was supposed to be the matrimonial catch of the season, I never liked Fergusson above half. Never could take to a man with a limp handshake. But Colin Frazer, now—a different kettle of fish, Isobel. A different kettle of fish entirely. Yon's a laddie I'd be proud to own as a son-in-law. A first-class shot, a good judge of horseflesh and carries his liquor like a gentleman—ay, and a pair of shoulders on him I might envy myself!'

A glance over his shoulder failed to reassure him of Isobel's appreciation of these qualities, but he was not a man to give up easily. 'I've known his father since we were boys together in Inverness, and Colin is as like his sire as makes no difference. Pig-headed devils, both of them, but the kind you'd like to have with you in an emergency. You'll mind the time the three of us were fishing at Falls of Cardoch—och, you were no older than Laughlan at the time—and old Johnnie slipped on the rocks . . .'

Isobel strangled a yawn and transferred her attention to picking at a blob of candlewax that was stuck to the desk-top. The story was an old familiar one, and it was clear that the incident had made a profound impression on her father, since he was never tired of retelling it. Even the phrases he used were so familiar that she could anticipate them: '. . . the pool they call the Devil's Stewpot . . . that cub of his was along the bank like a hare . . . into that black hole with a head of foam on it like your Aunt Euphemia's home-made ale . . .'

At the time, she too had thought Colin everything that was wonderful, and his dramatic rescue of his father only served to confirm him in her mind as the most desirable of men. If only he had remained as he was at twenty-three, laughing, inconsequential, totally volatile. But, of course, she too had grown up in the interim and now saw beyond a flashing smile and a romantic profile.

'. . . and plump in the pocket, too.' Her father was well into his stride now. 'Dunarras fell to Colin when his mother's brother died and, naturally, he is heir to Transk when old Johnnie goes. And mark this, both estates are close to Inverness, so you would see plenty of your own family while we are there for the summer months. What more could you ask for?' Receiving no reply to this question, he barked, with real irritation, 'I don't know what you think you are about—flirting with the lad and leading him on and then leaving it to me to send him away with a flea in his ear!'

'Flirting with him!' Isobel burst out, forgetting her vow of silence. 'I wouldn't *dream* . . . I never flirted with Colin Frazer in my life!'

Flirt with Colin Frazer! The very thought made her cringe! She could too well imagine the raised eyebrow, the amused glint in his eye, the half-hidden curl at the corner of his mouth. Flirt with him? Oh, *certes!*

Seeing that her father was waiting for her to elaborate on her retort, she muttered unwillingly, 'Colin is not that sort of person, Papa. He simply refuses to take part in light conversation or gossip or . . . Oh, I know it serves no real purpose, but it is the way I am used to deal with young men. But Colin Frazer will not be kept at a distance. No! He must know my opinions, my dreams, my innermost thoughts! He doesn't want to flirt with me—he wants to possess me utterly!'

It was only half the story, but she had no intention of going deeper into the subject. Even if she had wished to tell him, there were no words to convey the unnerving vulnerability she felt in Colin's presence. Without her accustomed shield of coquettishness she had no defence against his dissecting stare. Even in a crowd of people she was constantly aware of his presence, of his eyes on her face, and felt herself powerless to deny him her constant attention. She felt menaced by him. His very proximity was a challenge and an assault and, she was sure, he both knew it and revelled in it.

James blinked at her in perplexity. 'So—it is your own self he wants and not just your pretty face. Is that so terrible? Why should he not want to know what is in your mind? If that is all . . .'

'Well, it is *not* all,' Isobel snapped, casting around desperately for some reason that might make sense to a man. 'I simply do not see him as the paragon you describe, Papa. Am I to marry a man because he is a good shot or a good judge of horses? A man whose morals are of the lowest, whose appearance is quite unremarkable and whose shoulders'—she added out of pure temper—'are entirely of his tailor's contrivance!'

James seemed at first to be about to snigger at this, but changed his mind and returned to his seat at the desk. 'You *are* being flippant, I take it?' he said, frowning. 'What's all this about morals?'

Isobel bit her lip, regretting her outburst. 'I . . . I heard he cheats at cards.'

James's eyes rolled ceilingwards and his lips took on a grimmer line. 'I don't know why I suspect your brother Laughlan's hand in this. Mebbe because he was the one to start the rumours about Captain Armstrong's drinking habits, and young Fergusson's paramour. You heard this story from Laughlan, I'll wager?'

'No. From Fiona.'

'Who had it from Laughlan. I suppose your brother was able to devise some creditable motive for this behaviour? One is not, I imagine, expected to believe that Colin should find it necessary to supplement his income by these means?'

Isobel ground her teeth, mentally consigning her brother to perdition. Even at the time it had seemed an unlikely story, but now, in the cold grey light of her father's scorn, it was more so.

'I heard he does it to ruin influential people and then blackmails them into declaring for the Pretender.'

To her surprise, her father threw back his head and crowed with delighted laughter. 'Devil mend the boy!' he chortled, wiping his eyes with the lace at his cuff. 'I never suspected him of such a vivid imagination. Takes after his Uncle Andrew, depend upon it. You never heard such bouncers as he used to tell!'

'But the elder Mr Frazer is a Jacobite,' Isobel insisted. 'I have heard you say that he was condemned to death after the 'Fifteen rebellion.'

'Johnnie Frazer is not, and never was, a Jacobite,' James growled. 'What he was, was a daft laddie of about twenty years of age who got himself and his tenants involved in what he thought of as an adventure. In the end he went home to Transk with scarcely a penny to his name and his head feeling lucky to be still on his shoulders. It has taken him and his boy thirty years to rebuild Transk, and, I can assure you, neither of them is going to risk it again. Not for a hare-brained scheme like this rebellion, anyway!'

Isobel was forced to accept the logic in this, and her father, sensing a small victory, hurried to consolidate his position. 'Well, now. That disposes of objection number one. What was number two? Ah, yes. His appearance. Quite unremarkable, I think you said. Strange, considering that both your mother and Fiona consider Colin quite the handsomest man of their acquaintance.'

'Beauty is in the eye of the beholder,' Isobel returned, aware that she was becoming more sullen as her father waxed jocular.

'But surely an excellent set of teeth, regular features and a tall athletic figure are repellent to no one?' he insisted, and chuckled as Isobel acceded with a shrug. 'Which brings us to objection number three, his shoulders. "Of his tailor's contrivance", was it not? Ah, well, there you have me, my love. I fear I have no proof to the contrary, but, speaking from a wide knowledge of shoulders and of tailors, I should confess myself surprised if the pair concerned were to prove other than genuine. Perhaps you would care to lay a small wager? Shall we say five pounds?'

Isobel was becoming worn out by this verbal jousting but could see that her father, for all his changes of tactics, had not given an inch. Did he intend, this time, to wear her down till she finally agreed to marry Colin out of pure exhaustion? 'Please, Papa,' she said urgently, stretching out a hand to catch at his sleeve. 'I *beg* you will not tease me to marry Colin. He may be a very worthy man—indeed, I know he is—but our natures are too divergent for harmony. Are you so impatient to be rid of me that you will give me to a man I cannot love?'

James acknowledged the hit with a fencer's gesture, and grinned unwillingly. 'Never that, lassie!' He swung his chair away from his desk and held out his arms to her, catching her to him as she ran to kneel beside him. 'Never that. We'll find you a man to your taste yet, and mine too, God willing. A pity you didn't like young Frazer, for he's a lad I cannot but take to. A man's man, mebbe—och, it can't be helped. You don't think you might change your mind?'

Isobel's hands clenched involuntarily on the breast of his coat. '*No*. I do not think it. Nor must you allow Colin to think it, else I shall never be rid of him. I declare, I hope I may never clap eyes on him again!'

'Very well,' James sighed. 'I'll send him packing for you, but as for never seeing him again, that's another matter. His father is an old and valued friend—I can hardly close my door to the laddie. Forbye,' he added philosophically, 'he might take a fancy to Fiona, which would be the greatest possible good luck!' He pulled Isobel to her feet and gave her a gentle push towards the door. 'Away with you now, and you can tell Laughlan that I'll tan his hide for him if I catch him out in any more of his tarradiddles.'

She paused in the doorway to look back at him and was overwhelmed by a warm rush of affection and gratitude.

'Papa . . .' she said softly, 'I *am* sorry to be such a trial to you. Truly, I do not mean to be disobedient.'

He looked up at her, his hand arrested in mid-air halfway to his pipe-stand, and for a long moment he made no reply. Then he gave an unexpected grin. 'Girl, you'll be the end of me. Away and leave me in peace.'

Laughlan was waiting to pounce on her as soon as she stepped into the hall. He had been kneeling at the keyhole and now looked even untidier than usual, his red hair escaping from its queue and his neckcloth awry.

'What happened?' he growled, falling in behind her as she made for the stairs. 'I could hear him roaring like a stag and not a whisper out of you. Are you to be married to Colin Frazer?'

'No, I am not.' Isobel paused to look him in the eye. 'I never had the least intention of doing so, so you see there was never any need for you to tell me all those silly lies about him—or to tell Fiona, knowing she would be bound to tell me. Papa was not in the least taken in by them.'

'You—you told Papa?' Laughlan recoiled against the banister. 'He will skin me alive this time, for sure!'

'Which,' Isobel said pleasantly, 'is no more than you deserve, you miserable wretch,' and she resumed her ascent.

He followed in her wake, muttering sullenly. 'I cannot think why you must be in such a hurry to marry and leave home. Oh, I know Papa is a bit autocratic and Fiona is a real pain most of the time, but still—I dare say you might not *like* being married after a while. Had you thought of that? And then where would you be? No, you would be better to stay unwed. When I marry, you could make your home with me—for I shall have to marry, you know, to procure an heir—so you would have someone to look after you.'

Isobel halted with her hand on her mother's door and composed her features before she turned to smile at him.

'Well I don't suppose you will marry much before you are twenty-five, Laughlan, which gives me ten years to make up my mind. If I am still unmarried by that time, I imagine I shall be pleased to accept your offer.'

Much cheered, he gave her shoulder a fraternal pat and disappeared, whistling, in the direction of his own room, leaving Isobel pink with suppressed mirth.

There was one thing she would never need, she reflected, and that was someone to look after her. Indeed it was she, to a large extent, who looked after both Laughlan and Fiona. Even the small staff of servants that ran the Edinburgh house were more likely to turn to Isobel for direction than to her mother, who had no taste for domesticity and rarely concerned herself with any decision weightier than a choice of ribbons.

Isobel was made immediately aware, as she entered her mother's room, that her interview with her father was not to be discussed. The outcome was writ large on her unclouded brow, and was immediately apparent both to her mother and to Fiona, who was seated in the window-bay.

Fiona jumped up with an eager expression, but her mother forestalled her question by saying smoothly, 'I wish you will speak with Agnes, Isobel. I sent her to the Luckenbooths for some pins an hour since, and she is returned with all sorts of wild rumours and is frightening the other servants.'

'The rebel army is marching on Edinburgh!' Fiona was round-eyed with excitement. 'Everyone is saying they will be here within three days, and cook wants to run away to her brother's farm, and . . .'

'Oh, fiddle!' Isobel laughed, squeezing on to the window seat beside Fiona. 'He cannot be on the march so soon. It was only the other day we heard he was enlisting his army at Perth.'

'No doubt Agnes is exaggerating,' Mrs MacIntosh murmured, examining her still lovely face in a hand mirror. 'Did I not hear that General Cope is on his way to intercept the rebels? I'm sure he will do so long before they reach here.'

'But what if he does not?' Fiona insisted, determined to look on the black side. 'Will Papa send us away, think you, Mama? Not to Aunt Euphemia, I hope and pray, for nothing could be so out of reason dull as Inverness at this season. It would be like being incanted in a prison!'

'Incarcerated,' said her mother absently, smoothing an eyebrow with a licked fingertip. 'I cannot think we should be in any danger, do you, Isobel? From all reports the rebel army have treated civilians with respect hitherto, and, after all, their objective is London. Why should they tarry in Edinburgh above a day or two? And should there be any fighting, thank goodness our house is far enough away from the walls and the city gates to be safe from stray shots. At the worst we shall be constrained to remain within doors for a few days, no more.'

'But how shabby it would be if the Young Pretender were to pass through the city and we not see him,' Fiona objected, sticking the end of one red-gold ringlet into her mouth, a habit of which the entire family had been trying to break her since childhood. 'That *odious*

Catriona Blair told me that her cousin met him in Italy and thought him quite the most charming person, and as handsome as he can stare. Why is it always Catriona . . .'

She broke off as her mother's serving-woman, Miss Walkinshaw, entered with a tray of tea-things. Isobel smiled inwardly. Probably Miss Walkinshaw was the only person in the world who could silence Fiona.

'Ah, thank you, Miss Walkinshaw.' Mrs MacIntosh made room for the tray on her dressing-table by the simple expedient of sweeping all her bottles and jars into a heap in one corner. 'You may as well put my hair up now. I have a suspicion we may have callers, since everyone will want to discuss these dreadful rumours.' She waved to Isobel to pour out the tea. 'You don't think we have anything to fear, do you, Miss Walkinshaw?'

'We are in the hands of the Lord,' stated that lady repressively. 'If He sees fit to deliver us into the hands of a horde of murdering savages, no doubt He will have His own reasons for it.'

Isobel laughed aloud at this, and felt Fiona shudder as though she expected her sister to be struck by lightning.

'Oh come, Miss Walkinshaw—"murdering savages"? These rebel soldiers are no different from the Highlanders we meet every summer when we are in Inverness. Just ordinary clansmen, like the tenants on my father's estate.'

The waiting-woman's lip curled without humour. 'Men in a pack are not the same animal as the domestic variety! Mark my words, no woman will be safe in the streets if once they breach the gates.'

An air of depression settled over the room, as frequently happened in Miss Walkinshaw's company, and the conversation dwindled to a lengthy silence. Finally Isobel drained her cup and returned it to the tray, saying, 'I had better have a word with cook, I suppose, and see if I can put her mind at rest . . .'

'Why, Isobel!' her mother interrupted, jerking her head away from Miss Walkinshaw's busy fingers. 'Only look, my love . . .' She had picked up Isobel's tea-cup and was turning it round in her hands.

Isobel exchanged a laughing look with Fiona, but for all she pretended to scoff at her mother's predilection for reading tea-leaves, she was intensely superstitious. 'What is it, then?'

'A tall, fair man, Isobel, so very distinct that I am persuaded he will be greatly important to you. And very close to the top of the cup, which means you will meet him soon.'

'Oh, Isobel!' Fiona cried, her china-blue eyes sparkling with excitement. 'How exciting if it should be the Young Pretender!'

'I suspect the odds are against it!' Isobel laughed, making for the door, and, as she closed it behind her, she heard Fiona say,

'Oh pooh! Isobel is such a septic, Mama. Read my cup instead.'

The rumours of the encroaching rebellion were being taken much more seriously in the kitchen, where Agnes was enjoying being the centre of attention and was making the most of it. The original word-of-mouth reports with which she had returned from the Lucken-booths had long since been milked dry, and she was now embellishing them with material of her own, thereby reducing the cook to tears and the porter to drink. She had come originally from the family estate in Inverness, and her Highland origins not only provided her with inspiration but lent credence to her stories.

These were abruptly terminated by Isobel's entry, and in a very few minutes Agnes was refuted and the porter detached from his pot of ale and sent about his business. Cook was reluctant to abandon her hysterics and it took some time to switch the direction of her morbid thoughts. In the end, this was accomplished not by sympathy, which only increased the flow of tears, but by pointing out that the last order of tea had disappeared rather quickly. This insinuation concentrated cook's mind wonderfully, but Isobel was forced, in the course of the ensuing argument, to consult her household account-book which she had left in the drawing-room.

Had her mind not been almost entirely occupied with the kitchen situation, she would have been aware earlier that she was not alone in the room. Instead, she was already rummaging in her writing-desk when, from the shadows behind her, a man cleared his throat and she whirled to see Colin Frazer rising from a chair.

It was impossible not to be flattered to note that he had deemed the occasion worthy of his best clothes. A superb coat of dark grey fitted smoothly across his suspect shoulders, parting to disclose a waistcoat embellished with just the right amount of silver braid. He wore no wig, but his black hair was smoothly *en queue* and forbidden, by some means, to exhibit its usual tendency to curl.

'I startled you, Miss MacIntosh. Allow me to apologise.'

'Not at all,' she denied brightly, and could immediately have bitten out her tongue. What an inane thing to say! Of course he had startled her. A blind man could have seen it! *Certes*, her whole body had cracked like a whip! Clasping the account-book to her bosom, much as a frightened child might hug her doll, she began to sidle towards the door.

'I came to see your father,' Colin said. 'The manservant has gone to look for him. Will you not keep me company till he returns?'

'I fear not,' replied Isobel briskly. 'I have household duties to attend to, and cook to see before dinner.'

She reached the door only to find, unaccountably, that Colin was there before her, his hand on the latch but making no move to turn it.

'You know why I am here today, Isobel?' Close to her like this, his voice took on a quiet intimacy, deeper in timbre, seeming almost to throb in his chest.

'Yes . . .' she answered, dropping her eyes before the cool grey-green stare that looked into the deepest recesses of her mind.

'Then you know what my answer is to be?'

All at once she was ablaze with anger. 'How dare you, Colin Frazer? Have you no sense of decency? You make a hobby of embarrassing me, and I have had enough of it! If you are here to speak to my father, then *speak* to my father and spare me your inquisition! And . . . And stop calling me Isobel!'

She could not be sure how he was taking this, as, looking down at her, his eyelashes masked his eyes, but a corner of his mouth lifted in a smile, as he said softly, 'So the answer is "No". For the present.'

'For all time!' Isobel snapped, much more loudly than she had intended, just as the door opened between them and the porter's head appeared in the gap.

'Ye're tae come ben tae the maister's study,' he informed Colin elegantly, and Colin turned to Isobel with a half-bow.

'I trust we can continue this discussion at a later date,' he grinned, his eyes teasing her, challenging her to blurt out some ill-considered remark.

She said nothing, but with extreme difficulty; and her two eyes on his back as he crossed the hall should have burned a hole in his coat.

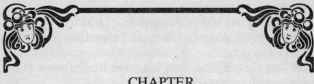

CHAPTER
TWO

DESPITE ALL predictions to the contrary, the rebel army
entered Edinburgh with the minimum of opposition, the
only noise being provided by the citizens themselves
who turned out to welcome the 'bonnie Prince' with loud
huzzas. Even the sun, which had been evasive for days,
showed fitfully between the clouds, like a young girl
flirting with her fan, glittering on the silver-hilted
broadsword of the handsome young man on horseback
and mellowing the garish tartans of the proud chiefs
beside him. White handkerchiefs fluttered in the hands
of the ladies, white cockades were hastily affixed to
every hat, while the flower of Edinburgh's young man-
hood did everything to ingratiate itself, short of actually
enlisting.

Forbidden, for the time being, to set foot out of doors,
Fiona and Isobel were reduced to spending the afternoon at their bedroom window. From this point it was
possible to see very little of what went on behind the
walls of the town, as the broadest part of the North
Loch, probably some four hundred feet across, lay
between the house and the Advocate's Close, directly
opposite. Several times Isobel told herself that it was a
waste of time to keep watching, but having earlier spied
three tartan-clad figures in the terraced gardens of Lady
Stair's Close, she did not dare to move away lest she
should miss seeing them, if they returned. Throughout

the afternoon she and Fiona remained faithfully at their post, but by the time the early dusk had blotted out all but the dim outline of the castle, they were forced to retire disappointed.

Fiona, particularly, found her thwarted curiosity hard to bear. Her imagination had been fired by Catriona Blair's description of the Prince, and it seemed to her that her father's action in forbidding her to go out was totally unjustified. During supper, she sulked openly and was even more hurt when her lack of appetite went unnoticed. Isobel, to all appearances, was not at all frustrated, and chattered quite contentedly about what she had seen from her window, unconsciously turning the knife in her sister's wound by declaring that she would not dare to cross the threshold until the town was well and truly quit of the invaders.

The sisters climbed the stairs together and were undressed by Agnes in a silence which Isobel, for one, noticed to be distinctly strained. She studied Fiona's set features closely, but could find no clue as to what might be the reason for her displeasure, and so decided to wait until the maid had left the room before setting enquiries in motion. Fiona, however, had no intention of waiting to be interrogated. She made it quite obvious that she had something to discuss by relieving Agnes of the hairbrush which the latter was about to apply to Isobel's hair, and saying, 'I shall do that, Agnes. You may go to bed now. Good night.'

Isobel met her maid's enquiring stare in the mirror with lifted brows, but nodded a dismissal and waited patiently to hear Fiona's grievance. It was some time before Fiona could bring herself to speak, but she filled in the time by venting some of her spleen on her sister's long hair. Presently she permitted herself a delicate sniff, and remarked somewhat enigmatically,

'I don't know how you can sit there, stimulating complete contentment. I really don't.'

'Presumably you mean "simulating",' Isobel suggested. 'But, even so, I cannot think what you are talking about.'

'Simulating, then.' Fiona tossed her head impatiently. 'I don't see that it makes any difference when you know what I mean anyway. How can you be so placid when I'll wager we have that odious Catriona Blair at the door first thing tomorrow morning, positively queening it over us because *she* has seen the Young Pretender and *we* have not. For you may depend upon it, her papa would not compel her to stay indoors, and when she discovers that we have been incant . . . incar . . . cooped up here like a couple of nuns, she will be in transforms of delight!' She dragged the brush through a heavy gold tress and glared at it as it sprang back sparkling, to curl softly on her sister's shoulders. 'And pray do not tell me that you could not have prevailed upon Papa to relent, for I know very well, and so do you, that did you ask for the moon he would never think of refusing you.'

Isobel turned to eye her perplexedly, but had the forethought to possess herself of the hairbrush before answering with a laugh, 'So that is why you are trying to drag my hair out by the roots? Come, now, are you not being a little unfair? How could I ask Papa such an unreasonable thing? For one thing, my credit is not very high with him at present, and for another, I would feel myself to blame if I were to persuade him to let us go out and something dreadful happened to us. But, in any case, I know he would never give his permission. What would all his Whig cronies say if he were to escort his daughters to welcome the Pretender's son?'

Fiona brushed this aside with a negligent lift of her shoulder. 'Laughlan . . .'

'Laughlan!' Isobel's eyes sparkled mirthfully. 'If you are about to suggest that Laughlan might have squired us, pray don't. If Papa had allowed him to go out, it would have been to his classes at the university, not to dance attendance on *us*. And, in the proximity of such wild-looking ruffians as we saw today, I prefer better protection than that afforded by a fifteen-year-old boy.'

'But you said yourself that they have never harmed a girl yet.'

'That does not mean I would deem it an honour to be the first!'

'Then Hamish could have taken us in the coach. If we had kept the curtains drawn, no one would have known we were there.'

'Very well, then,' Isobel sighed, defeated. 'Suppose we might have gone? It is too late now to begin complaining. If Catriona Blair does call on us tomorrow, you must simply say you have the headache and stay in your room. Her condescension will not bother me, I assure you. Perhaps we may catch sight of the Prince when he marches south.'

'But that is not the same thing at all,' Fiona wailed in obvious exasperation. 'Today's events were something I shall never, as long as I live, have the chance to see again. Don't you understand, Isobel? Papa has robbed me of something that it is not in his power to replace, and no matter how much he wished to, he could never call back the day to let me witness something that I should have been able to tell my grandchildren about. And you,' she added balefully, 'are equally to blame, for you might have made him change his mind.'

Isobel received a momentary picture of 'Time' moving inexorably forward, carrying with it the fruits that might have been plucked, and was stricken with remorse. 'I *am* sorry, love,' she said earnestly. 'I had no idea you felt so strongly about it. Why did you not speak to me about it earlier?'

Fiona might have admitted that her intensity of feeling was a product of her own eloquence rather than of any logical thought process, but wisely held her tongue.

'I know,' Isobel exclaimed, brightening. 'Shall I ask Papa to take us for a drive to Holyrood House? You would surely see the Prince there.'

'Oh, Isobel, would you?' Fiona hugged her sister ecstatically. 'It would not be quite so impressive as his actual entry into the city, but I expect my grandchildren will be content if I can say I have actually seen him. Do you think Papa will consent?'

Isobel was far from confident, but promised to exert all her powers of persuasion. Thus mollified, Fiona climbed into bed and was instantly asleep, leaving Isobel to extinguish the candle and snuggle in behind her.

The sounds from the street below had faded now into comparative silence, only an occasional clatter of hooves remaining to claim Isobel's attention as she lay staring blindly into the shifting darkness, envying her sister's instant and complete surrender to sleep. Possibly she dozed for a while, but suddenly she was completely awake, her ears straining for a repetition of the sound that had aroused her. The room, she knew instinctively, was empty, but she was equally certain that the noise had not come from beyond the shutters. Waiting, breathless in the darkness, she heard it again. The muffled clink of the chains that secured the kitchen door.

In a second, she had leapt from her bed and wrenched back the shutters, leaning far out to watch the road. A wind had sprung up, chasing the clouds across the moon and sending scurries of dry leaves rustling along the gutters. A skinny mongrel lay sleeping in the lee of the steps leading to the front door, but otherwise the road was empty. Isobel had almost decided that she had been mistaken, when she heard a yawning creak which she knew was made by the stable door. Torn between an impulse to rouse the household and a desire to know the identity of the prowler, she had drawn in her head, when a shadowy figure leading a horse appeared round the angle of the wall and moved down the road till it was swallowed up by the darkness. Isobel stared after it, open-mouthed, all thoughts of rebel thieves dying instantly. The appearance and demeanour of the silhouette was that of a felon, but the walk was unmistakably that of her brother Laughlan.

Without pausing to wake Fiona, who still slumbered peacefully, undisturbed by the icy draught that fluttered the bed curtains, she eased open the door and sped barefoot down the passage to her brother's room. The door stood half open, and one glance inside was sufficient to confirm her suspicions. The bed was empty, although the ruffled blankets suggested that it had lately been occupied, and propped against the pillow stood a large square of paper. Moving closer, Isobel picked up this missive, her knees trembling with a sudden dread, and by the fitful light of the moon managed to read, in Laughlan's large and laborious script,

Dear Father,

I am Sory if I bring Discrase to your Name but a Man must doe what he thinks is Right. I beleve that King James is our rightfull Sovrain so I have gone toe Hollyrood house toe enlist. Pleas give my Mother and Sisters my love and ask them toe forgive me.

Y'r obedt Son Laughlan.

Isobel sat down on the bed and groaned. 'Oh, you silly, *silly* boy,' she muttered, crumpling the paper into a ball and hurling it into the empty fireplace, in an access of impotent rage. Obviously the first thing to do was to rouse her father, but she hesitated, remembering the thrashing Laughlan had received only the day before for borrowing one of his father's fowling-pieces. The next time he misbehaved, her father had promised him, he would be sent to Aberdeen to complete his education.

Isobel loved her brother with a fierce, almost maternal, affection and would have grieved over the parting as much as he, but no alternative to betraying him was immediately apparent. How much worse it would be if Laughlan were to join the rebels and be killed in battle! Then her eye fell on a pair of old breeches which hung over a chair, and she caught her breath. Would it be possible, even now, to overtake Laughlan and bring him back before his absence was noticed? Dressed in Laughlan's clothes, she would be taken for a youth, no one would think to accost her and she would escape recognition by any acquaintance she might chance to encounter. It would be safe enough if she kept to the quieter roads, and if she galloped her horse . . . She bit her lip, struggling to think calmly, but every second was precious and a voice in her head kept insisting that it would be better to try and fail rather than to make no attempt to save her darling brother from the consequences of his own foolishness.

Even while she argued with herself, she was stripping off her nightdress and fumbling with the buttons of the breeches. The only shirt she could find was her brother's best, an elaborate garment with a great deal of lace about it. It contrasted oddly with the coat and waistcoat that he wore for fishing, but these were the first that came to hand, and she had no time to pick and choose.

They hung rather loosely on her narrow frame, and his brogues had to be padded with two pairs of worsted hose to prevent their slipping up and down, but having twisted her hair into a knot and covered it with a battered hat, she examined herself in the mirror and was not displeased with the result. The loose lines of the coat concealed any slight physical peculiarity which might have given away her sex, and by pulling forward her hat, she was able to throw the top half of her face into shadow. As long as she was not forced to speak to anyone, she told herself firmly, she had nothing to fear. Shivering, she crept down the stairs, not daring to pause long enough to let her better judgment catch up.

The kitchen was empty, but loud snores penetrated from the laundry, where Hamish the manservant was knitting up the ravelled sleeve of care, and the dull glow from the banked fire gave enough light to guide her soundlessly across the flagged floor. The door gave to her touch with a soft creak that made her dart through it like a frightened rabbit into the cobbled courtyard that gave access to the stables. The trees and bushes were alive with the wind, tossing frantic branches and moaning softly. The first step out into the dark night cost her an effort that left her with a curious emptiness in the pit of her stomach.

Laughlan had left the stable door ajar, admitting a bar of moonlight that picked out the gleam of metal trappings on the walls and lit the white star on the brow of Isobel's mare.

'It's me, Stella,' she whispered, but her voice sounded small and lost in the darkness, and Stella tossed her head and regarded her with open suspicion. The unaccustomed weight of the gentleman's saddle met with further disapproval, but Isobel tightened the girths determinedly, although with frequent pauses to suck at her torn

fingernails. She was panting with exertion as she led the
mare round to the front of the house, but she walked a
little way up the road before she deemed it safe enough
to mount. As she halted for a last look at the sleeping
house, the stray dog at the front steps awoke and, taking
one look at Isobel, set up a frenzied yelping that precipi-
tated her into the saddle and drove her heels against
Stella's flanks with a violence which almost cost her her
borrowed shoes. Unfortunately the faithful hound did
not consider his responsibilities discharged until he had
pursued horse and rider, in full cry, for the better part of
quarter of a mile. Gritting her teeth, Isobel did her best
to ignore the din, but was much relieved when it was left
behind at the dam which bounded the east end of the
North Loch.

Close to the wall of the town another danger
threatened, for the houses still showed a light here and
there, and at any moment a window might be thrown up
and a shower of refuse hurled forth with a nonchalant
'Gardyloo', which, as Isobel knew from past experience,
might easily be heard too late for comfort. Even at that
hour the streets were not deserted. The dark closes and
vennels were denizened by sundry vagrants and drunks
who either had no home to go to or had temporarily
forgotten how to get there, but those who noticed the
slim boy riding as though the devil were the pacemaker
were concerned less with importuning him than with
getting out of the way of his horse's flying hoofs. Again
and again Isobel kicked her mount to greater efforts and
gasped as Stella responded with a burst of speed
as gallant as it was uncomfortable. Oh, for a lady's
saddle with a pommel to crook one's knee over!
Happily, it soon became necessary to slow the pace a
little, as the road was deeply rutted after the recent
rain and the trees on each side dropped a great many

branches low enough to trap the unwary.

Forced to slow to a canter, Isobel's fears returned to plague her, and she became convinced that she was riding on a fool's errand. Laughlan would certainly have arrived at Holyrood House by now, for his usual pace when not hampered by his sisters' company was a break-neck gallop. Even if he had tarried on the way—which did not appear likely—there was no certainty that he would allow himself to be persuaded to give up this mad idea and return home. For all she knew, he might not have been headed for Holyrood House at all. It would have been just as easy for him to enlist at Duddingston Loch, where a large number of the rebels were camped.

She was trying to remember if Laughlan had actually mentioned Holyrood House in his letter, or if she had merely jumped to that conclusion in the heat of the moment, when she became aware of rapidly approaching hoofbeats in front of her. Prudently, she guided Stella to the side of the road and covered the velvet muzzle with her hand lest a whinny should betray her position in the shadows. Almost at once a riderless horse trotted aimlessly round a bend in the road, the reins swinging round its neck, and with a shock that struck her like a physical blow, she recognised Laughlan's gelding, Caesar. The beast knew her voice well enough to slow up when she called its name, and she was able to catch at the reins and bring it to a halt. Sick with worry now, she remounted and, leading Caesar, set off again as quickly as she dared on that treacherous surface.

What on earth could have befallen her beloved brother? Could he have been taken for a spy? Or had he merely dismounted for some reason and allowed Caesar to run off? She was not kept long in suspense. Rounding a corner with more speed than judgment, she was almost on top of him before she saw him. He was lying on his back on the grassy verge, his eyes closed and one side of his face streaked with dark blood. On one knee at his side was a tall figure in baldric and kilt, who was fumbling with the bloodstained neckcloth.

The latter looked up as Isobel dismounted, and remarked casually, 'Ah, I see you have caught his horse. Excellent! Is he known to you?'

Isobel chose to ignore this question until she had assured herself that Laughlan still breathed, but having done so, replied in as fair an imitation of her brother's gruff tones as she could affect, 'He is my brother, sir. I pray you will have the goodness to tell me how this came about. I take it he was thrown from his horse?'

The stranger shrugged with a palpable lack of interest, drawing the back of one hand across his brow. 'I am not sure,' he said. 'I was ahead of him on the road when I heard the sound of his horse falling, so I turned back. I expect the beast put its hoof in a rabbit-hole. He is not badly injured, as you will see for yourself, but merely stunned. There is a great deal of blood, to be sure, but it is all coming from his nose. You may depend upon it, his tumble will do him no harm and it will teach him not to ride so fast on a road like this.'

Isobel—who had already decided to say as much to her brother, as soon as he should recover his senses—bitterly resented hearing it from the lips of a total stranger. Biting back a crisp retort, she turned back to Laughlan and began to wipe his gory face with his own handkerchief, since she had none of her own.

There was a sizeable lump under his left eye, and another on his head, just above the hairline, but no sign of broken bones, so it remained only to wait till he recovered consciousness. Sitting back on her heels, in what she considered was a masculine attitude, she turned her attention to the tall Highlander.

There was nothing particularly warlike about him, although he was obviously one of the rebel army. For one thing, he was younger than Isobel had first taken him to be—in all probability no more than a year or two older than herself—and the narrow, pointed face and gentle eyes were those of a scholar rather than a soldier. He wore a fair peruke with his own hair combed over the front of it, but one lock fell across his brow, in spite of his intermittent efforts to push it back. He seemed in no hurry to take his leave, which did not suit Isobel's plans at all. If Laughlan recovered his senses in the presence of one of the Prince's men, there would be no dissuading him from volunteering, so the rebel must be got rid of quickly. He looked up at her at that moment and she gave a brief smile.

'Please accept my thanks for your assistance to my brother, sir,' she said, as pointedly as she dared. 'But now, since your business is no doubt urgent, I must detain you no longer.'

His eyes flickered slightly, as though he were taken aback by this dismissal, and then narrowed as he leaned forward to see her face more clearly. Slowly his eyebrows climbed till they were hidden by the truant lock of blond hair, while Isobel's heart stood still.

'Good God!' he exclaimed. 'I *thought* there was something odd about you.'

Isobel's mouth opened, but no words came. She scrambled to her feet and retreated a few steps, pulling down her hat-brim with a hand that shook badly. 'I . . . I don't know what you mean,' she stuttered.

The rebel was greatly amused. Rising, he made her a sketchy bow. 'Pray excuse me, ma'am,' he grinned. 'I had no idea that you were not . . . what you seemed.' He motioned to the tuft of grass which Isobel had just vacated. 'Will you not be seated? I give you my word, I would not dream of taking advantage of your situation, but I confess myself very curious to know the reason for your masquerade.'

Isobel studied his face, but finding there only amusement and puzzlement, she abandoned all pretence of innocence and sat down at a little distance, being careful to keep Laughlan's inert form between the Highlander and herself.

'If I may be allowed to introduce myself, ma'am,' he bowed again, as formally as if he were in the Assembly Rooms. 'Hugh Murray, of the Atholl Brigade, lately of Ravenscrag in Dunkeld.'

Isobel acknowledged this with a stiff inclination of her head. 'I am Miss MacIntosh of Shawbrae, and my brother's name is Laughlan,' she said, before her better judgment warned her that it would have been wiser to remain anonymous.

He spread a corner of his plaid on the ground and sat down, dashing her hopes of being quickly rid of him. A long silence ensued, uneasy on her part, plainly expectant on his, but she could think of no story to tell him other than the truth, which might be disastrous.

Finally he grew tired of waiting. 'I take it that you and your brother were bound for Holyrood House. But not together. One might be forgiven for wondering if, perhaps, you were pursuing him?'

Isobel closed her eyes, praying for an inspired lie, but she knew he could read the truth in her face.

'Ah!' he nodded, half to himself, and sat quietly for a moment, thinking. Then he said, 'He is young for a soldier, to be sure, but there are younger than he in the Prince's army. Do you not think he is old enough to fight for a cause in which he truly believes?'

It wasn't easy to decide on the best way to handle the

situation, but a distinct gentleness in his voice and manner gave her confidence. She studied him discreetly from beneath her hat-brim and rather liked what she saw. Really, he was quite romantic-looking with that high pale forehead and those shadowed eyes—a veritable Sir Lancelot. And what should appeal to a knight-errant better than a damsel in distress? Accordingly, she drooped a little as she said in a tremulous tone,

'Indeed, sir, I am persuaded that my brother has not given a moment's thought to the cause. His head is full of romantic notions . . . of Honour and Glory. Be assured, he will regret his decision to enlist within a week of doing so.'

Hugh Murray smiled at that, a smile of great sweetness and melancholy. 'Ay, there are many of that kind also in the Prince's army. But they will fight like the others when the time comes, and every one of them will be needed soon, whatever their reasons for enlisting.'

It was immediately crystal clear to Isobel that he himself already regretted being involved, and she was wholly sympathetic. War was not for people like Hugh Murray; sensitive, civilised people to whom violence and aggression must be total anathema. If he had possessed a sister as clear-sighted and determined as Laughlan's, perhaps he might be a happier man this night. The thought lent a nervous tremor to her voice as she said urgently,

'Mr Murray, my brother would not be much of an asset to the Prince. He is a very poor shot, and his swordsmanship—truly, he is the despair of his tutor! In fact, I do not scruple to tell you that, with Laughlan at my back, I would not be at all comfortable in a *mêlée*. He would be sure to get in the way or to trip me up. Forbye, he . . . he is my father's only son, and I would miss him most dreadfully if he were to be killed.'

In case the cogency of these remarks failed to sway him, she covered her eyes with a hand and sniffed piteously once or twice, whereupon, much to her gratification, he leapt up with an exclamation of dismay.

'Pray do not put yourself in a taking, Miss MacIntosh. Believe me, I would be ashamed to play the recruiting-sergeant in the face of your distress. God forbid!' Stepping across Laughlan, he dropped on one knee beside her, his eyes running over her features with an appreciation of which she could not but be aware. 'You are tired and frightened, and should not be abroad at this hour. Presently, when your brother is recovered, I will escort you both to your home.'

'Oh no, that will not answer at all.' Isobel cut him short, forgetting to wilt. 'For if Laughlan sees you here, he will insist on accompanying you to Holyrood. I would feel happier, I must confess, if you would allow me to speak privately with him.'

'Why, of course,' he said with a sideways glance at the insensible form at her feet. 'But, ma'am, I am afraid to leave you alone in such a potentially dangerous situation. Your disguise, as we have seen, is quite ineffective at close range, and the environs of an army encampment are no place for such a young and—forgive me—very beautiful young lady. Permit me, at least, to remain with you till your brother shows signs of regaining consciousness.'

He did, in fact, look seriously worried, and Isobel, quite charmed by his courtliness, found herself reluctant to dispense with his company. It made a pleasant change to be treated with such respectful consideration and to feel in control of the situation instead of constantly on the defensive. Colin would never have allowed her to get away with the 'helpless maiden' rôle. Nor would he be looking at her now with such well-bred reverence.

Unfortunately Laughlan chose that moment to move his head a little, bringing both onlookers hastily to their feet.

In some agitation, Isobel gave the rebel her hand, and said quickly, 'Goodbye, Mr Murray, and thank you for being so understanding . . .'

His eyes held hers as he carried her fingers to his lips. 'Miss MacIntosh, I am happy to have been of service to you. If your brother will not be dissuaded from enlisting, I hope you will direct him to me, and I will do my best to see him safely through the campaign.'

'How kind you are,' she murmured, as he turned away to catch his horse's bridle. 'Good luck!'

He lifted a hand. 'Goodbye, Miss MacIntosh of Shawbrae,' he said, as though imprinting the name on his memory, and, wheeling his horse on to the road, rode off at a brisk canter.

Laughlan groaned softly as she returned to kneel beside him. 'Lie still, you silly boy,' she said gently, laying a cold hand against his brow. 'You will feel more the thing in a minute.'

His eyelids flickered, closed, and opened again, and he stared at her without recognition.

She said, 'It's me . . . Isobel. I followed you. No, do not try to sit up yet awhile.'

He seemed to give this some thought, and produced at last, in drunken tones, 'Holyrood House . . . but I don't remember . . . were you with me?'

'I told you. I followed you, to stop you.'

'Oh, my poor head! You had better tell me—is there much of it missing?' He sat up, holding his head together with both hands, and his jaw dropped as his eyes focused on his sister's attire. '*Isobel!* That's my old fishing-jacket. Have you run mad?'

'It was necessary,' she stated flatly. 'If you force me to

ride out at all hours of the night to stop you making a fool of yourself . . .'

'Oh, have done, Isobel,' Laughlan groaned, rolling up his eyes. 'You may save yourself the trouble of nagging me, for it is of no use. My mind is made up. In a minute or two I shall ride on to Holyrood House and enlist in the rebel army. Being a woman, you do not understand these things, but when Duty and Conscience call . . .'

'I don't know where you hear such high-flown nonsense.' Isobel eyed him with strong disfavour. 'But I hope you are not intending to repeat it to Papa. That letter you left for him was the greatest piece of balderdash I have ever seen. I only hope and pray no one sees it before we get home.'

'I am not going home. I told you . . .'

Isobel drew a finger down his bloody cheek and held it before his eyes. 'You can't go to Holyrood House looking as if you had been dragged through a hedge backwards. Your nose has been bleeding, your eye is already going black, and just look at your clothes! Of course, if you don't mind Prince Charles Edward knowing that you cannot keep your seat on a horse!'

He explored his face with tentative fingers, and winced. 'Well, I dare say it would be better to wait till I have a whole suit to my back, for there is no saying when I may come by another. But, Isobel, if I go home with you, it will only be for tonight. Tomorrow I join the rebels, and you must promise not to warn Papa till I am well away.'

Isobel had no choice but to give her word to this arrangement, but reflected that, tomorrow being another day, she had every chance of devising an adequate deterrent before then.

CHAPTER
THREE

LATER, LOOKING back, Isobel realised that she had been over-sanguine in expecting her own and Laughlan's absence to pass unnoticed. Her sole thought throughout the proceedings had been to overtake her brother and bring him home again and, even as they dismounted at the end of the street and began to walk their mounts the last few yards to the stables, she had not given a thought to what tale they would tell if they had been missed. It was Laughlan who first noticed the lights in the stable-yard and as they turned the corner of the house a loud cry of relief and recrimination went up from the motley crowd assembled therein. Hamish, Agnes, the cook, two inebriated passers-by, a beggarwoman and the vociferous mongrel, who seemed to have adopted the house as his own, surrounded the misdoers eagerly.

Cook, dressed only in her smock petticoat (and most becomingly too, Isobel noted. Who would have guessed she had such a noble bosom?) ran towards the half-open kitchen door, shrieking, 'Here is Master Laughlan now, sir!'

Isobel realised instantly that she had not been recognised, but before her numbed brain could suggest any way of taking advantage of this fact her father had appeared in the doorway, his shoes unbuckled and his wig at a rakish angle over one ear. Never had she seen him look so angry.

'What . . .' he fairly choked. 'What is the meaning of this, you young devil? Where is your sister Isobel? Out with it, where is she?'

Laughlan cast an embarrassed glance at the ring of curious faces that hemmed him in, and answered in as firm a voice as he could manage, 'I think you would prefer if we discussed the matter in private, sir.'

The veins in James MacIntosh's forehead bulged alarmingly. 'Very well, bring your friend with you. I will wish a word with him.' He turned back into the house.

Without a word, his two children trotted after him as he charged through the kitchen and into his library, snatching up, en route, a branch of candles which stood on the hall table. Halting beside his desk, he swung to face them, his face white with temper.

'Now,' he said, venomously quiet. 'We will hear what you have to say.'

Laughlan cleared his throat awkwardly, in very evident perplexity, so Isobel took the bull by the horns and pulled off her hat.

'*Isobel!*' Her father shied like a startled horse, and cursed as his hand received a splatter of hot wax from the candles which he still held. 'What the devil . . .? Well, thank God you are safe home, at any rate.' He sat down heavily, removing his wig and running a hand over his cropped poll. 'Now, then! What has been going on? What do you mean by stealing out at this hour of the night, to say nothing of leaving the kitchen door unchained for all the thieves and murdering rebels in Edinburgh to come and go as they please? What are your reasons, I say, and by God they had better be good ones, or I'll have the hides off both of you!'

Laughlan slipped a protective arm around his sister's shoulders and straightened his own manfully. 'This whole business was entirely my fault, Papa.' he said loudly, but his voice was none too steady. 'I give you my word that Isobel was not to blame in the slightest. Will you not allow her to withdraw? As you can see, she is quite overwrought.'

Isobel was indeed feeling the effects of the tensions of the past few hours, but she had not believed the fact to be apparent. She was surprised, therefore, when her father, after one look at her drawn face, nodded his consent, and barked,

'Very well. You may go to your room, and stay there until you have my permission to leave it. Whatever fancy excuse your brother has in mind to give me, you will be punished for this night's work.'

She would have liked to warn Laughlan once again that their father would not appreciate an impassioned speech on the glories of Duty and Honour, but since she dared not open her mouth, she contented herself with throwing him what she hoped was an eloquent glance, and withdrew. Too late she remembered that her disguise was now incomplete, and could only turn her face away from the open-mouthed group of servants who had waited up in the confident expectation of witnessing mayhem. Their gratified whispers followed her to her room.

Fiona had been wakened by the disturbance, or perhaps by her mother, who was pacing the floor in an agitated manner, a scented handkerchief pressed to her lips. As Isobel entered, her sister sat up in bed and, fixing her with an accusing glower, said icily. 'There she is, the deceitful thing. Saying only last night that she would not dare to leave the house till the rebels had gone!'

Mrs MacIntosh interrupted her pacing to emit a small shriek. 'Merciful heavens! What is the girl wearing? Oh, God! This is surely a nightmare. Presently I shall wake up and find I have been dreaming.' She wilted gracefully into a convenient chair and fanned herself with her handkerchief, the picture of afflicted femininity.

Isobel went to kneel beside her, and patted her arm. 'Now, please do not put yourself in a taking, Mama. I promise you, no one knows of this but ourselves and the servants.'

This had the effect of throwing her mother into mild hysterics. 'The servants,' she wailed. 'As if they were not the worst possible scandalmongers. The tale will be all over town by daybreak, be sure of it.' After relieving her feelings with a burst of weeping, she demanded, with more martyrdom than curiosity, 'What in the world inspired you and your brother to do such a mad thing? I swear, it is a mystery why you must go out of your way to be such a trial to me. Is it nothing to you that your father and I have been worried to death about you? Oh, what have I done to deserve two such wicked children?' She dabbed affectedly at her dry eyes. 'What a positively *hoydenish* prank to play!'

Isobel groaned despairingly. 'I *am* sorry, Mama. *Truly* I am—But at the time, it seemed the only thing to do. I could think of no other solution.'

'Solution to what, pray? If you mean to explain, I wish you will do so, instead of talking in riddles.'

'I am trying to explain,' Isobel muttered, wondering what Laughlan was saying in the library and hoping that he would have the sense to tell the truth. 'It was Laughlan, you see. He ran off to join the rebels.'

Mrs MacIntosh gave a shocked scream and fell back in her chair, utterly prostrated. Fiona abandoned her huffy silence, which had not achieved any noticeable effect in any case, and beat her hands together with frustration.

'So that *is* where you were! I thought as much. Indeed I told Mama she might depend upon it—did I not so,

Mama? Well, of all the mean, selfish things to do! You might have taken *me* with you!'

'Oh hush, Fiona!' snapped her sister, rounding on her in real irritation. 'If you imagine that I have been enjoying myself tonight, you are much mistaken. It is very cold and very frightening out there in the darkness, all alone, and I can assure you of this—the next time Laughlan decides to run away, he can do so with my blessing! I shall stay in my warm bed and mind my own business!'

'There *is* a middle course, you know, Isobel,' put in Mrs MacIntosh faintly. 'I cannot, for the life of me, understand why you must do everything yourself. Anyone else would have thought to rouse the house. Your father would have ridden after Laughlan.'

'My father would have thrashed him soundly and packed him off to Aberdeen, as he threatened to do only the other day,' Isobel said, not mincing matters. 'Whereas, by going after him myself, I stood the chance of bringing him home again without other folk being any the wiser. As things have turned out, I might just as well have told Papa in the first place, but at least I managed to prevent Laughlan from enlisting, which was the important thing.'

'Well, I think it very interfering of you, Isobel,' Fiona stated, nibbling petulantly at the end of a ringlet. 'Why should Laughlan not enlist as a soldier if he wishes to? I dare say it is a very exciting life, and perfectly respectable. He might easily have done something heroic, and returned home in triumph . . .'

'More likely he would have something stupid and returned home in a coffin!' retorted his exasperated sister, at which Mrs MacIntosh cried out in horror.

'Heaven forfend! Isobel, I wish you will not say such dreadful things! But you are perfectly right, I would not for the world have the dear boy subjected to such dangers, and you did well to stop him. I cannot like your methods—but there, I shall say no more on that head. We must just be thankful that he is back home safe and sound, and trust to your Papa to ensure that he does not run off again.' She rose, and trod towards the door, pausing at the mirror to re-tie the satin ribbons of her nightcap and to inspect her face for traces of her recent tears. 'Ah me! How fortunate that I was not born to be a Roman matron. I could never take any pleasure in sending my sons to war. Only consider how very trying it would be, not knowing where they were or what was happening to them! No, it would have been quite insupportable if Laughlan had joined the rebels—and so I shall tell your father, Isobel, you may depend upon it.'

So saying, she exited with a faint, long-suffering smile, and Isobel heaved a sigh of relief. It was easy enough to make her mother see reason, but her father would prove a harder nut to crack. The indisputable fact that things might have been worse was unlikely to carry much weight with him since, indeed, things were bad enough as it was.

In saving Laughlan from his just deserts, Isobel had, she suspected, done her reputation considerable harm, and her father, knowing Edinburgh society as he did, could hardly fail to be aware of this. By morning the whole story of her midnight ride would be the talk of the town. Every mother with marriageable daughters of her own would speed the tale on its way, slightly embroidered, till Isobel became such an object of universal disapproval that it would be a miracle if an eligible bachelor were as much as to bow to her in the street.

This mattered to Isobel more than she cared to admit, even to herself, and she knew that it mattered a great deal to her doting father. For years now he had made no secret of his ambition of arranging a brilliant marriage for his elder daughter. Whatever he might say to the contrary, when it suited him, she was well aware that, until the advent of Colin Frazer, every applicant for her hand had fallen far short of her father's ideal. And now, so soon after turning down a catch like Colin, it would gall him unbearably to have to face the fact that his daughter's value on the marriage-mart had fallen appreciably. One thing was certain, Isobel thought as she climbed into bed. Her father, for the next few days, would be a man to be avoided.

But, perhaps fortunately, James MacIntosh proved to be in no hurry to see his wayward daughter. Isobel spent the following morning in hourly expectation of a summons to his study, but none came. Instead she was left wholly alone—bored, worried and exceedingly depressed—and even Agnes, who carried up her meals, could give her no news of what was happening.

Fiona had gone out to pay morning calls with her mother and the house seemed unnaturally silent, as though a death had occurred. There were no voices in the passage, no clattering of Laughlan's brogues on the stair, no distant tinkle of the spinet, and to Isobel, all alone with her troubles, the hours dragged by interminably.

It was almost dinner-time before Mrs MacIntosh and Fiona returned, and the latter lost no time in reporting to her sister. 'Well, my *certes*!' she cried, throwing her hat on a chair and seating herself on the bed with an energetic backward leap. 'I think the whole town is talking about your escapade. If you do not have a blot on your expulsion this time, I shall be most surprised. Mama says . . .'

'Moonshine!' Isobel put in crisply. 'You do exaggerate, Fiona. The whole town has more to worry about than my doings, and my escutcheon is unlikely to be blotted by such a minuscule offence. Try not to dramatise everything.'

'Well, anyway . . .' Fiona waved this criticism away with an airy gesture. 'Mrs Blair and Catriona had heard all about it from Catriona's music teacher, and they were so smug about it—especially Catriona—that I could have slapped their fat faces. Mrs Blair said . . .' She sat up, folding her arms atop her bosom in imitation of Mrs Blair's customary stance and speaking in that lady's well-corseted Edinburgh accent. She said, "I heard sech a *dam*aging story concerning dear Isobel, this morning. Not a *wirrd* of truth in it, naturally, but I felt you should know about it, Margaret, before it goes any *firr*ther." And all the time that *weasel* Catriona was smirking away behind her, as happy as though it were Christmas morning!'

'So what did Mama say?' Isobel asked, steeling herself. Some mothers might have been expected to rise to the occasion, to defend their offspring either by cunning or by sheer force of character, but Mrs MacIntosh was not of that kidney.

'She said . . . But first I must tell you what happened earlier.' Fiona slid off the bed and danced across the room to perch on a low chair at the fireside. 'This is me in my sedan chair outside the lending library. Mama had gone in to pick up that book you wanted—*Thirty Fables* or something—and I was waiting outside for her with the curtains drawn, when I heard a woman's voice say, very shrewishly, ". . . and quite comely, I won't deny—if one admires brown eyes—but a sad romp, you know. Why only last night, so I'm told, she arrived home in the small hours, accompanied by her brother and dressed in his clothes from head to toe. One cannot but be shocked by such ill-bred, totally reprehensible . . ." Then she stopped, because the man she was speaking to burst out laughing—and do you know who it was? I recognised his laugh immediately. It was Colin Frazer!'

'Oh, dear God!' Isobel spun away and stared unseeingly out of the window as a scalding blush crept up her face to her very scalp. If anything had been lacking to make her feel totally defeated, this was it. 'How dare he laugh!' she muttered, squirming. 'I'll never forgive him for that, if I live to be a hundred!'

'Don't be such a goose, Isobel,' Fiona said impatiently. 'It wasn't like that at all. He was laughing because he didn't believe a word of the story. He . . .'

'Didn't be*lieve* it?' Isobel stared at her, saucer-eyed. 'Are you sure?'

'Yes, and if you will hold your tongue for a minute and stop interrupting me, I shall tell you what happened.' With an admonitory shake of her head, Fiona flounced around in her chair and mimed the stealthy parting of a curtain. 'I peeped out, very carefully, and there was Colin standing there like this . . .' She jumped up and assumed a recognisably Colinesque pose, shoulders squared, legs comfortably astride and chin arrogantly tilted. 'And he was laughing so much he could scarce catch his breath—and, oh Isobel, you know the way his eyes crinkle and his teeth are so strong and white, my heart simply . . .'

Isobel gripped the arms of her chair. 'Just tell me what was said, Fiona.'

'I was just going to! Heavens, you are the most impatient jade!' Fiona compressed her lips furiously, and resumed her seat. 'Well, then Colin said, "I do beg your pardon, Mrs Anderson"—Oh, I forgot to say it was Mrs Anderson, Greta's mother, and she was looking at Colin like this—well, he went on, "I could not help laughing at the way these stories become garbled. In fact, Miss MacIntosh was not involved in this escapade at all." And then . . .'

'Not *involved*?' Isobel could not help gasping.

'That's exactly what Mrs *Anderson* said, and Colin laughed again, and said, "Not at all. The truth of the matter is—and I have it from a most reliable source— that the two delinquents were not Laughlan plus Isobel in *boy's* clothing, but Laughlan plus a friend in *Isobel's* clothing." What do you think of that?'

Isobel, for some seconds, was so stunned that she was unable to think with any clarity at all. Whether Colin had actually been told this less damaging version, or whether he had made it up himself to protect her reputation, was a matter for conjecture, but he would certainly be given credence. Whatever Isobel might think of him personally, she knew that he was one of the darlings of Edinburgh society and generally believed to know what he was talking about, so she could only hope that he would continue to refute the true story.

'Mama was as pleased as Punch when I told her about it,' Fiona was saying with great complacency, as though it had been her own idea all along. 'So, of course, when Mrs Blair started talking about the incident, we both laughed like lunatics and repeated Colin's version. You should have seen Catriona's face! Her mouth went all twisted like this, and she said, "But, of course, we *knew* it was all a tarradiddle, did we not, Mama?" Oh, it was lovely! And then we went to visit old Miss Cunningham, and the Flemings, and Lady McAllister, who is the biggest gossip in Scotland. Some of them had heard the story, and some hadn't, but we made sure they all knew *our* version before we left.'

'Oh, what a good idea!' Isobel exclaimed gratefully, giving Fiona's shoulders a hug. 'The two stories are so alike, I'm sure that most people will suspect that the nasty version—the one involving me—is only malicious gossip.'

In fact the two stories ran neck and neck in the popularity stakes for a day or two until they were both forgotten in the excitement of another, more serious, rumour. A Hanoverian force under the command of General Cope was, reputedly, on its way to the relief of the capital. It had already disembarked at Dunbar, and although a confrontation was thought to be daily more imminent, the rebel army showed no sign of making preparations to retreat.

As these rumours reached her, Isobel found her thoughts dwelling more and more on the gentle rebel she had met on the way to Holyrood House. In spite of the fact that her mind had been on other things, Hugh had made a very strong impression on her in the course of their conversation, and she was now conscious of a decided wish to meet him again. They had said nothing of any significance to each other, yet beneath the surface, totally unconnected to the words they spoke, had run another communication, as though mind spoke to mind.

She had known instinctively that he was a thinking man—perhaps even a dreamer—and that he was bitterly unhappy in a situation which forced him to face the brutal realities of war. She had sensed his fastidiousness and his sensibility and seen in his eyes a quiet, undemanding appreciation of herself. And if there had been the smallest hint of gallantry in the way he kissed her hand, he had been careful to cause her no embarrassment.

It was difficult to avoid contrasting him with Colin Frazer, who was anything but a dreamer, far from undemanding and who positively revelled in embarrassing her on every possible occasion. Hugh, by comparison, was so uncomplicated and so plainly in need of sympathy and affection that Isobel's heart went out to him. Here was a man with whom she could relax and be comfortable, and to whom she could bring a whole wealth of support.

So ran her thoughts in her leisure moments, and as her imprisonment extended into the second, and then the third, day, those moments expanded into hours. Laughlan, it transpired, was suffering a similar incarceration, but he, glad of a holiday from the university, had quickly adjusted to his situation and was perfectly content to pass his time in renovating his fishing tackle, tying flies, and swearing everlasting allegiance to King George.

Since this abrupt change of politics had been brought about by the persuasion of his father's riding-crop, it was felt by both his parents to be only prudent to keep him under restraint until Prince Charles and his followers should have quitted the neighbourhood. Yet there had been no mention of sending him to Aberdeen. Even Fiona sensed something ominous in this remission, since James MacIntosh rarely made empty threats, and the general feeling among the rest of the family was that an even worse fate might be hanging over Laughlan's head.

No one dared to speculate on what this might be and, three days after the transgression, Laughlan's father was still in such an evil mood that to ask him his intentions would be to court dog's abuse. Mrs MacIntosh did enter a plea for leniency, to which he replied with a singularly ill-chosen remark which was later to cost him two flowered muslin aprons, a length of green velvet and a pair of pearl earrings. After this incident his family composed itself, with varying degrees of patience, to await whatever retribution he might announce. This was not long in being revealed.

The evening being overcast and chilly, Agnes had obtained permission to light a fire in Isobel's grate, a

luxury that was seldom granted except in the case of illness. Isobel had just settled down in front of the blaze with
the new copy of Allan Ramsay's *Collection of Thirty
Fables*, when the door flew open and Fiona rushed
in and threw herself on the bed in an ecstasy of weeping.
Seriously alarmed, Isobel dropped her book and ran
to throw her arms about her, making soothing noises
and insisting that nothing could warrant such a passion.

It was some time before Fiona could be persuaded to
divulge a reason for this display of despair, being too
intent on drumming her heels and punching the pillows
with impotent wrath. Presently a small face emerged
from the chaos, very red and alarmingly contorted, and a
torrent of half-intelligible phrases poured forth.

'That wretch Laughlan! I hate him! And you, too! It's
all your fault . . . I won't go! Why should I suffer? I'll go
into a decline! I'll just *die*, and then he'll be sorry! He's
an ogre and a tyrant and . . . and a devil inculcate! It's
not fair!'

'Hush, now,' Isobel soothed her, smoothing back the
damp hair from her brow. 'If it's Papa you are talking
about, I don't think you should call him a devil incar-
nate. That's going too far, don't you think? Here, blow
your nose and tell me what has happened. I dare say it
will prove not to be the end of the world after all.'

'Yes, it is!' Fiona sobbed defiantly, glaring through
her tears. 'Or, at least, it's just as bad. Papa is taking us
all home to Inverness for the entire winter—perhaps
even longer—until the rebellion is over, he says. It's all
arranged. We leave tomorrow.'

Isobel was indescribably shocked. Inverness was bad
enough in the summer months, but in winter-time, when
most of the gentry migrated to the comforts and better
educational facilities of the capital, it would be a living
death.

'You must be mistaken, Fiona,' she said, with less

confidence than she felt. 'How could we possibly be ready to travel by tomorrow? Think of all the packing to be done, and the arrangements to be made. Depend upon it, it is all a hum!'

'No, it isn't! Agnes will be here directly to pack our things for the journey.' Fiona had stopped wailing now, but her lip still trembled ominously. 'We are to travel in the coach with Mama, and Laughlan and Papa will ride.'

'And the servants? Are they to be left here in Edinburgh?'

'No. They are to follow with the baggage. You see? Papa has it all arranged and will not hear a word against it.'

'It all seems very odd.' Isobel slid off the bed and paced to the fireplace, gnawing thoughtfully at her lip. 'If Papa means this to be a punishment for Laughlan and me, why should he be in such a rush? There must be another reason.'

'Well—He did say something about the likelihood of there being a battle when General Cope arrives, and perhaps fighting in the streets . . .'

'Ah—Yes, Fiona. That sounds more likely. I imagine Papa wants to be sure that we are well out of the way until either the rebels have been stopped or they have pressed on towards London. We must just hope that one or the other will happen soon.'

Yet, even as she spoke, she realised that whether the rebels won or lost the coming battle, the chances of seeing Hugh again were very slight. She was going north, he was headed south, but somehow she could not throw off the conviction that the Fates had brought them together for a purpose and that somehow, somewhere, their paths would cross again. It was a forlorn hope, she knew, and totally groundless, but it did provide one small ray of sunshine in a very gloomy outlook.

CHAPTER
FOUR

THE FIRST day of the journey was spent in a continuous downpour that leaked into the coach in several places and drenched its two attendant horsemen, affording James MacIntosh serious doubts as to the necessity of this evacuation. The innkeeper at Crieff, however, prophesied with conviction that there was better weather on the way, and indeed, on the morning of the second day, the clouds were discovered to have lifted slightly and the rain slackened to a soft mist, so it was agreed to press forward towards Glenalmond.

For the occupants of the coach the journey was one of unrelieved tedium. The constant jolting and swaying soon had a detrimental effect on Mrs MacIntosh, who was consequently obliged to lie back in her corner with her eyes closed and a hot brick, supplied by her host of the night before, at her feet. Fiona and Isobel conversed spasmodically in considerate whispers, but neither was at all convinced that their mother's unprecedented travel-sickness was not merely assumed in order to punish her inconsiderate husband. This suspicion was considerably strengthened by the invalid's remarkable recovery when, four or five miles from Crieff, they heard shouts from the road ahead and the coach began to slow down.

'Now, what do you suppose can have occurred?' Mrs MacIntosh exclaimed, sitting up and pressing her cheek

to the window in an effort to see as far ahead as possible.
'Your father and Laughlan are nowhere to be seen. How
discourteous of them to leave us in suspense like this.'

'I dare say it is only a fallen tree or something blocking
the road,' Fiona hazarded with an uninterested yawn, but
Isobel, who found even such an everyday occurrence
vastly entertaining after four of the most boring days she
had ever endured, let down the window and leaned as far
out as she could. At first, all she was able to discern was
an overturned coach slewed across the road some twenty
yards ahead of where they had halted, but as she relayed
this information to her mother and Fiona, three forms
materialised from behind it. The first two were easily
identifiable as her father and Laughlan, but the third, a
tall, slim gentleman wearing a coat and breeches of dark
blue, had his back to her and was partly hidden by the
wreaths of mist.

'What a bleak spot for an accident to occur,' her
mother remarked, as Isobel resumed her seat. 'But, you
may depend upon it, such is always the way. Nothing
ever goes wrong when one is within reasonable distance
of a town, but only in places where there is no help
available and there is little chance of meeting a fellow-
traveller. Only consider how awkward it would have
been for these poor people had we not come along. Did
you perceive, Isobel, how many were in the coach?'

'Only one gentleman, as far as I could see, and judging
from his attitude I don't think he was injured. The horses
have been cut loose and I imagine there to be some
damage to the coach, as they were examining it closely.'

'The gentleman . . .' Fiona had produced a hand
mirror and was tidying her hair. 'Was he young or old?'

Isobel exchanged amused glances with her mother,
but answered indulgently, 'I was not able to see his face,
love, but his stride and carriage were those of a young

man. I dare say I should not be proved wrong if I guessed him to be under thirty.'

Mrs MacIntosh could barely contain her curiosity. 'I wonder if it can be someone with whom we are already acquainted. Really, it is too bad of Laughlan not to think that we might wish to know the reason for the halt. Pray, take another look, dear, and see if you can discover why they are taking so long.'

Isobel obediently let down the window, and found herself literally eye to eye with the last person on earth she had expected—or desired—to see.

'*You!*' she uttered in accents of deepest dismay.

'None other, my dear Miss MacIntosh.' Colin Frazer made her a sweeping bow and straightened to meet her eyes, his own brimming with laughter. 'And how happy it makes me to find you so pleased to see me. Am I to be allowed to hope that absence makes the heart grow fonder?'

Isobel emitted a strangled sound and hastily made way for her mother, who had been tapping impatiently at her arm.

'Why, Mr Frazer!' cried that lady, as Colin rose from another bow. 'This is an unfortunate predicament we find you in. I trust you are not injured?'

'Not a scratch, ma'am. My fool of a coachman took the corner too quickly and the coach overturned, being heavily laden with plants which I am conveying to my father. It was only by the greatest good luck that my horses escaped injury.'

'By Jove, it was luck indeed,' agreed James Mac-Intosh, appearing wraith-like out of the mist, with a stony-faced Laughlan at his elbow. 'If anything had happened to those beautiful animals it would have been a tragedy.'

Under cover of her mother's back, Isobel threw her

sister a glance that made plain her opinion of men whose first thought was for their horses, but Fiona had again brought out her mirror and was intently nibbling her lips to redden them.

'Will you try and talk some sense into this laddie, my love?' her father was saying to his wife. 'I have told him that there is a place for him in the coach, but he will insist on sending one of his grooms back to Crieff for help, and waiting here till it arrives.'

'Leave you here in this weather?' Mrs MacIntosh's voice floated back to her elder daughter's horrified ears. 'I declare I never heard of such a thing. Why, what would I say to your father, if you caught an inflammation of the lungs, as you very likely would? Pray, do not be so foolish.'

Colin laughed gently. 'Forgive me, ma'am, but I warrant that I am so wet already that another hour or two will make little difference. As for the inclement weather causing me to take ill, I give you my word that I am quite used to it and will take no hurt from a soaking.'

'Fustian!' Mrs MacIntosh disposed of this with an imperious gesture, ignoring the frantic tugging at the back of her skirt, and, turning to her husband, said calmly, 'Pray, have Hamish let down the steps, my dear, for I do not intend to move from this spot without Mr Frazer shall accompany us. My *certes!* How could I tell his father that we left him stranded here?'

The steps were accordingly lowered, and Colin, having supervised the removal of his crippled equipage to the side of the road, mounted them with palpable reluctance. He was, as he had warned them, extremely wet. From his limp neckcloth to his squelching boots, he was completely saturated, and his hair was plastered to his brow in half-curling wisps that dripped water into his eyes. If he was aware of his bedraggled appearance, he gave no evidence of being embarrassed by it, but Isobel was conscious of a wicked glow of satisfaction. Fiona, who had chosen not to advertise her presence until she was satisfied with her appearance, was greeted with enthusiasm.

'My word,' Colin cried, raising her fingers to his lips. 'This is indeed a pleasure! Both the celebrated Misses MacIntosh all to myself for at least half an hour. I am almost grateful to my coachman for overturning me.'

Fiona simpered, and dropped her lashes seductively. 'Why, Mr Frazer,' she fluttered coyly. 'Such compliments! I declare, I am quite decomposed!'

Colin's face froze. 'Oh, surely not?' he managed to reply with only the slightest twitch of his lips, but was immediately obliged to sit down beside her and envelop his face in his handkerchief in the pretence of drying the raindrops that still clung to it.

Throughout this exchange Isobel had kept her eyes steadfastly on the window, although in spite of frequent rubbing it steamed up so quickly that it was impossible to see much of what went on outside. As the coach moved off, her father edged his mount closer and, stooping to catch her eye, sent her a pointed look that said, as clearly as if he had spoken aloud, 'If you are rude to Colin Frazer, you will have *me* to answer to.'

She ducked her chin submissively, but kept her head turned away from Colin, whose eyes she could feel on her face, as though their unobtrusive regard were warming her averted cheek. It should have been perfectly obvious that she was disinclined to engage in conversation, but he did not seem to have noticed this, and, after a brief discussion with her mother on his reasons for returning to Transk, he turned to Isobel and remarked, 'I had hoped to meet you at Mrs Cockburn's musical evening last Friday, Miss MacIntosh. Mrs Cockburn assured me that you had been sent an invitation.'

Isobel eyed him with undisguised suspicion. Did he know that she had been forced to miss the musical evening because she had been confined to her room? Or had he truly been taken in by the story Fiona had overheard him repeating? There was a smile in his eyes as he waited for her reply, but she could not decide whether he was teasing her or not. The devil fly away with you, Colin Frazer, she longed to say aloud. Can you never open your mouth but to put me in an awkward position?

'I had intended to go,' she said, forcing a tight smile. 'But I was indisposed.'

'Well, I'm glad *I* did not have to sit through it!' Fiona interjected kittenishly, her voice several notes higher than normal. 'We went to hear Corvetti sing last month, and I was in a constant fret in case I would laugh out loud! He strikes such poses and pulls such strange faces . . .'

Fearing a possible demonstration, Isobel said hurriedly, 'Ah, but he was in excellent voice—he gave us an aria by Monsieur Lully, you know. One might have heard a pin drop.'

But Fiona would not relinquish Colin's attention so easily. 'I dare say even a musical evening will appear wondrous exciting to us after a few weeks in Inverness,' she said, pouting outrageously and making great play with her eyelashes. 'There is nothing whatsoever to do there except go to church twice on Sunday and discuss the sermon the rest of the week.'

Colin's hazel eyes crinkled appreciatively, as he asked her mother, 'Do you mean to stay long in the north, ma'am?'

'I do not expect to see Edinburgh again before next autumn,' Mrs MacIntosh sighed. 'Perhaps not even then, if this horrid rebellion is not brought to a swift conclusion. But, of course, it will be, for General Cope is bound to catch up with the rebels any day now, and that will be the end of the affair.'

Colin appeared to give this his consideration. 'Such is, I believe, the opinion in the capital,' he agreed. 'But I have recently come from my cousin's house at Doune, where they are not so sure that the government forces would have the advantage over the insurgents in an engagement. Admittedly, the rebels are, in the main, underclad, ill-fed and indifferently armed, but on the other hand your average Highlander has been raised on a diet of blood and slaughter. The McGregors, Camerons and MacDonalds are all cattle-rievers and sheep-stealers, neither of which is exactly a peaceable occupation, whereas a large proportion of Cope's soldiers are raw recruits who have never faced anything more alarming than a tavern brawl. It will be interesting to see how they stand up to a Highland charge. Perhaps General Cope will have to look to his laurels.'

'Oh, never say such a thing!' protested Mrs Mac-Intosh, looking horrified, while Fiona, with an affectation that chilled her sister to the bone, caught hold of Colin's sleeve and wailed,

'Surely not, Mr Frazer? Why, Papa promised that the revolt would be over in no time and we might return to Edinburgh! Supposing it should drag on and on? *Two* winters in Inverness would be beyond bearing. I should die of torpordity!'

'I sincerely hope you will not, ma'am,' Colin assured her with suspicious gravity. 'I am depending on you and your family to help preserve my own sanity. My father is hopeful that, if the alterations we are planning to the great hall are completed in time, we might extend our hospitality to those of our friends that are still in the district and enjoy a few days of festivity to welcome in the New Year. I do hope you won't disappoint me?' His smile included them all. 'I fear I cannot offer you entertainment such as you might have enjoyed in Edinburgh, but perhaps, by that time, half a loaf will appear better than no bread.'

Fiona and her mother cried out with pleasure, protesting, with an enthusiasm that only partially covered Isobel's frozen silence, that a visit to Transk was a treat to be anticipated with pleasure at any season. But the invitation was not one that could be expected to fill Isobel with elation. There would be little pleasure in avoiding Colin every waking hour, and unless his feelings for her had undergone a radical change, it would be a constant game of hide-and-seek.

But perhaps he had abandoned all hope of winning her round? Isobel considered this for a moment, her eyes on the misted window, and discovered that this possibility would not necessarily make her visit any less trying. She might not want Colin for herself, but it would be too mortifying to have to watch him pay court to someone else. Fiona, for instance.

Irritated by this thought, she sent him a malevolent glance and found him smiling at her, the picture of smug satisfaction, as though he imagined her to be as delighted at his invitation as were her mother and sister. Since politeness prevented her from enlightening him on this point, she maintained a discreet silence till Aberfeldy was reached, where, much to her relief, their passenger was set down. Even then her trials were not at an end for, after sending back assistance for his stranded coachman, Colin insisted that his good Samaritans must join him for such sustenance as the inn could provide, and it was over an hour before they took the road again.

Isobel did not enjoy the meal, but with Colin at her

elbow and her father's basilisk stare across the table, she had no choice but to act with complaisance and was uncomfortably aware that Colin regarded this attitude as encouraging. There was not the least sign in his demeanour that he regarded himself as a rejected suitor. On the contrary, he could not hide the fact that he was supremely happy to be with her, and each time he spoke to her his eyes moved over her face as though they were starved for the sight of her.

As always, she shrank from this attack on her modesty, berating herself for the way she coloured up so easily and trying to ignore the uneasy fluttering beneath her ribs. She hated him for making her feel like this, constantly at a disadvantage and, surely, a figure of fun to all who witnessed her discomfiture. Hugh Murray, she had no doubt, would never have put her to the blush with such ardent looks, nor would he have leaned so close that her tongue stuttered and stumbled over her words, making her want to throw herself on the floor and drum her heels with vexation.

Before the meal was over, she had whipped herself into a shocking temper. This was exacerbated by the suspicion that her father had not sent Colin packing with the finality she had demanded of him but had actively encouraged him to bide his time and try again. This so incensed her that when they emerged into the inn yard to wait for the coach to be brought round, she moved away from the others and stood with her back to them, trying to calm herself by gazing out across the now sunlit hills.

But it was too much to expect that Colin would respect her—surely quite obvious—desire for solitude. He was at her shoulder almost immediately, standing just that little bit too close for comfort and speaking with the warm-toned intimacy that affected her breathing so detestably. 'You look pale today, Isobel, and there are shadows about your eyes. Perhaps a few weeks' rest away from the diversions of Edinburgh will be a blessing in disguise.'

Isobel could neither look at him nor bring herself to make reply, but he continued easily, toying with a stray curl which had escaped from her cap,

'I must say, I am greatly looking forward to having you virtually all to myself for a while instead of sharing you with all your Edinburgh beaux. We shall see if I cannot make you think a little more kindly of me than you do at present.'

He was trying to provoke her again. She could tell by the barely suppressed chuckle in his voice, but she was determined to remain calm. 'Your optimism does you great credit, Mr Frazer,' she said very sweetly, her eyes on the cloud shadows racing across the strath. 'But, really, I feel you would have done better to remain in Edinburgh and take your chance with the rebels.'

This appeared to strike him as amusing. 'It was not the impending battle that sent me hot-foot northwards, Isobel! There is only one bait that could lure me to Inverness at this time of year, and I'm sure I don't need to tell you what *that* is.' He leaned forward to bring his lips momentarily close to her ear. 'I'm afraid you don't shake me off so easily, my love.'

She drew in her breath to disabuse him of this assumption, but made the mistake of turning to look at him and discovered that he was awaiting her reaction with eyes brimming with hilarity. She looked him straight in the eye, knowing that her face was stained with a blush of quite volcanic proportions, but determined not to be outfaced. 'Ah! But I *will* shake you off, Colin Frazer!' she hissed passionately. 'I shall take leave to tell you that I find your company distasteful. I don't like your manners, I don't like your horrid teasing, and I—do—not—

like—you! Is that clear?'

He gazed at her in mixed horror and amazement. 'Such lies!' he said, shaking his head sadly. 'And in one so young and fair! Do you believe them yourself, I wonder?'

'Indeed I do!'

An incredulous smile tilted one corner of his mouth. 'Truly? But, darling, you are too virginal for words! Won't you admit to being just a little attracted? Don't you feel the Pulse of Life beat a little faster when we are together?'

His eyes still sparkled with laughter, and she was sure he was playing with her like a cat with a mouse. 'I wish you will just go away and leave me alone!'

'Oh come, now. Why should you be afraid of me?'

'Afraid?' she gave a short laugh. 'What rubbish!'

He tilted his head to one side and lifted one specu-lative eyebrow. 'Is it possible, then, that you are afraid of *yourself*, Isobel?'

Isobel drew in her breath with a gasp of pure exasper-ation, and, rather than rise to his taunts, she turned with a swirl of skirts and strode back to where her mother was about to join Fiona in the coach. She was seriously put out, but so determined to hide it that she was able to respond with a distant smile when Colin bade her farewell with the assurance that she would be seeing him soon. It was not until the inn was left far behind, however, that she was able to look out at the glories of the passing scenery with equanimity.

Mrs MacIntosh, by that time, had quite forgotten her travel-sickness and sat up in her corner with every evidence of enjoyment. 'What a lucky chance to run into Colin Frazer like that,' she beamed. 'You may be sure of it, Isobel, he has heard nothing of your escapade, so if you will only treat him with a little more civility and stop behaving like a spoiled child, all may not yet be lost.'

Isobel sighed and looked out of the window at General Wade's five-arched bridge, which they were crossing at a spanking trot. 'My opinion of Mr Frazer has not changed, Mama,' she said wearily. 'I would rather spend my days in comfortable spinsterhood than marry him.'

'If you imagine spinsterhood to be at all comfortable,' said her exasperated mother, 'you are much mistaken. I cannot think your Aunt Euphemia's position to be enviable, for instance, for she is hemmed in by convention on every side and is dependent upon your Papa for a home. Only consider how lonely it must be for her when we are in Edinburgh.'

Isobel pointed out that if her aunt were lonely, she would accompany them, instead of insisting on being left at home in Inverness, but her mother ignored her.

'As a married woman, you would have much more freedom, and Colin Frazer has wealth enough to guarantee that you would want for nothing. All this nonsense about not loving the fellow!' she tut-tutted irritably. 'How can you possibly know whether you love him or not until you are married? Good heavens, you hardly *know* him!'

'But you were in love with Papa . . .'

'What is that to the point, pray? I assure you, that fact did not influence your grandpapa in the slightest, when he agreed to the match.'

'I only wish he might offer for *me*,' Fiona put in dreamily. 'Is he not *the* most attractive man? Have you noticed the length of his *eye*lashes? And his *voice* . . . ! Oh *certes!* It makes me feel as though I were floating in warm honey! Only his eyes look so . . . so *amused*, sometimes. I can't help wondering—just the teeniest bit—whether he could be laughing at me.'

'If you *will* insist on describing yourself as "decomposed" when you mean "discomposed", it's not really surprising, is it?' Isobel snapped, with such uncharacteristic acidity that both Fiona and her mother blinked at her. 'Indeed you may count yourself lucky that he chose to be amused by your affectations. I would not dare to put on airs with him for fear of a severe damper.'

'He treats Fiona with the indulgence he would afford a younger sister,' Mrs MacIntosh said placatingly, patting Isobel's arm. 'I am persuaded he had no intention of making you jealous.'

'*Jealous?*' Isobel repeated incredulously, and gave a burst of rather brittle laughter. 'Oh, really, Mama! You do let your imagination run away with you sometimes!'

'Mmm . . . well,' Mrs MacIntosh changed the subject forcibly. 'I must say I take it very kindly in him to invite us to Transk. I'll wager the idea of a house-party has never entered his father's head . . . yet. I do not doubt for a minute that Colin hit on the idea only in order to further his suit with you, Isobel. Mark my words, we shall find him on the doorstep before we are properly settled in.'

'I sincerely hope we shall not,' Isobel stated trenchantly, but without much confidence. 'I have already told Papa that I do not wish to marry him, and I take it ill in you both that you thrust me into his company and allow me to be harried from pillar to post . . .'

'Will you stop talking such fustian?' Mrs MacIntosh exploded, flushing bright pink. 'I have decided that you must become better acquainted with Colin Frazer. Only then will you see what a charming person he is. No, do not argue with me, I know all your objections off by heart already. It is high time you learnt to do as you are told.' She plied her fan agitatedly for a few seconds before she was able to continue in a changed tone, 'But, how satisfying to have a little gaiety to look forward to, even if it is so far away. We must definitely have something new to wear for the occasion, for the dresses you have are not suitable for anything but the Assembly Rooms. Not that Transk is not worth dressing up for, but Edinburgh fashions might be thought a trifle ostentatious in the country. Perhaps a nice flowered satin for you, Fiona, and for you, Isobel . . . white, I think. I am determined that you shall look your best, whatever you may say to the contrary.'

Isobel listened with half an ear, her eyes on a glistening stretch of the Tay, just visible through the trees, and her mind on Hugh Murray, who might already, for all she knew, be dead on the field of battle. Colin Frazer's view of the rebel army was immensely cheering. Virtually everyone else had dismissed the insurgents' chances with a laugh, almost as though it were a foregone conclusion that General Cope would squash the rebellion at a stroke. But now it seemed possible that Prince Charles Edward might, after all, manage to bring off his wild gamble and gain the throne. And, if that were so, his followers, instead of ending up as dispossessed renegades, would be in positions of preferment.

This was a comforting thought, not only because it boded well for Hugh, but because it might make him more eligible as a husband, and, despite all the promptings of common sense, it was as a husband that he was beginning to figure in Isobel's thoughts.

She held her long, introspective confinement to blame for this foolish fancy, and in her more rational moments she tried resolutely to banish him from her mind. Yet it was impossible to rid herself of the hope of seeing him again. The tall, fair man whom her mother had seen in her tea-cup was retrieved from the mental rubbish-dump to which she had instantly consigned him and reassembled in Hugh's image—foreordained, inevitable—and therefore of an importance that was yet to manifest itself.

In the meantime it gave her a warm and comfortable feeling just to think about him and to use the memory of their one meeting to blot out the thought of the months of boredom that lay ahead.

CHAPTER
FIVE

INVERNESS HAD not changed for the better during the
short absense of Isobel and her family. For all that the
sun came out to welcome them home, it was with
somewhat jaundiced eyes that they viewed the familiar
gaunt shape of the castle, perched on its hill above the
river; and the pervading odour of fish and tar that drifted
up from the harbour evoked no answering twinge of
nostalgia. None the less, it was a welcome relief to go to
bed at night between one's own well aired and sweet
smelling sheets, knowing that one might lie abed next
day if one chose, instead of rising, ill-rested and stiff, to
re-enter a coach that had taken on the nature of an
instrument of torture, rather than a means of transport.

The MacIntosh residence in Church Street was larger
than most of its neighbours, because James's father had
been possessed of a large family of girls, whom it was
necessary to keep in the public eye. As it was, he had
managed to marry off only four of them, and the other
three were still living together with one of their sisters,
now widowed.

The small staff of servants was supervised mainly by
Mrs MacIntosh's unmarried sister Euphemia Logan, a
deceptively mild woman in her middle thirties, who
justified her existence by harrying the maids unmerci-
fully and polishing everything within reach. She had
come to Inverness ten years previously on the death of

her mother, and had made herself so unobtrusively indispensable that her periodic visits to her brother in Dalnacardoch caused havoc in her sister's house. Shy and retiring by nature, she was not totally at ease among the many visitors who called at Church Street when the family was in residence, and for that reason was relieved when her sister now showed signs of living quietly for a change, spending much of the day in her room and making no plans for any large-scale entertaining.

One visitor who was always made welcome, however, was Colin Frazer. As Mrs MacIntosh had predicted, he arrived on the doorstep barely a week after the family had arrived home, but, being informed (quite truthfully, as it happened) that Mr MacIntosh had driven his wife and daughters into Nairn, he sat quite happily, drinking tea with Euphemia, for upwards of an hour. Naturally, Euphemia was charmed.

'Not the least sign that he was disappointed to find only me at home,' she informed Isobel on the latter's return home, 'and, although I told him that it would be some time before you might be expected to return, he was in no hurry to leave. *Such* an interesting boy. I shall never understand why you dislike him, Isobel.'

She could have informed her aunt that she was aware how ingratiating Colin could be when there was something to be gained by it, but she merely shrugged. After all, even if he managed to win over all her family with his insidious crawling, she herself knew him too well to be swayed by their opinions. A week later she was given another opportunity to observe his subversive tactics.

He arrived an hour before supper, but spent so long closeted with James MacIntosh that courtesy demanded, as Isobel's mother later defended herself, that he be invited to share their repast. Under the watchful eyes of her father, Isobel was forced to be civil, if not exactly effervescent, but it seemed to her that the meal would never end.

Laughlan also preserved a disapproving silence for most of the meal but, when the conversation turned to the excellent shooting to be had at Transk at that season, he so far forgot his prejudices to exclaim, 'By Jove! That sounds like famous sport. Papa will never take me shooting, you know, Mr Frazer. He says I am like to blow his head off. But how am I to learn to handle a gun if I never get any practice?'

His father silenced him with a glare, but Colin nodded sympathetically. 'Then you must certainly come down to Transk for a few days and allow me to give you a few tips.' He turned to his host with a lifted brow. 'You would have no objection to that, would you, sir?'

'Objection? No, no.' James pursed his lips and sent another glare at Laughlan. 'The boy couldn't have a better tutor. But, good God, you don't want to saddle yourself with a scruffy schoolboy. He will have you in Bedlam before the day is out.'

'I trust not, sir.' Colin exchanged grins with an elated Laughlan. 'Besides, I assure you, I do not consider him a scruffy schoolboy. Shall we say Saturday, then? Perhaps you would care to join us, sir? I know my father would be overjoyed if I could persuade you. He is greatly missing my mother at present, as she has gone on an extended visit to my sister, whose first child is expected at Christmas.'

'Mebbe I will at that!' James's eyes glittered appreciatively. 'Ay, why not? It is time I saw Johnnie again and had a sup of that excellent brandy he keeps. I'll wager it tastes all the better for not having paid tax!'

Colin coloured slightly at this and shot an embarrassed glance in Isobel's direction, but was saved from having to reply by Mrs MacIntosh, who remarked,

'See that you wear your heavy stockings then, Laughlan. We do not wish a recurrence of that nasty cough that you took last autumn.' She turned to Colin and added confidentially, 'I know I can rely on you to look after him, Mr Frazer, but he has always been subject to chills and will do nothing to avoid them.'

Laughlan was blushing to the roots of his coppery hair, but Colin did not look at him. 'You may be quite easy on that score, ma'am,' he smiled. 'I will engage to return Laughlan to you intact. I only regret that lack of a hostess precludes my inviting ladies to Transk but, as my grandmother intends to take up residence with us shortly, I hope to remedy that in the near future. I believe you are acquainted with my grandmother, Miss Logan? She frequently enquires after you in her letters and asks me to deliver her good wishes.'

Euphemia started, and dropped the piece of orange which she had been conveying to her mouth. 'Why—Oh yes. How very kind . . .' she stammered, blushing. 'She enjoys her customary good health, I hope?'

'Yes, indeed. Her constitution is remarkable for one of her years, but only the imminent advance of the rebels to Glasgow persuaded her to undertake the journey north.'

'*What?*' Isobel did not realise that she had spoken aloud till Colin turned to her with raised brows, but she went on, spurred by a consuming curiosity, 'I mean . . . are the rebels still advancing? Surely General Cope has caught up with them by now?'

Colin laid down the walnut that he had been absently cracking between his long fingers and gave her the full benefit of his appraising stare, under which she felt her cheeks flaming guiltily.

'There was an engagement, of course,' he answered, after what seemed a long silence, 'just a day or so after

we left Edinburgh. The two forces met in the neighbourhood of Prestonpans, where General Cope's army was
completely routed in a conflict which lasted less than a
quarter of an hour.'

Isobel could not trust herself to speak, but Fiona
cried, 'Routed? Cope? You did not tell us of this, Papa.'

James was viewing both his daughters with suspicion.
'Had I realised with what interest you were following the
campaign, I should naturally have informed you immediately. Regrettably, I did not, until this moment,
fully appreciate the aura of romance that surrounds the
Young Pretender.'

Mrs MacIntosh laughed lightly. 'One cannot but take
an interest, my love,' she reasoned, 'when the length of
time we must remain in Inverness is entirely dependent
on the duration of the rebellion. But I am persuaded that
the outcome of the battle must have been due to some
stroke of luck. Surely, Mr Frazer, that rabble of hillmen
could not otherwise have withstood an organised
attack?'

Colin reflected for a moment before answering.
'Would that I might agree with you, ma'am, but I fear
that was not the case. I have received a letter from my
cousin Gillies Frazer, whom I believe you have met. He
was actually engaged in the battle, on the government
side, and he admits that the rebels charged with such
ferocity, and with such a hideous noise, that the less
experienced soldiers were thrown into a panic and even
the veterans were taken aback. The battery of which
Gillies was in command fired one round—which took a
reasonable toll—but before they were able to reload,
they were overcome by Camerons, sword in hand, for
they had thrown away their muskets without firing them.
In places, he swears, the Pretender's line was ten deep.'

James nodded in agreement. 'That tallies with what I

heard, from various sources. A disgraceful business, but it will not happen again, take my word for it. Next time Cope will know what to expect and be prepared for it.'

Isobel fingered her knife, striving not to appear too interested. 'But the rebels did not escape without losses? Were there many killed?'

'I heard one estimate of fifty killed, eighty wounded,' Colin said, turning to his host for confirmation.

'Ay. That's near enough what I heard. But Cope lost ten times that amount, they tell me, and nearly a thousand taken prisoner. If that's true, I am glad I got my family away when I did. Those rebels sound like an army of butchers.'

'Yes, indeed,' Mrs MacIntosh agreed. 'We would not have been as safe in Edinburgh as we are here.'

'There was some alarm in the capital about that time, I believe,' Colin remarked. 'The Pretender's son ordered a blockade of the castle, and General Guest—who, you must admit, is as game as a pullet for all his eighty-five years—retaliated by threatening to fire on the town.'

Fiona threw up her hands in alarm. 'Oh, but he would never have done so. Why, such an act would be in-human!'

'Nevertheless, shots were fired,' Colin assured her calmly. 'Whether anyone was injured I cannot say, but I do know that some windows were shattered and the neighbouring residents considerably alarmed.'

Mrs MacIntosh digested this in silence for several seconds and then, with an abrupt change of ground, leaned across Laughlan to eye Isobel sternly and say, 'You hear that, my dear? Now let us have no more talk about going back to Edinburgh until we know we may sleep safely in our beds!'

Since this unprovoked rebuke left Isobel momentarily at a loss for words, the subject was dropped in favour of a discussion on a horse that James had seen and was of a mind to purchase, so she was able to close her ears and give some thought to the subject uppermost in her mind, namely Hugh Murray.

During the weeks that had passed since their meeting, scarcely a day had gone by when she had not spent some time in contemplation of the strange attraction he held for her. How very different from Colin Frazer he was, she thought idly, viewing that gentleman through her lashes. Could it be that very difference which drew her? It seemed unlikely, for instance, that Hugh would marry a girl who did not love him, as Colin seemed willing to do. There was something about Hugh, a gentleness of expression about his eyes and mouth, that told Isobel he would need to be loved, and, to a certain extent 'looked after'. The girl he married would have to be sensible and practical as well as affectionate, and she knew where such a girl was to be found.

'These must be happy thoughts, Miss MacIntosh. Do you smile so sweetly when you think of me, I wonder?'

The teasing voice so close to her ear made her start, but she had no need to turn round to know who had spoken. Looking about her, she realised how abstracted she had been, for the table was deserted and the rest of the family were just disappearing through the door at the far end of the room, her father bringing up the rear and talking over his shoulder, as though he believed his daughter and his guest to be just behind him. Realising that Colin was still waiting for an answer to his question, she rose and gave him an icy smile.

'I'm afraid I don't think of you at all, Mr Frazer,' she said sweetly, and had the satisfaction of seeing him blink.

'Not at *all*?' he rallied, clapping a dramatic hand to his heart. 'You are too severe by half, ma'am. Pray, what have I done to be thus excluded from your thoughts, as well as from your heart?'

Isobel willed herself not to blush, and said pointedly, 'Shall we join the others? The servants will be in presently to remove the covers.' She turned towards the door, but Colin's tall frame and the chair which he had drawn back for her blocked the passage between the table and the wall, and he made no attempt to move aside.

'Must you always behave like a bird in a trap every time I speak to you?' he queried plaintively. 'What harm could I possibly cause you, here in your own home with your parents on the other side of that door? I only want to know why you refuse to marry me.'

'Mr Frazer, please . . .' She tried to look outraged, and her now flaming cheeks and heaving bosom were evidence of her mortification. 'My father—Surely he made my feelings clear? Why can you not accept the fact that I do not wish to marry you, instead of hounding me in this shameful manner?'

'Because I love you, Isobel,' he said softly, smiling a little. 'I have never given up anything I really wanted without a fight, and I have never wanted anything as much as I want you.'

Frantically she looked past him to the door, praying that her father was not so lost to propriety as to leave them alone together. Apparently he was. Turning to Colin, she said coldly, 'May I go now?' But he only looked at her as if she had asked for his head on a plate.

'No,' he answered, without the slightest trace of shame. 'Will you not sit down? What I have to say may take some time.'

Isobel almost gasped at his audacity, but deducing from his manner that he was in no expectation of being interrupted, she was too aghast to make any reply other than a curt refusal. Colin merely shrugged and leaned one shoulder against the wall in a negligent attitude.

'As you choose. It seems a pity that I must trap you into letting me speak to you alone, but you leave me no alternative . . . Was there ever a more trying wench?' he burst out suddenly. 'What, pray, is so very terrible in wanting to know why you dislike me? Am I to let myself be sent packing without a reason?'

Isobel looked away from him stubbornly. He might talk as much as he chose, but he could not compel her to answer him. His shoulders came away from the wall impatiently.

'You liked me well enough once,' he insisted. 'I know you did. Will you tell me what I have done to merit this animosity?'

'The hour is late,' Isobel could not resist retorting. 'I have no time to begin cataloguing your failings.'

'Are they so very many?' His lashes drooped momentarily, but Isobel had seen her shaft go home, and turned away quickly, ashamed of her quick tongue.

'Are they not remediable faults, perhaps?' he probed determinedly, ducking his head to see her downcast face. 'If so, I shall remedy them. Call me a rabbit and you shall have your lion. Say I am too forceful and you may lead me by the nose. Tell me I talk too much and I shall take on the appearance of a Trappist monk.'

Isobel suppressed a smile and lifted her eyes, but finding his face aglow with laughter, she was immediately incensed. 'Can you never be serious about anything?' she demanded in a piqued tone.

'But I *am* serious, my love.' He sobered instantly, laying a hand on his heart. 'Never more so in my life. If I am flippant it is only because I cannot resist trying to make you smile. Will you not take me at my word?

Mould me closer to your heart's desire, Isobel, for without you I care not what I am. Listen to me,' he added with a whimsical smile. 'Do you realise what it costs me to say that? I am putting my very soul into your hands, and you will not even meet my eyes.'

Isobel looked down at the lace handkerchief that her hands had been methodically shredding. 'You can never be the man I would wish to marry, Mr Frazer. The leopard cannot change its spots, and I fear our natures are too divergent for harmony. I can only hope that it will not be long before you meet a girl who will make you a better wife than I ever could.'

Judging the matter to be closed, she gently put aside the chair which he had forgotten to guard and made to pass him, but he moved with the disconcerting rapidity of a striking snake. His arms encircled her, pinning her against him with a strength that rendered futile her puny efforts to disengage herself. As he bent his head, she jerked her own away, snapping, 'Don't dare.'

'No,' he said equably, his mouth all but touching hers. 'But you see how easy it would be? Don't play with me, Isobel. Let us have no more talk about another girl. There will be no other wife for me and no other husband for you, let that be understood. I shall wait for you if I must, but in the end you will be mine.'

He let her go abruptly and, finding herself free, she did not delay to give utterance to the fury that consumed her, but made straight for the door. His voice halted her with her hand on the doorknob.

'Your hair, my love. It looks enchanting falling down like that, but don't you think your parents might view it with suspicion? I would hate them to think you might have been kissing me.'

She flushed crimson, grinding her teeth with vexation, but paused to pin up her tumbled curls. 'My parents would think no such thing,' she told him rudely. 'They *know* my opinion of you!'

He ignored this remark and came towards her, holding out his hand for the pins which she was hurriedly replacing in her hair.

'Here, let me help you. You are making it worse than ever and, remember, my reputation is at stake as well as yours. No, I am not going to kiss you, so you may stand still . . . There, that is a little better. Probably not up to your maid's standard, but if you can now do something with your facial expression, it may escape notice.'

Isobel's mortification had sufficiently cooled by this time to allow her to say 'Thank you' with only a hint of stiffness but, a moment later, it blazed into life again as he remarked, with unmistakable intent to shock her,

'There, now. No one would guess that a moment ago you were in my arms.'

'Oh—you . . .' she exclaimed, whisking away from him. 'Oh, what a despicable creature you are, Colin Frazer! If I were a man, I would run you through!'

'What have I done now?' he spread his arms in counterfeit dismay. 'I only said . . .'

'I heard what you said. Will you kindly stand away from that door?'

'I wouldn't dream of it.' he told her with finality. 'Not if you intend to satisfy your family's curiosity by joining them with such an eloquent expression on your face. If your father sees you looking like that, he will assuredly call me out without putting himself to the trouble of asking any questions.'

'You seem very confident that I will not report to my father that you treated me like a tavern wench!' Isobel flared, but he only smiled coolly.

'Well, will you?'

Knowing full well that she would not, Isobel answered

not at all, and marched through the door, which he was now holding open. But as she entered the drawing-room, she made an effort to compose her features. Things were embarrassing enough as they were without her father making a scene—if, indeed, he would—for it was now evident that he was on Colin's side.

Her parents' complicity was immediately apparent in the way they barely looked up as she entered, but Fiona and Laughlan took no pains to conceal their curiosity and only took their eyes off Isobel's face to scrutinise Colin's. Finding nothing in either of them, they began to converse with each other in hushed whispers that made their sister long to bang their heads together. Only Euphemia appeared uninterested and immediately engaged Colin in a conversation that lasted until he took his leave.

As soon as the door had closed behind him, Isobel found herself fixed by four pairs of expectant eyes. Seething with indignation, she returned their gaze in a defiant silence for a moment and then, rising, said in a tone of unmistakable restraint, 'If I may be excused, I think I shall go to bed now. Good night,' and made a hurried exit.

CHAPTER
SIX

By CONSTANTLY pumping her father and Colin, Isobel was able to keep her finger on the pulse of the rebellion. Although the news was almost a week old when it reached her, she was beside herself with jubilation when she heard that the rebels had crossed the border and were at last on English soil. That they had by-passed Glasgow on their march south was as much a bone of contention to Colin's grandmother, after her long journey to escape them, as it was a relief to the inhabitants of 'the second city', but the people of Jedburgh were not so lucky. Rumour had it that every able-bodied man in that town had gone into hiding to avoid being pressed into service with the Young Pretender, and only the ladies, whose sentiments Isobel could understand, remained to welcome the 'bonnie Prince'.

It seemed incredible that the half-naked, undisciplined rabble who had invested Edinburgh should have won so far, but by the end of November it was known that Carlisle had fallen to the insurgents, not only the town this time, but the well-manned garrison as well, and a fortnight later they were reported to be almost at Derby. Inverness was agog with the news, but it was widely felt that the further south the rebel army marched, the more comfortable it would be in the north.

The weather continued dry but bitterly cold, with

brief flurries of powdery snow that capped the hills and
lodged in the gullies, but Isobel and Fiona rode out every
day, accompanied by Laughlan or Hamish. This was not
so much that they needed the exercise, but to escape the
bustle that Colin's forthcoming entertainment had
caused in the house in Church Street.

Fiona's pale lemon dress had already been made up
and trimmed to her own and her mother's satisfaction,
but Isobel had caused a major upheaval by refusing to
wear white satin and choosing a chocolate-brown velvet,
which was as becoming as it was unsuitable. Deaf to all
remonstrances, however, she allowed herself to be dissuaded from having the underdress tailored in a match-
ing satin and settled for pale apricot silk embroidered
with roses, but the extra work that this had involved held
up production to an alarming degree. Her father even
suggested that she should have a hooded cloak to match,
although the dress allowance that he permitted her had
long since evaporated. The long hours of fittings and
discussion were inexpressibly tedious to both girls, and
after one particularly trying morning they dislodged
Laughlan from his eternal target-practice and demanded
his escort for a canter over the moors.

The sun was well past the zenith before the town was
left behind, but the sky was clear and there would be
three or four hours left before the early dusk would
overtake them, so they rode along the shores of the Firth
before turning inland across the vast expanse of heather
called Drummossie Moor. Here the going was safe
enough to give their horses their heads, and they raced
across the barren plain and up the slight incline at the
other side with the crisp breeze whipping the colour into
their cheeks and stinging their eyes so that the tears ran
in horizontal streaks across their temples. Laughlan
breasted the rise a little way ahead of his sisters, clutch-

ing his hat and whooping with exultation, but he drew rein so suddenly that Fiona, who was just beside him, was forced to swerve to avoid a collision.

'Hey—Look out, Laughlan!' she shouted indignantly. 'You shouldn't stop so suddenly. You might have had me out of the saddle! What are you looking at?'

'The door has been replaced,' he explained, indicating a small bothy just visible through a clump of rowans. Isobel brought Stella to a halt beside him, and followed his pointing finger with her eyes.

'Why, so it has. That used to belong to old Angus Urquhart, did it not? I remember thinking, last time we passed, that it was becoming very tumbledown. Now you mention it, the door *was* lying on the ground. But, what of it? Someone must be using the place as a store for wood or something. Come on, it's time we were turning back.'

She touched a knee to her mount and moved forward, but Laughlan, after starting to follow her, changed his mind.

'I must just take a look. Wait here for me, I shall not be more than two minutes.'

Before Isobel could open her mouth to argue with him, he had set Caesar at the slope and was soon out of earshot.

'Oh—Really!' she exclaimed. 'What a trying boy he is, to be sure. We must sit here freezing while he goes nosing about for mysteries where there are none. I hope no one has put a bull in there out of the snow.'

'Serve him right if he did blunder into a bull!' Fiona replied through chattering teeth. 'But, who knows, he may find something interesting.'

They watched listlessly as Laughlan disappeared behind the trees, to emerge a few seconds later in front of the part of the bothy that was visible. He dismounted and went to peer in at the doorway, holding aside the rotten door that had been propped up in the opening. Suddenly he leapt across the threshold with an agility that made him appear to have been plucked inside by an unseen hand.

Isobel stiffened with surprise, hearing Fiona's sharp intake of breath. 'It's all right,' she calmed her. 'He has just gone inside for a closer look.' But when at the end of a few minutes Laughlan did not reappear, she said sharply, 'Come on,' and urged Stella up the hill.

The bothy, on closer inspection, was even more dilapidated than it had appeared from a distance. Parts of the surrounding dyke had crumbled away, and what fallen masonry had not been removed for the repair of near-by farms was covered with moss, but the walls were still standing and the roof was intact. As Isobel dismounted, Laughlan appeared in the doorway, his face the colour of an underdone bannock.

'Isobel . . .' He grasped her sleeve and began to draw her towards the door. 'There is a man inside! I—I think he is dying!'

She stopped short, and Fiona, behind her, gave a despairing wail.

'Dying . . .?' Isobel whispered. 'Dying of what?'

'A wound.' Laughlan swallowed hard and drew a hand across his mouth. 'A great gaping wound in his thigh. It was covered with a piece of dirty rag, but . . . I looked.'

From his face, Isobel could see that he wished he hadn't. Her courage failed her at the thought of going in, but since Laughlan could not be trusted to know what to do and Fiona was half-fainting already, she had no choice. Drawing a deep breath, she nodded to her brother, and followed him through the doorway.

It was dark inside, but as her eyes grew accustomed to

the gloom, she picked out a huddled figure lying on a pile of heather against one wall. Pushing past Laughlan, she went to kneel beside the sorry couch. Its occupant was a youth of about nineteen, fair-haired and pallid, a faint film of sweat about his brow and upper lip. His short jacket was torn and muddy and his kilt had been pushed up to bare the jagged wound that ran diagonally across his thigh. The ragged piece of tartan that Laughlan had removed lay where he had dropped it, wet and sticky with blood, and a similarly sodden plaid was draped across the youth's chest. Isobel looked away quickly as a wave of nausea passed over her, and her eye fell on a bashed pewter bowl lying on the floor. Pointing to this, she said,

'That must be his. Take it and fill it at the nearest burn. Give it a thorough rinsing first, as it is very likely filthy. Be as quick as you can and don't let yourself be seen. If this man is a rebel, there would be no point in saving his life only to have him taken and hanged.'

'Perhaps he is not a rebel after all,' Laughlan suggested. 'I only thought that he might be because he has a gun. The rebels are all in England, but he might be a drover.'

His sister fixed him with a stare. 'Do you mean to stand there chattering all afternoon?' she snapped. 'Do you imagine a drover would be at such pains to conceal himself when he was in such urgent need of a doctor? Be off with you, and run all the way.'

He folded his lips in a hurt manner and hurried out into the already failing light, while Isobel turned back to her patient. He was quite insensible, probably from loss of blood, but his breathing seemed strong enough, so perhaps he was not so close to death as Laughlan had feared. The wound was still bleeding sluggishly in a slow trickle that seeped into the heather. It would have to be bathed and bound tightly, but with what? Quickly she hitched up the skirt of her habit and tried to tear a strip off her petticoat. It should have been easy, but the fine cambric resisted the efforts of her shaking fingers and she was forced to use her teeth to make the first rent. After that, the rest was simpler, and by the time Laughlan returned with the water she had enough to make a start.

'That Fiona,' her brother snorted derisively. 'She has been as sick as a cat, so I told her to stay where she is and mind the horses. We don't want her fainting in here. Is he going to die, do you think?'

'I don't think so.' Isobel swabbed the wound carefully, afraid to dislodge the clot that was beginning to form. 'It doesn't look so deep now, but I am not sure. I have never seen anyone so badly injured before, so I cannot judge. I don't even know if I am doing the right thing in bathing it, but since I hesitate to tell anyone about him until we are sure whether or not he is a rebel, we must just do what seems best. There doesn't seem to be any pus, but I cannot remember if that is a good thing or not. Now, then, do you raise his leg very gently while I bind on this pad. Steady, now . . .'

Tenderly, Laughlan eased the cold limb off the ground, his lips compressed with compassion, but, for all his care, the youth moved his head slightly on his bracken pillow and a low, sobbing moan escaped from between his parted lips. Isobel winced in sympathy, but continued to apply the bandage, clenching her teeth. The pad in position, she motioned to Laughlan to lower the limb, and, when she put up a hand to brush back her fallen hair, she found her brow damp with sweat.

'Put the plaid over him again,' she said in a voice that sounded faint and far away.

'But it is soaked with blood—Feel it,' Laughlan held out the plaid for her inspection.

She nodded, without touching it. 'It may be, but we have no spare coats to leave him, and if you go home without yours there will be a lot of explaining to do, so it must be the plaid, blood or no blood. The wind whistling through that doorway would freeze him. I only wish we might light a fire for him before we go, but it will not be dark enough to conceal the smoke for some time yet.'

Dampening her handkerchief in the last of the water, she began to sponge the youth's face and the fine, strong column of neck that his torn jacket exposed. She had turned to Laughlan to bid him refill the bowl in order to leave some drinking-water beside the bed, when a faint sound at her elbow made her start. The boy's eyelids were half-lifted and he was making soft, semi-intelligible noises in his throat.

'Hush, now,' Isobel whispered soothingly, forcibly reminded of Laughlan in a similar condition.

His eyes opened completely and he looked past her at Laughlan, trying to raise his head, and muttering, 'Must leave me . . . please go on . . . I'll manage . . .'

Isobel pressed him back gently. 'You are safe now. But you must lie down and rest, for you have hurt your leg, and if you move it it will start to bleed again.'

He stared at her uncomprehendingly, frowning slightly as though struggling for recognition. 'Who are you? Where is my brother?'

Laughlan had moved closer to Isobel's shoulder and now leaned over the youth, grinning reassuringly.

'We haven't seen your brother; but don't worry, we shall take care of you. My name is Laughlan MacIntosh and this is my sister Isobel. My other sister, Fiona, is outside being sick,' he added conversationally, and would have continued, had not Isobel dug him in the ribs.

'No doubt your brother will soon return,' she smiled. 'But, since we are not able to wait till he does so, do you think you could remember to tell him that we shall not give away your hiding-place? When he sees that your wound has been bandaged, he may be afraid to stay here. We are not Jacobites, but neither would we wish to see you taken. That is, if you are indeed a rebel?'

The youth looked from brother to sister doubtfully. 'I thank you, but . . .' He broke off as a sharp cry from Fiona floated in from outside.

Isobel and Laughlan leapt to their feet and turned in the direction of the sound, but were brought to a halt by the sight of a man in the doorway. He was silhouetted against the pale blue twilight, but Isobel's eye caught the gleam of brass on the pistol that he held, cocked, in his right hand. For the space of several seconds they faced each other across the room, silent and immobile like figures in a tableau, and then the man in the doorway laughed. It was the merest ripple of sound—little more than a chuckle—and yet its effect on Isobel was devastating.

'Surely . . .' said Hugh Murray's well-remembered voice. 'Can it really be Miss MacIntosh of Shawbrae again?'

Receiving only a faint gulp in reply, he advanced further into the room and, having assured himself that his eyes were not deceiving him, he pocketed his gun and made an elegant leg.

'My most sincere apologies for frightening you, ma'am,' he said humbly, luckily taking Isobel's dazed silence for that of fear. 'I had no idea—That is, when I saw the horses, I was afraid it might be the soldiery.'

Fiona's ashen face had appeared in the doorway behind him, tremulously inquisitive, but Isobel ignored it and made a valiant effort to recover her composure. If Hugh Murray had looked out of place in baldric and kilt at their last meeting, he looked even more so now.

She was shocked by the change of him. His jaw was unshaven, his clothes filthy, and the spiritless droop of his eyelids spoke of a disillusionment and despair that made her throat constrict with pity. The tatters of his gentility still hung about his slouched body like a ragged ball-gown on a scarecrow, and his soft voice was incongruous in a man with the appearance of a vagrant. She was at once ashamed and embarrassed to confront him in his degradation, and tried to cover up by saying, rather too brightly,

'Mr Murray! This is indeed a surprise. We have just made the acquaintance of your brother.'

'Ah, yes? Is he awake, then?' He stepped closer to the pallet and dropped on one knee beside it. 'How does it feel now, Adam?' He pulled aside the plaid to examine the wound, and his eyes widened as they fell on the neat bandage. '*Dhia!* Is this your work, Miss MacIntosh? I am indeed indebted to you. Neither Adam nor I have anything about us as clean as this bandage—nor have had for many weeks.'

'These are grievous circumstances we find you in,' Isobel said tentatively. 'How come you to be in this part of the country and in such dire straits? I had thought the Prince's army to be well into England by now.'

'Alas, no.' Hugh straightened, pushing back his wilful lock of hair. 'The promised support of the English Jacobites was not forthcoming, so the chiefs advocated a return to Scotland until our numbers might be augmented from other sources. That is why Adam and I are here now. We left the Prince at Kendal and rode north with three others in order to see various chiefs who are at present undecided, but who might be persuaded to come out for the Prince.'

Laughlan, tired of waiting for an introduction, gestured at the now sleeping Adam. 'How did your brother come by his wound?'

'We had the ill-fortune to run into some of Loudon's men four days ago. The others managed to get away in the darkness, but I had been unhorsed and, as I had to carry Adam, we became separated from our comrades. With such an important mission to carry out, of course, we cannot expect them to return to look for us and must rely upon our own resources.'

Laughlan, with a disdainful glance around the bothy, seemed about to comment on the evident lack of success their resources appeared to have enjoyed thus far, but Isobel interposed. 'It may be days before your brother can walk, Mr Murray. I confess I am uneasy about your safety here. Is there no better place of refuge near by?'

Hugh shrugged, rubbing a hand across his jaw. 'There is an old kiln about a mile nearer Nairn. It might shelter us well enough, but it is rather closer to the road and might also be seen from the big house on the hill.'

'Transk.' Laughlan nodded. 'It belongs to a friend of ours, but I think you would do better to remain here. Although Colin is the best of good fellows and would not dream of giving you away if we asked him not to, his father might deem it his duty to do so for the sake of his tenants, who might be implicated.'

'Yes, indeed,' Isobel agreed. 'For my part, I would trust neither father nor son. You must stay here till we can find you a more secure hiding-place. Think, Laughlan. Are there any Jacobite families near here who might give Mr Murray shelter?'

Laughlan's eyes went blank with thought. 'James Brodie is no use. He has taken his family to Edinburgh for the winter. So have the Jamiesons and the Mc-Kenzies. How about the Dowager Lady MacIntosh? Is her house too close to ours, think you? We dare not risk any word of this reaching Papa.'

'Papa need never know,' Isobel retorted. 'But old Lady MacIntosh could not help us anyway. She has gone to spend Christmas with her daughter-in-law at Moy. Can you think of no one else?'

They fell silent while Hugh watched their faces hopefully, but at last Isobel was forced to admit at least temporary defeat.

'Don't worry,' she told Hugh sunnily. 'If we cannot find someone to take you in, we shall at least do our best to make your stay here as comfortable as possible. To begin with, we can procure you a warm plaid or two. And how will you do for food?'

'We do have a pistol apiece and a good supply of balls and powder,' Hugh replied. 'But with game so scarce in these parts, we have eaten but scantily these past few days.'

'Oh fiddle!' Laughlan exclaimed contemptuously. 'Colin and I were out with our fowling-pieces only yesterday and brought home a fine bag of woodpigeons and two hares.'

'Not many of which were brought down by you, I'll wager,' his sister snapped waspishly, her hand itching for his ears. 'Tomorrow, Mr Murray, we shall bring you as much as we can assemble without arousing suspicion. No one will think it odd if we are seen in this vicinity, as we are quite in the habit of riding here every other day. But now we must be gone. Come, Laughlan, it will be dark soon, and the road is treacherous.'

Fiona was discovered in the doorway, sucking a ringlet, her pinched face eloquent of her feelings at being left alone in the cold. She acknowledged Isobel's introduction of Hugh with a pleasant smile, and waited till he had been left behind before commenting, with a severity reminiscent of Miss Walkinshaw at her most grim, 'You seem on uncommon good terms with that uncouth rebel, love. Although I would not have expected you to report him, I cannot see it at all necessary for you to be so affable.' She thought for a second and then substituted 'effusive' as being more worthy of her. 'One cannot but perceive that he is a person of quite inferior position.'

'Pray do not talk such utter fustian, Fiona,' her sister returned with a light in her eye that made Fiona wish that she had kept her opinion to herself. 'How can you possibly judge Mr Murray from the little you have seen of him? Do you imagine you would look like a lady if you were forced to live in a derelict bothy for days on end?'

'Well, I dare say I should make better shift than he appears to do, at any rate,' Laughlan asserted positively, nudging Caesar in between his sisters' mares. 'I'll wager I could feed myself at any rate—if not off the land, then by stealing a chicken or some kail out of a cottage garden. There's no shortage of water to wash in, forsooth, and another thing . . .' He caught sight of Isobel's choleric eyes and changed tack abruptly. 'Who was the fellow, anyway? I must say I thought it very ill-mannered in you not to introduce me.'

Isobel turned to look at him, uncomprehending, and then laughed. 'Oh, Laughlan, forgive me! I had quite forgot that you never saw him. It was when you ran off to join the rebels in Edinburgh. When you fell off your horse, Mr Murray turned back to help you, but I made him go away since I knew you would have insisted going on to Holyrood in his company.'

'*What?*' Laughlan dropped his reins so suddenly that Caesar took the action as an invitation to gallop, and shot away with an agility that took his rider some moments to curb, allowing Isobel to escape her brother's ire by riding away at a tangent.

All in all, she reflected, watching the first stars appear overhead, the day had not turned out too badly after all.

CHAPTER
SEVEN

DURING THE next few days Isobel contrived to keep the two fugitives adequately supplied with creature comforts. Laughlan donated two pairs of thick stockings and also succeeded in appropriating a bottle of his father's brandy without being detected, an achievement which was the source of much secret pride to him. Even Fiona, although she steadfastly refused to set foot inside the bothy, did her best to make up for her 'lack of bottom', as Laughlan termed it, by purloining such a quantity of eggs, cheese and oatmeal that her aunt was forced to keep a suspicious eye on the maids.

'The water-woman would seem to be the most likely,' Miss Logan complained on the day of their departure for Transk, 'although I have watched her these last three days and have seen her take nothing. One must expect a little shortage here and there, of course, but of late it has become quite impossible to overlook.' She threw her sister an impatient frown, compulsively polishing the top of Isobel's washstand with a corner of the bed-hangings. 'Really, Margaret, something must be done about it before it gets quite out of hand.'

Mrs MacIntosh lifted a negligent shoulder, but was more interested in watching the final fitting of Isobel's velvet gown. 'If you feel you must speak to the maids, by all means do so, love. But pray do not ask me to do it. You know how much I hate unpleasantness of that kind.

Do you really wish it to be so high at the bosom, Isobel? It *is* a ball-gown, after all, and by the time we have the lace inserted it will look quite dowdy. Just drop the neckline another inch, Mrs Gunn. If that is too low, we may fill it in with lace.'

'Oh, Mama . . .' She looked at her reflection in the mirror, and blushed. 'Surely it is low enough as it is? I shall freeze to death.'

'Nonsense. If you *will* insist on wearing velvet, you will soon be glad of a little ventilation. One reel in that dress and you will be fainting away. Still, the colour suits you better than I would have expected, and I must say I am glad to see that you are not totally dispassionate about how you will look to Mr Frazer tomorrow night.'

'Mr Frazer's opinion is a matter of no importance,' Isobel disabused her with a twitch of her shoulders that caused the sewing-woman to stick a pin in her. 'My sole reason for choosing this material in preference to the white satin was that it will be a long time before I get another such dress, and I shall be able to wear this on more occasions. If I can avoid Mr Frazer entirely, you may be sure I shall do so.'

'Oh, you cannot do that,' Euphemia put in, in shocked tones. 'Mr Frazer is your host, in a manner of speaking, since it was he who invited you, not his father. How very rude it would be in you to avoid him.'

'Of course she will not do so,' Mrs MacIntosh replied. 'Depend upon it, her father will be on hand to see that she does not disgrace us with her missish ways. Now, do you hear me, Isobel? Your Papa will not countenance such behaviour.'

'But *he* does not treat *me* as he should. I told you—he treats me most improperly. He . . .'

'If I stay here, I shall lose my temper,' her mother stated, rising and moving towards the door. 'Such a

blatant untruth I never heard. Mr Frazer, of all people.'
She turned in the doorway and addressed the sewing-
woman with a total disregard for her daughter's muti-
nous face. 'When you have the lace sewn in, Mrs Gunn,
you may give the dress to Agnes to pack. We must be
ready to leave directly after luncheon.'

She whisked her voluminous skirts through the doorway very much the *grande dame*, leaving Isobel in two
minds whether or not to acquire some malady that would
necessitate her staying at home, but the thought of
missing the festivities was too much for her. Colin Frazer
or no Colin Frazer, she would go to Transk and enjoy
herself. The only drawback was that at Transk it would
be impossible to slip away to visit Hugh and Adam. This
worried her, because Adam's wound was healing with
such astonishing rapidity that she was afraid that he and
his brother would be gone before she could see them
again. Laughlan, being the only member of the household who was not rushed off his feet with preparations
for the visit, had ridden out that morning, but he did not
arrive home until the family were sitting down to
luncheon and Isobel was unable to converse privately
with him.

It was noticeable that he was big with news but, as the
coach was full, he and his father rode beside it, and
although Isobel could see him sending her obscure
signals which only worried her all the more, she was
forced to contain her curiosity as best she might. Even
when they reached their destination, luck was against
them. Colin and his father came out on the front steps to
meet them, and having handed Isobel down from the
coach, abandoned her to a bevy of female cousins who
kept her chattering until it was time to dress for dinner.

In the end it was Fiona who was the bearer of the evil
tidings. Luckier than Isobel, she had managed to waylay

her brother on the stairs, and only waited till Agnes had left the room to whisper, with unnecessary drama, 'They are ready to decamp.'

Isobel dropped her patch-box with a clatter.

'The rebels? When do they leave? Tonight?'

'Tomorrow night. Laughlan says that Adam is able to walk quite well already, and his brother thinks another day will suffice to make him fit enough to move on.'

'Then we must try to get some food to them before they go. If they are forced to live off the countryside at this season they will starve.'

'Hush! Here is someone coming.' Fiona cocked an ear towards the door, and added in a rush, 'We must get what food we can. Laughlan says he will take it to them tonight when everyone is asleep.'

She broke off as her mother entered, and there was no opportunity to say more, but Isobel descended the stairs with a heavy heart. She was placed next to Colin at the table, but was so dazed by disappointment that most of his teasing remarks failed to find their mark and she quite forgot that she was expected to smuggle away some food for her two dependent rebels. Fortunately, Fiona more than made up for her sister's defection by hiding behind the curtain of a near-by window those choice morsels which she could resist eating, and going back for them later when the room was empty.

They took stock of their spoils in their room and then got into bed to await the arrival of Laughlan, who had arranged with Fiona that he would call to collect the food on his way out. Three minutes later, Fiona was sound asleep, but Isobel lay awake listening to the slowly diminishing noises as the house settled down for the night. One by one the faint sounds died away, and still Laughlan did not come. Isobel would have risked conjecture by going to look for him, but she had no idea which room he had been allocated, and the house was so full of guests that he might be sharing a room. Comforting herself with the reflection that there was really no need for her to stay awake since Laughlan would waken her when he came in, she snuffed out the candle and fell asleep. In the morning, the food was still there.

Laughlan came down to breakfast looking sheepish and as heavy-eyed as his sister, but after the meal he allowed himself to be cornered in the ornamental wilderness and subjected to a thorough cross-examination.

'I don't believe you.' Fiona dealt him before he had the chance to open his mouth. 'So it is of no use to put on that martyred expression. I *know* you fell asleep.'

'I did *not*,' Laughlan protested, looking indescribably maligned. 'Why must you always believe the worst of me? I have had the most dreadful night. Isobel, would you believe it, one of Colin's friends arrived unexpectedly last night—he was not due to arrive till this evening—and had to be put in beside me. And it is such a tiny room, even for one; little more than a cupboard.'

'You do not mean to make that your excuse, surely?' Isobel asked crisply. 'If you had but stayed awake until he fell asleep, you might easily have crept out!'

'Yes, but that is just *it*,' Laughlan interrupted triumphantly. 'He did not fall asleep. All night long he paced the floor with a hot brick clapped to his cheek. Toothache, poor devil. Never shut an eye until dawn, and neither did I.'

'You foolish boy!' Fiona berated him. 'Have you no imagination? There must have been something you could have said to account for your absence. Why did you not tell him that you had an assignation with one of the maids?' She found herself immediately the focus of two pairs of astounded eyes and shrugged, blushing, 'Well, for goodness' sake! Everyone knows that such things happen, after all.'

'Not in this house, I hope,' Isobel managed to utter faintly. 'Nor is it at all the thing for you to say so.' She turned to Laughlan, who had still not recovered from his astonishment, and added, 'In that case, you must go tonight. This afternoon is out of the question as Papa will have his eagle eye on all of us, but tonight everyone will be tired after the dancing, so perhaps your room-mate will have a better night's rest.'

'I intend to make sure of that,' Laughlan assured her confidentially. 'He is not much older than I am and really rather a baby, so it should not be too difficult to make him drunk. If I can contrive to do so, he will sleep like a log. Don't worry about it, I promise you it will be all right tonight.'

On this assurance Isobel was compelled to pin her hopes, but she spent the afternoon in an increasing despondency, which was not alleviated by a growing conviction that Colin's grandmother regarded her as practically one of the family. For three long hours she was forced to simulate an interest that she did not feel, while that redoubtable old lady recounted anecdotes of her descendant's youth; his extraordinary prowess with horse and gun; his early genius at school; his bravery and endurance when he broke two ribs in a riding-accident when he was barely out of petticoats. In mounting embarrassment Isobel heard her out, but all her covert appeals for rescue were studiously ignored by both her parents, and at last she could stand no more and escaped to her room on the rather flimsy pretext of recouping her strength for the ball that evening.

She had been looking forward to the festivities with no small degree of pleasure, having had time to make the acquaintance of several personable young men to whom she had promised dances, but the imminent departure of

Hugh Murray had blown dark clouds across the sun of her anticipation. Even the prospect of donning her new velvet gown for the first time and having her hair dressed by Miss Walkinshaw had lost its appeal. But, once dressed, with her hair powdered and a small patch set seductively at the corner of her mouth, it was not easy to remain downcast. The girl who stared back at her from the mirror with those enormous long-lashed eyes was such an improvement on the old, work-a-day Isobel that her old self, with all its attendant worries, seemed to have been shed, rather in the manner of a snake's sloughed skin.

Mrs MacIntosh seemed slightly stunned by her daughter's transformation, but, having noted the somewhat awe-stricken expression in the eyes of sundry dowagers with marriageable daughters of their own, she became convinced that Isobel's entire ensemble had been of her own conception.

The ballroom had undergone a complete change since Isobel had last seen it, four years previously. Gone were the glaring yellow hangings and the striped settees. Now the windows were draped with a dark blue brocade that echoed the paler hue of the silken cushions and shimmered in the glow of the candles burning in burnished sconces along the walls. It was a long narrow room with a wooden ceiling painted with heraldic devices. By the time the last of the guests had arrived, it was filled with a voluble, elated crowd; the ladies shimmering in jewel-coloured silks and brocades, the gentlemen only slightly less flamboyant in velvets and silver braid. Head-dresses of flowers and feathers bobbed like flotsam above a tide of hooped skirts that ebbed and flowed in time to the music.

Isobel's hand was claimed immediately by a stocky young man rejoicing in the name of Elphinstone Mac-

Martin, a distant relative of her host, who had clearly been lying in wait for her. He proved to be a singularly talkative person, but his sense of the ridiculous appealed to Isobel and she was glad to dance with him if only to escape the attention of Colin Frazer, whose watchful eyes she seemed to meet every time she turned her head. When the dance was ended, Mr MacMartin returned her to where her mother and Aunt Euphemia were enviously watching the proceedings and stayed to talk to them for some time. It would have been thought improper for Isobel to dance with him more than once or perhaps twice, but every time she returned to her seat after dancing with someone else he materialised at her elbow, eager to relieve her of the necessity of plying her fan with her own fair hands and giving her a short biography of those of his relations ill-advised enough to pass beneath his gaze.

On returning to her seat after a particularly energetic reel, she found that both her mother and Aunt Euphemia had stood up to dance, the music being a minuet, the only dance thought suitable for a married lady or spinster to take part in. Elphinstone MacMartin, however, was still at his post.

'I have taken the liberty of procuring you a glass of lemonade, Miss MacIntosh,' he greeted her, handing her a tall, misted glass. 'It is become so hot in here . . . and you have been dancing such a lot . . . You must be very thirsty.' He possessed himself of her fan and began to ply it solicitously. 'There goes Lady Vane, my mother's cousin. Did you ever see such a monstrous hoop? I'll wager it is nine feet in circumference if it is an inch. How on earth did she manage to get it through the door? She was a sad romp in her youth, you know. I have heard my mother say that she and her sister—that was Colin's mother, you know—caught a pig and . . .'

Isobel's eyes wandered away to look for her mother, who would certainly stop dancing if she noticed her daughter in solitary converse with a young man, but, when located, she was too engrossed in treading a measure with the elder Mr Frazer to be interested in her charge. Her husband was not so forgetful of his duty, but he was on the other side of the room talking to Colin and, although he was watching Isobel like a hawk, it would take him several minutes to skirt the dancers to where she was sitting. Fiona was dancing with a thin young man in green who had successfully laid claim to her earlier in the evening, and was holding her against all comers with a disregard for propriety that would have earned him a sharp set-down from her mother, had she not been too intent on watching Isobel. Judging from Fiona's glowing countenance, this arrangement was entirely to her liking.

Laughlan was nowhere to be seen. Absently returning suitable replies to her companion's incessant chatter, Isobel scanned the floor for him without success. She had just decided to dispose of Mr MacMartin by sending him for another glass of lemonade, when a shadow fell across her. Expecting this to be cast by her father, she looked up with a smile that died on her lips as she recognised Colin.

'I hope you will forgive me, Miss MacIntosh,' he smiled, sketching a bow. 'But I am come to deprive you of Mr MacMartin's company.' He turned to his relative, who had risen at his approach. 'Elphy, my friend, Nemesis has caught up with you at last. Miss Carswell informs me that you are neglecting your promise to stand up with her for a country dance, and I have given her my word to see that you remedy this immediately. No, don't worry about Miss MacIntosh.' Mr MacMartin had flushed, and opened his mouth to speak. 'I shall

deem it an honour to look after her till her mother
returns.'

For the space of several seconds there was an awful
silence, and Isobel felt her breath flutter in her throat. If
there were to be a scene . . . But at last Mr MacMartin
dropped his eyes from Colin's bland gaze, and muttering, '. . . servant, ma'am,' stalked away, his shoulders
stiff with anger.

Isobel's bosom heaved with suppressed indignation.
What a cock-and-bull story! Did he really expect it to be
believed? As if any lady would complain to her host
because one of her partners had forgotten to keep his
promise! She threw him an icy look, but he only lifted an
eyebrow at her as though inviting comment. Realising
that he could annihilate her with sarcasm if she were to
accuse him of jealousy, she rose, and gave him a stiff
bow.

'If you will excuse me,' she said through stiff lips. 'It is
rather hot in here.'

He fell into step beside her, with every appearance of
having considered himself invited to do so.

'I agree with you entirely,' he nodded suavely, cup-
ping a hand to her elbow. 'It seems to become hotter and
hotter, does it not? And the music gets louder and
louder until it positively throbs in one's ears and escape
becomes imperative. I mentioned to your sister just now
that the garden room has lately been completed, and
should she feel the need of a little—Ah, here it is. Allow
me.'

He pushed open a door, and Isobel found herself in a
small room with long unshuttered windows, filled with a
profusion of plants and shrubs. A wooden bench ran
round three walls and through the windows could be
seen the moonlit garden, the trees stretching out bare
black arms across a silver-blue expanse of snow-covered

lawn. But what made a most immediate and lasting impression on Isobel's mind was that it was completely empty. She turned on her heel with a half-formed protest on her lips, but Colin had already closed the door behind him and was saying,

'I am persuaded you will be more comfortable in here, Miss MacIntosh. This room is always airy and cool and, besides, I have been looking forward to showing it to you, as it was my own idea. Here my father and I are able to grow our most treasured seedlings without being put to the trouble of a half-mile tramp every day to keep an eye on them. We have decided to lay out a plantation of firs on the hill beside the river, and my father is very keen on trying some alders as well.'

Isobel relaxed slightly, and sat down on the edge of the bench, comforting herself with the assurance that if she could keep him talking about his beloved garden it would divert him from less unexceptional topics. 'I think I noticed a new bowling-green this morning,' she remarked invitingly, and was gratified to see his eyes glow with the light of proud ownership.

'Did you see it?' he asked happily. 'It is not quite established yet, but when it is I hope to surround it with some statues that I brought home from Italy. It is a trifle exposed to the north-east wind at present, but we have put in a line of trees at the far side which should provide a little shelter when they are bigger.' He strode to the window and looked out. 'No, it is too dark to see them from here, but you may be able to make out some of the statues down there at the end of the lawn.'

Isobel went to stand at his shoulder and nodded politely, although she could see only some pale shapes in the darkness. 'I did not know you had been in Italy,' she said idly. 'I have never heard you speak of it before.'

He shrugged, still looking out into the night. 'I have

always thought it a great bore when young men start prosing about their travels. I did a tour with my tutor when I was a boy, of course, but I have been back to Italy since then. Last year I set off again, bound for Venice, but I only got as far as Edinburgh.'

'What halted you there?' Isobel prompted before she had time to appreciate the meaning of his words.

'I met a girl I hadn't seen for years,' he said sombrely. 'A girl with hair like heather honey and eyes like polished chestnuts. After that, Venice would have been a sad anticlimax.'

Isobel had spun round towards the door, but halted, blushing, as she realised that he had not referred to her by name and would certainly reply to any rebuke with a sly 'I don't think you know the lady', or some such remark. Keeping her back turned, she said instead with bland innocence, 'What happened? Did she marry someone else?'

His answer was so tardy that she glanced at him over her shoulder, and encountered a look that held her eyes like a magnet. 'No,' he said at last with a smile that held more than a touch of grimness. 'Nor will she.'

Isobel's face flooded with colour, but before she could think of an adequate rejoinder, Colin added in a changed tone,

'Listen. Is not that a minuet? Do you feel sufficiently refreshed to stand up with me? Come, it will be thought odd in you to spend the evening in here with me.'

Gasping with exasperation, Isobel moved towards the door. Insufferable wretch, she thought angrily. Need he always make it seem that she was pursuing him, instead of *vice versa*? Perhaps he actually believed it—he was just conceited enough.

Their absence from the ballroom had not gone unnoticed. They took the floor under a battery of calculating eyes, which made Isobel's teeth clench. In a row sat Mrs MacIntosh, complacent; Euphemia, delighted; Colin's grandmother, approving; Mrs Johnstone of Kinloch, outraged; and Miss Johnstone of Kinloch, green with envy. Ignoring all of them as best she could, Isobel stared straight ahead with such self-consciousness that it was several seconds before she fully comprehended at what she was staring.

A small anteroom opened off the main hall—there were several of them, in fact, mostly occupied by gentlemen who had deserted their ladies for the pleasure of 'taking a trick at the cards'—but through the half-open door of this one Isobel was to perceive her brother Laughlan and—supposedly—his room-mate, in a scene that swept all other thoughts from her mind.

So shaken was she by what she saw that she left the floor at a brisk trot, without so much as a word to her partner, and threw wide the door. There on the threshold she halted, her mouth open and one hand pressed to her sinking heart, temporarily at a loss for words. Slouched half across the table, his neckband untied and his head on one arm, lay Laughlan, while opposite him in an armchair stretched his victim, in an attitude of deepest unconcern, his eyes closed and his mouth inelegantly open. Between them on the table, in mute evidence of the cause of their collapse, stood an empty brandy-bottle and two glasses.

Uttering a cry of dismay, Isobel strode forward, and grasping her brother's flaccid shoulders, shook them with all her strength. 'Wake up,' she ordered him desperately. 'Oh, Laughlan, you odious, untrustworthy beast, how could you? Wake *up*, I say! Do you hear me?'

Laughlan's only reply was a loud and unbecoming belch.

'Er . . . excuse me.' Colin had entered the room

behind her, and now closed the door against a battery of curious eyes. 'I honestly believe you are wasting your energy, Miss MacIntosh. If you will permit me, I shall have Laughlan and my foolish young friend put to bed, for until they have slept off the effects of their . . . er . . . excesses, they will not be able to stand.' He examined her glittering eyes with a puzzled frown. 'I hope you do not mean to be angry with your brother? It would be a deal too bad if you were, for this was bound to happen some time, you know. Every young man must discover his own capacity for brandy, and a small miscalculation now and then is surely permissible. No one will think anything of it, I assure you.'

Isobel whirled on him, beside herself with rage and frustration. 'You must think me the greatest possible ninnyhammer,' she began, her voice heavy with scorn, and then stopped, biting her lips as she realised that she had almost given herself away. It cost her a good deal to continue, in an effort to cover up, '. . . as indeed I am. It is just that—well—he is so young, and I have the headache a little. Perhaps I should go to my room. Will you excuse me?'

She swept past him, seeing the veil of inscrutability which he hurriedly drew across the naked disbelief in his eyes, and without giving him time to reply, sped across the ballroom and upstairs to the sudden silence of her room.

The strong desire to give way to tears of pure temper was not easy to overcome, and she was compelled to take a turn about the room before she felt composed enough to sit down on the bed and attempt to think logically. One fact was evident. Laughlan could no longer be relied upon to carry out his mission, since it was already well past eleven and he would, presumably, sleep for hours yet. Therefore, it being unthinkable that

Hugh (and, of course, Adam) should be allowed to set off on a long tramp through the snow without sustenance, she would have to go herself. If her mother should notice her charge's departure from the ballroom, Colin would inform her that she had gone to bed, and Fiona would know better than to betray her if she found the room empty when she came up. Having finally decided that there was no alternative, she divested herself of her restricting hoop and, picking up her new velvet cloak and the package of food, stepped out into the darkened passage.

CHAPTER
EIGHT

AT THE opposite end of the corridor from the main staircase was another flight of steps used mainly by the servants and, remembering from her last visit that these ended in a door out to the kitchen garden, Isobel turned in that direction. Faint strains of music floated up from the ballroom, mingling with a buzz of laughter and conversation which deadened the sound of her footsteps as she sped across the wooden floor. Hardly had she taken a dozen steps, when a figure stepped out of a doorway into her path. The face was in darkness, but she caught a gleam of white teeth as he laughed softly.

'You are about to be angry with me again, I fear, Miss MacIntosh,' Colin Frazer whispered in despairing tones. 'And this time with good reason, I must admit, for I have been spying on you in what I feel sure you are about to tell me was a nasty, underhand and despicable manner. As if this were not enough, I am about to antagonise you further by refusing to let you go out without giving me an adequate and, if possible, truthful explanation.'

'You have no right to stop me,' Isobel blazed, breathing heavily.

'Admittedly. But, on the other hand, as your host, I am in some way responsible for your safety, and if you refuse to honour me with your confidence I would be in duty bound to inform your parents which, I suspect, would please you even less.'

Cornered, Isobel racked her brains to think of a convincing excuse for slipping out at night, but since it seemed unlikely that he would believe her to be interested in astronomy, she decided that only the truth would suffice.

'Do you swear to me on your honour that you will speak of this to *no* one and will do nothing to hinder me?' He nodded. 'Very well, then, I shall trust you. But if you betray my trust, I shall never speak to you again, I promise you. There are two rebels in hiding not very far from here. They have been there for some days because one of them was wounded and unable to travel, so Fiona and Laughlan and I have been helping them. At first light tomorrow they are going away, and we promised that they should have enough food to keep them going until they reach their friends. But Laughlan was to have taken it, and—Well, you saw for yourself that he could not have gone anywhere tonight.'

Colin covered his eyes with his hand, and his shoulders shook soundlessly.

'So, being what you are, my little heroine, you came to the conclusion that everything depended on you? I see. The rebels, I might point out, are no news to me. I have suspected their motives for hiding in that bothy for almost a week, and so has at least one of my neighbours. Fortunately for them, neither of us was sufficiently patriotic to have them apprehended, but you must warn your friends to be a little more circumspect next time they take to the heather. Smoke can be seen quite clearly against a clear sky even at night, you know, and a door that has been off its hinges for several weeks does not leap back into position of its own volition. However, we are wasting time. We must not keep your friends waiting. Shall I take your parcel?'

'But . . . No!' Isobel retreated a pace, clutching the

bundle to her breast. 'I cannot—That is—*You* are not coming with me!'

'Assuredly I am, my love,' he told her confidently. 'If only to procure you a horse without my entire household becoming aware of your nocturnal habits. Did your unfortunate experience in Edinburgh teach you nothing?'

He stretched out a hand for the package, and Isobel, hurt by his needlessly cruel reference to an episode about which she had imagined him to know nothing, relinquished it without a murmur and allowed him to guide her down the narrow stairway and out into the kitchen yard.

A strong wind was blowing in from the sea, singing eerily among the trees to the accompaniment of dance-music which was clearly audible, even here. Colin, bidding her wait in the shadow of the doorway, strode away in the direction of the stables, to reappear minutes later leading a big chestnut horse that shied as Isobel stepped out from her hiding-place.

'I thought it wiser not to invite comment by asking for a second mount with a side-saddle,' he apologised, but without obvious regret. 'But if you don't mind riding pillion? I know I can trust you not to take advantage of the situation.'

He hitched her up behind him and they set off diag-onally across the yard to where a small postern opened on to the drive. Here, safe from view from the house, he gave the restless horse its head. Isobel's hood was immediately blown back, but, precariously perched as she was, she did not dare to loose her grip on Colin's coat to replace it. She cowered in the shelter afforded by his back, feeling Miss Walkinshaw's artistry being de-stroyed by the wind and illogically blaming it on her companion. It had been her one regret, on viewing her radiant reflection in the mirror that evening, that Hugh could not see her in all her finery, and now that the opportunity had presented itself, Colin Frazer seemed bent on nullifying it. Had she gone on foot, as had been her intention, she might have arrived looking much less dishevelled.

Colin spoke only once during the brief ride, to warn her to hold fast as they cleared a rushing burn, but as they dismounted near the bothy, he drew her attention to a distant flicker of fire high in the hills behind Transk.

'See, the bonfire has been lighted to herald in the New Year,' he said in a solemn voice. 'It is now the year of our Lord seventeen hundred and forty-six, and you, Isobel MacIntosh, have welcomed it with malice in your heart. Are you not ashamed?'

Isobel laughed unwillingly, waiting for him to tie up his horse. 'Malice? Oh, pray acquit me. You have admitted yourself that your treatment of me deserves that I should be angry with you, but I am not so ungrateful of your escort that I still bear you malice. If you will only cease trying to embarrass me, I shall engage to be everything that is conciliatory.'

'But you blush so delightfully,' he objected. 'I am not at all sure that I could resist the temptation. Besides, when we are married . . .'

Isobel did not wait to hear the rest of this remark but hurried away from him quickly towards the bothy. Firelight flickered warmly from within—surely it could be seen from a distance—and as Colin rapped smartly on the door-jamb Hugh appeared in the opening with a foot and a half of dirk in his hand.

'Put up your steel, my friend,' Colin remarked laconically. 'Had we come for your blood, we would not have bothered to wake you first.'

Hugh looked past him into Isobel's eyes, and his

expression softened into a smile of recognition. 'In such company, sir, you are welcome.' He bowed briefly. 'Your servant, Miss MacIntosh. Adam and I had despaired of seeing you again. Will you not come in?'

Isobel stepped past him and indicated Colin with a movement of her hand. 'This is Mr Frazer of Transk, of whom I spoke to you before. But you may be at ease, as he has given me his word not to betray you. Indeed, he has been aware of your presence here for some days. The smoke shows even at night, you know.'

The two men exchanged bows as she continued into the room where Adam was standing beside the fire, watching them. After making him known to Colin, she bade him sit, so that she might examine his wounded leg. The gash had knit cleanly in a red and puckered scar, but although she could see no reason why it should reopen, she replaced the bandages and warned him to save it as much as possible.

'We have no intention of travelling a great distance in the first few days,' Hugh told her, standing beside her in the red glow of the fire. 'It will be enough if we make a start, and perhaps we may make better time when Adam is stronger. I don't like staying in one place longer than we can help, and we must make haste to rejoin the Prince, who is short enough of men as it is.'

Colin had seated himself on the floor with his back against the wall, from where he had watched Isobel's ministrations with strong disapproval, and now he put in softly, 'It is, I think, just as well that you do not intend to prolong your stay here. Although you have apparently not been reported to the authorities up till now, there is no saying when one of my neighbours or one of the guests at present under my roof may take it into his head to do so. If you will take my advice, you will lose no time in making your departure.'

Hugh frowned slightly into the fire, the corners of his mouth pulled down as he considered this. 'It seems we have not been as careful as we might have been,' he admitted, casting a swift, grateful smile at his uninvited guest. 'As you will appreciate, sir, my brother and I are not in the habit of skulking in the heather like animals and are consequently somewhat inept at the game. In fact, had it not been for the kindness of Miss MacIntosh and her brother, we would have been in a sorry state, game being so scarce in these parts . . . to say nothing of the admirable care my brother's wound has received.'

Colin nodded grimly. 'Certainly it would have been as unchristian to have refused to help you, knowing your desperate situation, as it would have been to have handed you over to be shot, and yet I cannot think it to have been necessary to involve Miss MacIntosh. Surely it was sufficient to let Laughlan . . .'

'I have brought you some food,' Isobel interrupted hurriedly, pulling forward the bulky package. 'There is not a great deal, but perhaps it will serve to supplement what you may procure for a day or two.'

'You are a great deal too kind, ma'am,' Hugh murmured, looking very red about the cheekbones. 'We had not intended to put you to so much trouble.'

Adam leaned forward out of the shadows, the firelight lending colour to his still pallid cheeks. 'Fruit, Miss MacIntosh!' he exclaimed, laughing. 'I'll wager I have forgotten what it tastes like. You can have no conception of how weary one becomes of a restricted diet. Oh, for one of my Aunt Sophie's dinners, with a big bowl of broth and a sheep's head and plenty of . . .'

His voice tailed away as he turned to look at Colin, who had risen and was standing in the doorway, staring out into the darkness in an attitude that made Isobel say shortly, 'Is something wrong, Mr Frazer? What do you see?'

He did not answer for a moment, but tilted his head and seemed to listen intently. 'See . . . ?' he said absently, his attention still focused on the still night outside. 'I see nothing unusual, but I heard, or thought I heard . . . but no, I must have been mistaken.' He made as if to turn away, but froze instantly, his eyes on a belt of pines that fringed the road. 'Did you hear it? The jingle of a bridle.'

The other three jostled each other to get to the door, but Isobel, a poor third, could see nothing over the broad shoulders that blocked her view except for a patch of starry sky and the bald dome of a near-by hill.

'Look!' It was Adam who spoke, and although his face was hidden, the word shivered with an intensity that made Isobel's heart leap into her mouth. 'Down there in the hollow. There must be half a dozen of them at least, and definitely coming this way.'

'Redcoats?' Isobel croaked, but was ignored as Hugh pushed past her to snatch up his plaid and the bundle of food.

'Quick, lad,' he urged his brother, his face a pale oval in the dim light, 'we must make a run for it. They are too many for us. Hurry, they are only a few minutes away from here.'

'Wait.' Colin spoke quickly over his shoulder, his eyes fixed on the group of redcoats which Isobel could now pick out among the trees. 'Where can you run to? If you break cover now, you would be shot before you could run ten yards. These men are mounted and armed, and the moonlight is as bright as day. Your only chance is to hide in here. Miss MacIntosh and I will try to head them off.'

'Hide?' Hugh halted in the act of picking up his

baldric. 'There is no place to hide in here. Not even a chair to crouch behind.'

Colin turned away from the door and scanned the room. It was perfectly true. One glance sufficed to show that there was not enough cover for a cat, nothing but the bare walls and the smooth packed-earth floor. He raised his eyes to the rafters and stretched up an arm to test their strength.

'Up there,' he said tersely. 'As close in above the doorway as you can get.'

'Will they hold us?' Adam wondered, and for reply his brother grasped one in each hand and hoisted himself up with an agility which Isobel could not help but admire.

When they were both balanced somewhat precariously under the eaves, Colin handed them up such articles as might betray their presence and returned to his position beside the door to check on the progress of the advancing soldiers.

Isobel joined him, trembling and lightheaded with sheer terror. 'What are we to tell them?' she asked. 'Will they not think it odd to find us here alone, together? They will certainly suspect an assignation.'

'I sincerely hope they will.' Colin slid a glance at her along his shoulder. 'But there should be no need for them to discover your identity. Pull your hood well over your face and go and lie down on the pallet. And pray, do not look at me like that. Your friends are just above us and will be witness to my admirable restraint.' He raised his voice to include Hugh and Adam. 'If anything should go wrong, leave me to do the talking. Go on now, Miss MacIntosh. I shall join you presently.'

Isobel did as she was bid, blushing hotly, and drew forward her hood to cover her face and the bright hair by which she might be identified. In a moment Colin left his post and lay down beside her.

'They are almost at the edge of the wood,' he said softly. 'Remember, don't speak unless you are forced to do so.'

He made as if to put his arms about her, but she stiffened and pulled away, whereupon he remarked in a voice just loud enough to reach the low rafters,

'Come now, Miss MacIntosh. Your acting must be better than this if we are to deceive His Majesty's troops. I must ask you, no matter how distasteful you may find it, to put your arms about my neck . . . That's better.'

He held her trembling body firmly, but the abject dread which engulfed her filled her consciousness to the exclusion of all other emotion—even distaste. Straining her ears for sounds of the redcoats' stealthy approach, she heard a branch rustle, and instantly a cold sweat broke out on her brow and palms. The strain of waiting for the curtain to rise on the hastily stage-managed scene was excruciating. A taut cord of tension in her throat seemed to stretch and stretch, and had almost reached snapping-point when Colin murmured in a whisper which she barely caught,

'Are you aware, my love, that you have the most delectable little hollow just behind the lobe of your ear? Assuredly I must kiss you there the minute you give me permission.'

Isobel's teeth came together with an audible click. Fear was forgotten in a hot surge of contempt and dislike. 'Beast,' she mouthed at him. 'How can you think of such things at a time like this?'

'I confess, I can think of little else,' he said huskily, grinning at her quite unabashed.

Beyond him, in the shadows, Hugh and his brother had evidently heard nothing of this exchange. Craning her head to peer over Colin's shoulder, she could make out the faintest outline of their bodies in the gloom, but their attention was riveted on the doorway and the stealthy but still distant rustle of the approaching soldiers.

The sound was unbelievably menacing, and as it grew gradually more distinct she felt a scream begin to grow inside her, filling her chest and rising into her throat. Her mouth opened, but as she drew a breath to give the tension release, Colin laid a hand to her cheek.

'Sh . . .' he breathed, running his thumb along her cheekbone. 'Don't be afraid, Isobel. You must know me very little if you can think that I would allow you to come to any harm. You are my woman, and I know how to protect my own!'

Isobel's eyes quitted the doorway and clung to his face, battening on the quiet confidence of his smile and the strength of purpose in his shadowed eyes. She wanted to tell him that she was *not* his woman and never would be, but the words stuck in her throat. She needed, at that moment, to have his arm cradle her and his hand caress her cheek, and when he dipped his head to kiss her on the lips, she made no move to stop him.

His mouth was warm and undemanding on hers, and she felt her body relax against his with a languor that seemed to turn even her brain to liquid. There was no room in her thoughts for Hugh and Adam in the rafters, or for the Hanoverian patrol outside. The question of whether to push Colin away or not simply didn't arise. She had stepped, for a moment, outside the world she knew, and was in no particular hurry to return. Even the scrape of a booted foot on the threshold failed to affect her, and she gasped with surprise as Colin leapt up to stride towards the sound. With her head reeling, she watched him halt the burly figure in the doorway.

'What is this?' he demanded, his voice a convincing blend of surprise and anger.

The redcoat stepped back a pace, the better to see his face. 'Mr Frazer?' he asked, incredulously. 'We—We did not expect to find *you* here, sir.'

'Then who *did* you expect to find? This *is* my property, after all.'

'Why, two rebels, sir. A report came in earlier this evening that two men had been seen lurking around this bothy, and I was detailed to investigate.'

'Two rebels? Oh, I see. Good God!' Colin drew a hand down his face and rubbed a long finger under his nose in a rather embarrassed gesture. His shoulders seemed to shake slightly with suppressed laughter. 'I . . . um . . . I fear I owe you an apology for having you dragged out on a wild-goose chase, Captain, and on a night like this.' He glanced over the officer's shoulder at the interested troopers, and dropped his voice confidentially. 'It would appear that *I* have been taken for a rebel—I, and a . . . friend of mine.'

Isobel, miraculously sensing her cue, emitted a vulgar giggle which had a galvanising effect on the young captain.

'I—Good God!—I never . . .'

'Quite,' Colin nodded understandingly. 'The mistake was a natural one, of course. One would not normally choose such a spot to . . . er . . . meet one's friends, but my friend is in rather exceptional circumstances.'

The captain was acutely embarrassed and had obvious difficulty in overcoming a strong desire to bolt, but he averted his eyes from Colin's and muttered doggedly, 'Deeply as I regret having to disturb you, sir, I fear it is my duty to take a look inside.'

There was a brief silence during which Isobel's breathing became totally suspended, and then Colin replied with the greatest geniality, 'But, of course. Your thoroughness is most praiseworthy. Major Menzies is of your regiment, is he not? I must commend you to him next time we dine together, Captain . . . ?'

'Ogilvie, sir. Captain Ogilvie. Yes, sir, Major Menzies is my superior officer.'

'Excellent. He is lucky to have men like you under him, and I shall certainly tell him so. But by all means look round, Captain Ogilvie. As you will see, the room is entirely devoid of cover, so I hope you will respect my friend's modesty and look from here.'

To Isobel's straining ears came the redcoat's mumbled, 'I would not wish to embarrass the lady, of course, sir.' He thrust his head through the doorway and cast a cursory glance around the bare walls before retreating with a brisk, 'Thank you, sir. I hope you will forgive the interrup . . . er . . . the intrusion.'

'Not at all, Captain. I am much indebted to you for your delicacy and understanding. Good night.'

There was a sound of creaking leathers and retreating hoofbeats, and from a short distance a ribald laugh floated back to make Isobel's cheeks burn. Colin returned to the pallet and would have resumed his former position, had she not sprung up.

'They might come back,' he suggested hopefully, but Isobel gave him a scathing look and went to stand by the fire, shivering with the release of tension.

'Are they gone?' Adam muttered from above the doorway. 'Is it safe to come down now?'

'Not yet,' Colin said. 'Stay where you are till we are sure they do not suspect anything. They may only be waiting for Miss MacIntosh and me to leave before coming back to make a more thorough search. Captain Ogilvie might not dare to call me a liar to my face, but that does not prove him entirely gullible.'

In silence, he and Isobel watched the road until the soldiers reappeared on it, no longer bothering to keep to the scant cover of the bare trees, but making what speed they could towards the warm beds that awaited them at Fort George. Not until the last gleam of moonlight on stirrup-iron had been swallowed by the darkness did Colin permit the two rebels to quit their hiding-place.

Swinging himself to the floor, Hugh advanced on his protector with outstretched hand. 'How can I thank you, sir?' he said fervently. 'If it had not been for your presence of mind, and you, Miss MacIntosh . . . I hope you were not recognised, for if you were, I shudder to think . . .'

'Never mind that,' Isobel pushed the thought aside quickly. 'You must be on your way now, this instant, for it is not safe for you here.'

'I agree entirely with Miss MacIntosh,' Colin emphasised. 'It seems that we have succeeded in fooling Captain Ogilvie, but I fear Major Menzies does not deem me as ardent a Whig as he would wish and may, in consequence, not be so willing to accept my story. It would be safer if you were to leave immediately, in case the troopers return.'

'If I might make a suggestion?' Adam put in hesitantly. 'It would appear a better plan if you, sir, and Miss MacIntosh were to leave first. That way you could keep an eye open in case any redcoats have been left behind to watch this place, and, if so, warn us of it.'

'An excellent idea!' Colin clapped him on the shoulder approvingly. 'Come, ma'am. We have tarried over-long already. The ball will be over and we have still to effect an entrance to Transk without being apprehended.'

'Yes, indeed. We have been much longer than we intended.'

Isobel felt drained by the events of the past hour. Now that the moment had come to take leave of Hugh, she could feel nothing but a vague irritation at the brevity of his stay. Tomorrow, no doubt, she would weep and worry, but for the moment her emotions, were exhausted. She gave him her hand and a rather wan smile. 'I wish you God-speed, Mr Murray, and hope that the next time we meet it will be in happier circumstances.'

He touched his lips to her wrist, and when his eyes met hers they were lit with warmth. 'You have been the one shaft of sunlight to enter our hiding-place, Miss MacIntosh,' he said gently. 'I shall never forget your courage and your generosity. If ever you need a friend, remember you have one, always, in Hugh Murray.'

Colin chafed visibly as she made her farewells to Adam, and when she had done, tossed her up on to his horse with an impatience that brooked no delay, so that she could do no more than raise a hand to the man who had lived so long in her thoughts and whom she might never see again. In spite of this, her thoughts on the ride home were totally concerned with what had happened between Colin and herself in the bothy. The incident now seemed so incredible that she could scarcely bring herself to believe that it had really happened.

If some fortune-teller had told her that she would one day lie happily in Colin Frazer's arms and let him kiss her—and with Hugh no more than feet away, to boot— she would have cried out in utter repudiation and horror. Yet she had not only permitted such intimacy, she had luxuriated in the experience to a level which left her extremely shaken. No one had ever dared to kiss her like that before. From time to time an audacious beau had taken advantage of an opportunity to essay a hasty buss, but those experiences had done little to prepare her for Colin's assault. Naturally, the question arose—If kissing Colin Frazer was so pleasurable, how would it feel to be kissed by Hugh?

Surprisingly, she could not bring herself to consider this seriously. Hugh was Hugh and Colin was Colin; totally different people. She simply could not imagine Hugh kissing her with such tender, yet such overwhelming passion, nor would she wish him to do so. Their relationship was, she told herself, on a higher level, a more spiritual level, and if the realisation brought a touch of regret, she refused to recognise it. The fact that she had responded to Colin's kiss did not mean that she could ever look on him with any degree of preference, and it would be altogether too uncomfortable if he were to assume otherwise.

With this in mind, she waited until they halted in the Transk stable-yard before saying, with a good deal of resolution, 'I would not wish you to think me ungrateful for your help tonight, Mr Frazer—indeed, my friends would be in custody now were it not for your quick wits, and I would be beyond redemption did I not feel beholden to you. But I do not feel under any obligation to submit to the indignities to which you subjected me tonight. Any repetition of such behaviour will be reported to my father without delay, and in the strongest possible terms.'

He lifted her down to the cobbles but remained close to her, holding her by the elbows so firmly that she could neither step back nor bend her arms to push him away. Tipping his head on one side, he regarded her with his usual amused and loving tolerance, and said softly, 'Isobel, my one love, you fight like a salmon for your liberty, refusing to admit that the hook is already embedded. Very well, I shall give you a little time, but, believe me, when I draw you in, *you'll come!*'

CHAPTER
NINE

FOR THE remainder of her stay at Transk, Isobel did her best to avoid Colin. Grateful to him as she was for the part he had played in helping Hugh and Adam to escape, she had no desire to be left alone with him, since he made it clear that he intended to pursue her relentlessly. Mrs MacIntosh was no great help in this matter, refusing point blank to believe that John Frazer's son could behave in a manner unbecoming to a gentleman, and insisting that Isobel had become either sadly prudish or over-imaginative, or both. Admittedly, in her mother's presence, Colin behaved with perfect propriety, hardly daring to raise his eyes to Charlotte's face and addressing her in such an exaggeratedly respectful tone that she was hard put to it to maintain her gravity.

Since he was playing on his home ground she did not always succeed in foiling his attempts to separate her from her chaperons, and by the end of the week she had formed a healthy respect for his ingenuity. By that time also, Elphinstone MacMartin was considerably more Colin's relative than his friend, for the moment he approached Charlotte, Colin would pop up like Orpheus from the underworld and send him packing with a calm suavity which could not be challenged in the presence of a lady, but which left his rival seething with impotent wrath.

Isobel could no more ignore these exchanges than she

could prevent them, and on one occasion burst out, as soon as Mr MacMartin was out of hearing, 'Really, Mr Frazer, you go too far. For how long am I to suffer this tyranny?'

'I don't expect it will be necessary when we are married,' he said reassuringly. 'Not, at any rate if we take up residence at Dunarras, as I expect we shall. It is those Edinburgh dandies who are the biggest problem. They *will* play with fire and, kinsman or not, Elphy is becoming rather a nuisance. I really must ask you, my love, not to encourage him so assiduously.'

'Encourage . . . ?' Isobel choked. 'How dare you? Why, we were only talking about . . .' She stopped and drew a deep breath, reminding herself that she had resolved not to let his taunts inflame her. 'Am I then to be prevented from speaking to any members of the opposite sex?'

'Only when they are as blatantly enamoured of you as Elphy is,' he comforted her. 'Much as I admire his discrimination, I fear I cannot allow him to marry you.'

Isobel clutched at her head in despair. 'I can think of no reason in the world why you should suppose he wishes to marry me, just because he chooses to talk to me once in a while,' she exploded. 'And if he did wish to marry me, you would have no right to stop him.'

'No right,' Colin agreed equably, 'but a very strong inclination.'

Perceiving her arguments to be falling on deaf ears, Isobel rose and walked away from him to the refuge of a group of dowagers near by. Elphinstone MacMartin might be a gossiping old woman, she thought spitefully, but he was better company than a jealous despot. Thus, when Mr MacMartin requested permission to call on her in Church Street on the following Monday, it was granted to him with more grace than Isobel's attitude towards him had, till then, given him cause to expect.

Fiona was also expecting a visitor that Monday, and was in such a state of excitement that she could not keep still for a minute. She had fallen *inextricably* in love, she confided to Isobel, with Andrew Melville, the green-clad young gentleman who had claimed her at the ball. Since he was not one of the favoured few who had been invited to remain at Transk for an indefinite period, he had coolly overstayed his welcome until Fiona went home, and then moved in with an uncle in Inverness in order to be near her.

'I must say he seems quite a well-bred young man,' Mrs MacIntosh conceded, as they sat in the drawing-room waiting for their callers to arrive. 'But the Melvilles of Dundas are not personally known to me. Did you elicit, my dear, whether or not they are related to Lady Melville?'

'No, Mama. I never thought to ask.' Fiona paced nervously to the window to scan the street. 'But their estate is quite exhaustive, and he is the eldest son.'

Isobel looked up from the magazine she was leafing through, and exchanged glances with her aunt. 'I feel sure you mean "extensive", Fiona. Please do not stride up and down like that. You make me feel quite jittery, and if Mr Melville sees you at the window he will think you dreadfully forward, as well as being perfectly sure that you have never had a gentleman to call on you before. You must sit down with your embroidery and pretend that you had forgotten he was coming today.'

'Perhaps it is he who has forgotten,' Fiona fretted, sitting down reluctantly but with care, that she might not crush her silken skirts.

'He is hardly due yet, dear.' Euphemia smiled soothing-ly, giving a final rub to the already glossy surface of the tea-table. 'After all, it would not be at all the thing for him to arrive too early, would it? It will be time to begin worrying an hour from now if he is still not here. But, of course, he will be.'

'How cold it is become,' Mrs MacIntosh stated, in a determined effort to change the subject. 'Just look at those dark clouds gathering. You may depend upon it, we shall have a heavy fall of snow, if not this afternoon, then certainly some time tonight. It is to be hoped that Laughlan gets home before it starts. I wish now that I had never given him permission to remain at Transk over the weekend. Poor Colin must be heartily sick of him by now, for Laughlan has spent more time at Transk since we returned from Edinburgh than he has spent at home, but still Colin allows the boy to wheedle him into inviting him. However, he will at least have Mr MacMartin's company on the ride home this time.'

Her eyes flickered momentarily to Isobel, but having already said all she had to say on the subject of Mr MacMartin, his finances, his lineage and his total inferiority to Colin Frazer, she contented herself with giving an eloquent sniff and addressed herself to Fiona, who was again showing signs of restlessness.

'Fiona, if you go to that window again, I shall be forced to send you to your room.'

'But, Mama, I hear horses at the front door.'

'If you hear more than one horse, it is more likely to be Laughlan and Mr MacMartin. But, no matter who it is, you will sit still and await them being shown in.'

But when the door opened it was, after all, Andrew Melville. His scarlet coat might have been thought a trifle vivid, but it was well cut and embellished with a quantity of Flanders lace, gold buttons and gold buttonholes. Fiona, at least, was frankly impressed, and sent him such a radiant smile of welcome that it was several seconds before he recovered his composure enough to make his bows to her companions.

'Come and sit by the fire, Mr Melville,' invited Mrs MacIntosh. 'I am sure you are frozen half to death in that wind. Do you think it will turn to snow this evening?'

He sat down beside her, quite at his ease, and crossed one booted leg over the other. 'It does seem likely, judging from the sky, but it has been overcast all day, and although there was a light fall of snow early this morning, it soon melted.'

Euphemia laid down her knitting and looked surprised at this. 'That must have been very early,' she murmured, 'for I was out at half-past eight, and saw nothing.'

Andrew looked slightly embarrassed. 'Yes, it was just after the dawn.'

'What an unearthly hour to be abroad,' Fiona giggled. 'I thought the only people who were awake at dawn were duellists and insombulists.'

Before he had time to unravel this, her mother put in roguishly, 'A *duel*! But how romantic! You must tell us all about it. Did you kill your opponent?'

Mr Melville flushed darkly, and seemed at a loss for words. Isobel caught a strong impression that the joke had struck nearer the mark than he liked, but he said, 'I fear I must disappoint you, ma'am. I have never fought a duel in my life. Nor do I ever intend to do so, if I can avoid it, for it seems to be a foolish practice and one which never yet solved an argument. If one is forced into it, of course, one has no honourable alternative, but from the antagonist who can understand nothing but physical violence, may the good Lord deliver me.'

He smiled engagingly, and Isobel, watching the way his eyes kept sliding to Fiona, felt herself drawn to him. He was probably very little younger than his friend Colin, but compared to the latter he was attractively boyish and very much more straightforward.

'You make me glad I was not born a man,' she told him, laughing. 'For sure, I would much rather be called a coward than rise at crack of dawn to let someone shoot at me. But I do agree with you that it is a most heathen custom. Rather like hunting for pleasure, I always think. I hate to think of all the beautiful birds and animals killed only to satisfy some uncivilised instinct that should have been outgrown ages ago.'

Andrew seemed more at ease with this subject, but chose to disagree with Isobel, whereupon a lively discussion ensured which was only interrupted by the arrival of the tea-tray. While the cups were being passed round, Euphemia's sharp ears caught the sound of the arrival of their visitors from Transk, and in a minute Laughlan walked in, accompanied not by Elphinstone MacMartin, but by Colin.

'I trust you will forgive this intrusion, ma'am,' murmured the latter, bowing over his hostess's hand. 'I would not have dreamed of calling on you without first ascertaining whether it would be convenient for you to receive me, but I have a message for Miss MacIntosh, and Laughlan insisted that you would not object.'

'Object? Of course I do not object, you foolish boy!' Mrs MacIntosh dealt his knuckles a playful rap with her fan. 'We are always glad to see you, as you are well aware. Sit down, and I shall give you some tea. Laughlan, love, have them send up two more places.'

Colin seated himself beside Isobel on the sofa, but before he could speak, she said tightly, 'Pray do not bother to deliver your message, Mr Frazer. I think I can guess it only too well. "Mr MacMartin presents his apologies, but finds himself unable to visit you today as Mr Frazer has so arranged things that he must be engaged elsewhere." Am I right?'

He laid an arm along the back of the sofa and crossed

one booted leg over the other. 'Not entirely,' he said, smiling at her with his eyes and making his customary minute study of her face, her hair, and the expression in her eyes.

Isobel withstood this scrutiny without flinching. She had become quite inured to his teasing but when, as now, his gaze focused on her lips and his lashes drooped lazily across his eyes, she felt her cheeks burn. He was, she knew, remembering that night in the bothy and the abandoned way she had clung to him—a memory which she had tried assiduously to put out of her own mind—and the thought made her look away hurriedly. Although he had never referred specifically to the incident, the consciousness of it loomed large between them every time their eyes met, colouring their relationship and causing Isobel no small amount of soul-searching.

She felt, rather than heard, him chuckle as he said in a resigned tone, 'Mr MacMartin is, indeed, unable to call on you, but the reason is that he is indisposed. I do hope you are not too disappointed.'

'I see.' Isobel ignored his last remark with an indifference which was a recent acquisition. 'He is not seriously ill, I hope?'

'No. No, I expect he will be up and about in a couple of days. Unfortunately, by then it will be necessary for him to return to Edinburgh, so it seems unlikely that he will be able to see you before he goes, much as he would like to.'

'Mr Frazer,' Isobel said quietly, with a restraint that was almost saintly, 'will you please go and sit elsewhere? I do not wish to speak to you.'

Colin gave this his consideration. 'Do you know,' he decided at last, 'I don't believe I will. It would look most odd, don't you think? And, besides, I cannot allow you to think me a liar. Mr MacMartin *is* indisposed, I give you my word. See, your mother is looking at us. It is time we stopped whispering together and took part in this ridiculous discussion. What a silly thing to argue about. No one but an idiot could possibly be against hunting for sport.'

Naturally, Isobel was not greatly mollified by this remark. For the remainder of Colin's visit she refused either to look at him or to speak to him, being somehow convinced that if Elphinstone MacMartin were really ill, his illness had been induced by Colin in order to prevent him from calling at Church Street. Just how this had been accomplished she could not decide, but suspecting that Laughlan knew something about it, she cornered him as soon as the visitors had gone and demanded to know the exact nature of Mr MacMartin's illness.

'Oh, it is just a slight fever. The surgeon came and bled him, and he will be up and about in a few days,' he rattled off, running his words together in a suspicious manner that made his sister look at him with narrowed eyes.

'You have learned that off by heart very well, Laughlan,' she said suddenly. 'But it is not the truth, is it?'

Laughlan's face went one shade redder than his hair. 'What do you mean? Of course it is the truth. Why should I lie about a silly thing like that?'

'Because Colin Frazer told you to, of course. Do you imagine me to be completely brainless? I am quite sure that it is his fault that Mr MacMartin was unable to come here today, and I know that you are trying to shield him.'

'What a lot of rot,' Laughlan retorted unconvincingly, and turning on his heel, made for the door.

Isobel leapt at him and hung on to his arm with both hands. 'Laughlan MacIntosh,' she cried desperately, 'you low, treacherous hound! After all I have done for you, after all the beatings I have saved you, you turn against me for this . . . this unspeakable cad! Just because he takes you shooting, you conspire against me with him, and tell me whatever lies he wants you to. How could you, Laughlan?'

He tried to loosen her fingers from his sleeve, shaking his head and stammering, 'No, Isobel—Let me go! . . . I cannot tell you—I gave my word. Please, Isobel, I tell you, it is a matter of honour.'

Isobel's fingers went numb suddenly and she fell away from him, gasping, as a dreadful suspicion struck her. 'A *duel*! Then it was Colin and Mr MacMartin? Oh God!'

'I never said it was a duel,' Laughlan howled, horrified. 'I never told you! How did you know?'

Isobel clung to the back of a chair and turned a white face to her brother. 'It was this morning, wasn't it? At dawn? And Andrew Melville was Colin's second?'

Laughlan stared at her with round eyes, plainly unsure of his position with regard to his honour. 'I don't know who can have told you, but that's right. Colin had no choice. MacMartin forced it on him in front of witnesses. Called him a coward because he refused to fight a guest in his own house, and then packed up and went off to stay with friends last night so that Colin would not be able to make *that* his excuse.'

'But why?' Isobel asked. 'What was their quarrel?'

Laughlan shrugged. 'I don't know. They tried to keep me in the dark about the whole affair, but I heard MacMartin saying he wouldn't have Colin dictating to him about his choice of friends. He was a thoroughly nasty character, you know, forever biting Colin's head off.'

Isobel sat down suddenly and leaned her head against the back of the chair, shocked, but curious in spite of herself. Now she realised that Colin's treatment of his relative had been bound to end in an explosion sooner or later. But a duel . . . even Colin could not have expected that. 'Did you see the duel?' she asked fearfully. 'What weapons did they choose?'

'I wasn't there, but I heard all about it. Colin chose swords. Andrew says this was because he is an excellent swordsman and could prevent either of them being hurt, which would have been impossible with pistols.'

'Well, he didn't prevent either of them being hurt,' Isobel objected. 'Or why is Mr MacMartin indisposed?'

'Oh, that is nothing but a scratch. He will be all right in no time. He even wanted to go on fighting, but the seconds stepped in and put an end to it. It would have been a much more chancy business with pistols.'

He looked thoughtfully at his sister's closed eyes and reflected that it was just as well Elphinstone MacMartin had been unable to call, since the interest Isobel was showing in the state of his health was too keen to be merely friendly.

Isobel was horrified. Colin's methods might be thought unorthodox, but it was frightening to realise that they might also be successful. After all, if he were able to dispose of all her future suitors with the same ease as he had disposed of Mr MacMartin, there might come a day when James MacIntosh would not be so patient or so considerate of his daughter's wishes and would give her to Colin out of sheer desperation.

With a shiver, Isobel prayed that Colin Frazer would never discover the depths of her feelings for Hugh Murray.

CHAPTER
TEN

IT VERY SOON became apparent that Andrew Melville's
interest in Fiona was no passing fancy. His visits to the
house in Church Street were, from the beginning, so
frequent that James MacIntosh was heard to predict
sourly that he would be bringing his bed next, and as
January gave way to February, scarcely a day passed but
he would arrive at the door with some small love-token
or a posy of flowers.

Fiona burgeoned like a rose. She could speak of
nothing but Andrew, and did so with such frequency and
at such length that Isobel found herself beginning to
avoid her sister's company altogether. She was happy for
Fiona, but a little of her besotted maunderings went a
long way.

The romance put Isobel in rather an awkward
position, since her father made it quite clear that he
was reluctant to marry off Fiona before he had Isobel
comfortably settled.

'And how long will that take?' Fiona demanded,
gnawing angrily on a ringlet. 'You have rejected everyone who ever offered for you, even Colin Frazer, and if
you insist on being an old maid, I don't see why I should
have to be one also!'

'Now don't make a mountain out of a molehill,' Isobel
sighed, laying down the embroidery which, so often
these days, constituted the high-spot of her afternoon. 'I

have no intention of being an old maid, and forbye, you know Papa will not keep you hanging on for long. Give him a month or two, and he will relent.'

Fiona received this with strong scepticism. 'If I were you, I'd have Colin Frazer, Isobel, honestly I would,' she said earnestly. 'You're not likely to get such a chance again. After all, you will be twenty-two in August, and, who knows . . .' Isobel's warning stare gave her pause, but she swallowed and went on doggedly, 'Well, he must love you very much or he would not be still calling on you every other day, after all this time. And, when you think about it, there isn't anyone else, is there?'

'As a matter of fact, there is!' Isobel bridled, seriously put out, and immediately cursed her quick tongue.

'*Who?*' Fiona whirled round on her so abruptly that her skirt spun about her legs, but Isobel pressed her lips together and refused to meet her eyes.

A short silence ensued, during which Fiona studied her with determination. 'I know who it is!' she produced finally. 'It's that rebel—Murray—whom we found in the bothy at Christmas. I knew all along there was something between you and him. You used to look at him so . . . oh, you know! Yes! And the other day at dinner, when Papa said there was a rumour that the rebel army was marching on Inverness, I saw you go as red as a lobster and put salt on your pudding!'

'I did not!' Isobel retorted, and then burst into a fit of giggling. 'Yes, I did, and Papa was looking at me so suspiciously that I had to eat it! It tasted like seaweed! But—oh Fiona!—The very thought of seeing Hugh again almost took my breath away. Do you think there can be any truth in the rumour?'

'Andrew thinks there is, yes. And I heard Papa telling Colin this morning that he might take us all to Shawbrae. But never mind that.' She drew forward a footstool and made herself comfortable on it with her arms folded across Isobel's knees. 'I want to know all about Hugh. I can't think why you have such a partiality for him, for he seemed to me such a . . . Oh, all right, there's no need to scowl at me! I dare say he is quite pleasant-looking in a poetic sort of way, but not at all the sort of person I would have expected you to choose. Is he like to offer for you, do you think?'

Isobel spread her hands. 'Not right away, no. After all, we've had hardly any time together—only the ten days he spent in the bothy, really. But if the rumour is true and the Pretender's army is on its way here, he must surely call and pay his respects—if only out of gratitude for the aid we gave him—and I know that he does not find me altogether repellent.'

'And you? Do you really like him enough to marry him?' Fiona wrinkled her brows incredulously. 'I mean—You really prefer him to Colin?'

'I wish you will stop referring to Colin as though he were some sort of demigod!' remarked Isobel nastily, flushing with annoyance.

'Well, I *like* him! He is a lot nicer to me than you are! We talk about words together, and when you are too moody to receive him we play at word-puzzles together—he knows a great many, you know.'

'Indeed?' said Isobel crisply, raising her brows. 'I perceive Mr Frazer has charms I knew nothing about. If he is good at word-puzzles, I must marry him without delay!'

'Well, it's a great pity if you *don't* marry him, for I shall miss him dreadfully if he should stop coming to call. So will Laughlan, I'll warrant. The two of them are as thick as thieves, and Laughlan—did you ever see such a change in him since he started going shooting with Colin? Suddenly he is so grown up.'

'Well, I dare say he would have reached the age of

sixteen without Colin's assistance!' Isobel picked up her embroidery and made several wrong stitches, wishing that she had never started this conversation, but unwilling to leave Fiona with the impression that Colin was in any way superior to Hugh. 'You see all of Colin's virtues and none of his failings. And what do you know about Hugh? Nothing! You hardly exchanged two words with him all the time he was in the bothy, yet you are sure he is not the man for me. Let me tell you, Fiona, he is a perfect gentleman. So considerate of my feelings, so undemanding. I feel I can relax and be comfortable in his company, which, I assure you, I can never do in Colin's. Perhaps, when you meet him next, you will judge him differently.'

Fiona raised a derisive eyebrow. 'I can't wait!'

But wait she did, and so did Isobel, while the days became weeks and the rumours of the rebel advance became established fact, but still there was no sign of Hugh.

In the middle of February, Prince Charles Edward, with only a small part of his following, took possession of Inverness. No one quite knew how this had been accomplished without a fight, but it was generally believed that General Hawley, who commanded the garrison, had been fooled into believing that he was being attacked by a vastly superior force. Certainly he retreated with great speed across Kessock Ferry with all his men, leaving the capital of the north to the rebels.

It had all happened so unexpectedly that there was no question of Mr MacIntosh evacuating his family to Shawbrae. Even if he had been forewarned it would have been impossible, since he was laid low with a cold, which subsequently developed into a harsh cough that kept him housebound for a month.

Isobel could not but feel that it was an ill wind that

blew nobody any good. She knew that if Hugh were to ask for her at Shawbrae he would be directed to Church Street, and besides, as long as she remained in town she could watch for him among the growing number of fighting men who daily passed her window. She and Fiona were, once again, constrained to remain indoors, but Andrew's visits broke the monotony a little and Colin continued to be a frequent, and not always unwelcome, caller. He was still inclined to press his suit a trifle too forcefully, but Isobel could not help but be reassured by his regular attendance during the invasion.

Throughout the month of March, more and more clansmen poured into the town; not like that jaunty company who had invested Edinburgh half a year ago, but threadbare and haggard after their winter campaign. Isobel watched them from her window, hour after hour, studying each man that passed lest, beneath this blue bonnet or behind that grizzled beard, she should miss the one face she longed to see.

But there was no sign of Hugh, and she began to be seriously worried. There had been at least one major battle since she had last seen him, and the possibility that he had been killed returned again and again to haunt her. If she had not been afraid to run the gauntlet of the ragged clansmen in the streets, she would have sallied forth in search of him forthwith, but she forced herself to wait till she might devise some way of providing herself with an escort.

Finally, in collusion with Fiona, she managed to make her father agree to allow both girls to go to church on the following Sunday, provided they were accompanied by Laughlan, Andrew and Colin. This plan did not allow for great scope, as far as combing the town was concerned, but she was determined to make the most of the opportunity.

All through the service her eyes moved ceaselessly over the congregation, scanning the grim-faced soldiers and uneasy townsfolk, but without success. Yet the ritual itself was a solace to her, and she emerged into the pallid sunshine afterwards armed with a new confidence.

'It's such a lovely morning,' she ventured, as they started for home. 'Let's go round by the New Wynd. It's only a step further, and I hear Gavin Lang has new lambs in his field.'

Fiona clapped her hands and looked wistfully at their three escorts. She was well aware of Isobel's ulterior motive, and had been well primed. 'Oh, do let's! I feel as though I had been immured in that house since time *in memoriam*, and had almost forgot the feel of the sun on my face.'

'I don't know, dear,' Andrew murmured unhappily. 'I did assure your father that I would bring you straight home. What do you think, Colin?'

Isobel studied the budding branches overhead as though their decision were of no moment to her, but she knew that Colin was looking at her, and there was a stillness about him which she had come to distrust. It was faintly surprising, therefore, when he said easily,

'I don't suppose five minutes extra can signify. If Laughlan agrees, I won't cavil.'

Laughlan started, in the manner of one who had not expected to be invited to express an opinion, but appeared to be quite in favour of the motion. He fell in beside Fiona and Andrew as they turned in the direction of the New Wynd, leaving Isobel with no alternative but to take Colin's proffered arm and follow.

For once, however, Colin did not seem to be disposed to pay court to her. After a short, abstracted silence which Isobel made no attempt to break, he began to speak about the groups of rebels who were everywhere—lounging in doorways, spilling out of taverns and putting every unescorted young lady to the blush in time-honoured soldierly tradition.

'These are mostly Camerons and Clan Gunn around here,' he said, indicating the sombre-hued tartan of a group they were passing. 'Your own kin, Clan Chattan, are down along the river, and round the corner there the Atholl Brigade is quartered, with the officers lodged in the inn.'

Isobel stared at the inn across the road, and forcibly relaxed her fingers which had begun to tighten on his arm. If Hugh were anywhere in Inverness, he was in that inn, and she would die rather than turn on her heel and walk away without seeing him. There must be some way of getting Colin to take her inside. She had inadvertently closed her eyes to concentrate her thoughts on the problem, when she heard Colin say sharply,

'Miss MacIntosh? Are you all right?'

The other three, walking only a pace ahead of them, turned to look at her, and Fiona cried, 'What on earth is the matter, Isobel? You look as white as a sheet!'

'Nothing . . .' A thought occurred to her, and she swayed a little, raising a hand to her head. 'I felt a little faint . . .'

'It's the cold, probably.' Colin put an arm round her shoulders. 'This wind is freezing you to the bone. We'd better get some warmth into you. Fortunately there is an inn over the road where you can sit by the fire and have some mulled wine to thaw you out. Come.'

Isobel could simply not believe her luck. If he had been schooled to the part he could not have played more faultlessly into her hands. If only—if only he were not so still. As if he were listening to some conversation which only he could hear. His face gave nothing away, but his ways had become familiar to her over the last few months, and as they crossed the road, she was strangely ill at ease.

It was crowded inside the inn, and as the private parlour was at present occupied by rebel officers, they were forced to install themselves in a corner of the taproom. Isobel had no fault to find with this arrangement, as it gave her ample opportunity to observe the company as well as to keep an eye on all the comings and goings at the doorway. It took only moments to be sure that Hugh was not present, but she sipped her hot wine slowly and waited. If an opportunity to speak to one of his fellow-Athollmen should arise, she would be ready to take it. Let Colin think what he chose, she would ask for word of Hugh and, at least, discover whether he were alive or dead.

The others, apart from Colin, were uneasy under the stares of the other patrons of the inn and were waiting impatiently for Isobel to finish her drink, when Laughlan swung round in his seat and said, 'Look, Isobel . . . That man in the doorway of the private parlour. Is it not Mr Murray?'

Something violent and cataclysmic happened in Isobel's chest, something so powerful that it seemed to bruise her rib-cage. For a second or two her eyes refused to recognise Hugh, although he stood only feet away from her with one hand on the door-handle. His face was, somehow, empty of character, almost vapid, like a pencil drawing half-erased. Then he saw Laughlan's wave and smiled, and once again he was the Hugh she remembered.

'Miss MacIntosh! And Miss Fiona! What happy chance brings you here?' He shook hands with Laughlan and Colin, and bowed in response to Laughlan's unusually polished and mature introduction of Andrew.

Laughlan it was, also, who drew forward a chair for

him and called for more wine, while Isobel sat silently trying to control the ragged unevenness of her breathing. With Fiona's eyes upon her, and Colin, alert and possibly undeluded, at her elbow, she was cautious about speaking to him, but his attention was clearly drawn to her and she met his look with a smile.

Although he looked less haggard than he had done at their last meeting, the privations of the intervening weeks had drawn deep grooves beneath his eyes, and there was a bitter twist to his mouth that had not been there before. As he answered questions about his part in the rebellion, Isobel leaned back in her chair, barely listening to the conversation, content to look at him and to know that all her worries about his survival were unfounded.

As he threw back his head to laugh at something Fiona had said to him, she saw a small scar under his jaw and was immediately thankful for the circumstances that had kept her in ignorance of the wound. In all conscience, her heart bled for him enough as it was; she had no need to torture herself with details.

'You think there *will* be a battle, then?' Laughlan's voice intruded into her thoughts, sounding sharp with excitement. 'We had heard that the Duke of Cumberland was on his way, of course, but it seemed more likely that the Jacobite army would retreat rather than make a stand. Where will it be fought, do you think? Oh, if only I could be there!'

Hugh afforded him only the barest flick of a glance. 'You wouldn't like it,' he said shortly, and turned his back to address a remark to Andrew, oblivious to the quick chagrined blush that flooded Laughlan's face.

It was a tiny incident, and Isobel could not blame Hugh for continuing to treat Laughlan like the boy he had been so recently, but she could see that her brother's pride had been stung. She sent him a sympathetic smile, but was grateful to Colin for saying, with quiet camaraderie.

'I dare say Andrew and I share the same bloodthirsty thoughts, Lachie, but we are trying to preserve a civilised front before your sisters.' He shook his head with a rueful chuckle. 'There's a cruel streak in all of us that is never far beneath the surface, and although the sight of bloodshed horrifies us, still we seek it as the dog seeks the coarse grass that makes it sick.'

'Ay, indeed. If it were not so, the practice of making war would have died out generations ago,' Andrew put in, with a spurious heartiness that showed that he too had noticed the exchange.

Laughlan looked heartened by this show of solidarity, but his mouth remained noticeably grim and it was quite clear, as they rose to take their leave some minutes later, that Fiona too was as cross as crabs, although what could have irritated her was a mystery to Isobel.

She had, till that moment, exchanged scarcely a word with Hugh, but there was really nothing she wanted to say that could be uttered in such a situation. His eyes told her that he was drawn to her, and he would have had to be vastly less sensitive than she knew him to be to have missed the fondness in her own glance. His fingers pressed her hand as he bent to kiss it, and she took the opportunity to say softly, 'We are in Church Street now, Mr Murray. If your duties permit you time to call on us, or if we can be of any service to you, anyone will direct you to the house.'

His eyes lingered on her face and he smiled a little wistfully, forgetting to release her hand. 'One day, Miss MacIntosh. One day soon, God willing.'

The words stayed in her head during the walk home, and indeed there was very little conversation to distract her from her thoughts. Both Laughlan and Fiona were silent and tight-lipped, and even Andrew seemed to be forcing himself to respond to Colin's chat. On arrival at Church Street, all three young men refused the offer of tea and took themselves off on some ploy of their own, leaving Isobel to follow Fiona indoors with a puzzled frown.

'Whatever is wrong with you, Fiona?' she said with a touch of impatience as she closed the door. 'You've been looking as grim as a mustard-pot all the way home. Have you quarrelled with Andrew?'

Fiona paused on the bottom step of the stair, and turned to glare at her as though she were experiencing great difficulty in believing her ears. 'No, I have not quarrelled with Andrew! You know perfectly well what's wrong with me, and if you mean to imply that I should not be annoyed by your wonderful Mr Murray's lack of good breeding, then I'm sorry but I must disagree.'

She swung away and trod with awesome dignity up the stair, but Isobel caught at her arm. 'I don't know what you are talking about, you silly goose! Why are you at such variance with Hugh?'

'Oh indeed? I perceive I am to set no store by his insulting behaviour. Is that it? You expect me to pay no attention when he laughs me to scorn for making the merest slip of the tongue?'

Isobel felt her own colour rise as she remembered Hugh's back-tilted head. 'What did you say?'

'That,' replied Fiona with a haughty lift of her chin, 'is nothing to the point. He had no need to make a jack-pudding of me as he did, and Andrew would have told him so to his face if Colin had not caught at his sleeve and hushed him.'

'You know, Fiona,' Isobel mentioned gently, 'some of

the things you say can be very funny, at times. I would not wish to hurt your feelings, but Hugh is not used to your way of speaking, and if he were caught unawares . . . Well, I could imagine he might find it hard to hide a smile.'

'It wasn't a smile, and he didn't even try to hide it!' Fiona said hotly, resuming her ascent as far as the landing, where she paused to add, 'You may think Mr Murray a perfect gentleman, but I think him the most boorish, ill-natured wretch imaginable! And, forbye, we helped to save his life last Christmastime, and he has not had the common civility to come and pay his respects! I hope he never does!' With which, she flounced into her room and slammed the door.

Isobel was quite upset by this scene, largely because she was disappointed that Hugh had not done himself justice in either Fiona's or Laughlan's eyes. She tried, several times in the following day or two, to make them see Hugh's point of view, stressing the tensions he had been, and still was, under, but without any noticeable success.

She was by then under considerable tension herself, as news had arrived that the Duke of Cumberland had crossed the Spey unopposed and had made his camp at Balblair, a little to the west of Nairn and a scant sixteen miles from Inverness.

The following day, April the fifteenth, the rebel army was mustered in the streets and marched out of Inverness to the wild, stirring skirl of the pipes, the bright colours of their standards glowing against a leaden sky. Towards Nairn they marched, with their proud stride and disillusioned eyes, and the word filtered back that they had taken up position on Drummossie Moor, that bleak stretch of heather near the bothy that had sheltered Hugh and Adam three long months before.

CHAPTER
ELEVEN

ISOBEL SPENT the afternoon and evening of that day in mounting anxiety. Every slammed door sounded like the distant roar of cannon, and the black clouds that hung low in the eastern sky were tinged with pink as though they reflected a burning town. By noon she found herself rushing to the window every time she heard hoofbeats in the street below, lest it should be some fugitive from the battle. Just as she was about to send Agnes in search of news, Colin Frazer was announced and she ran downstairs to greet him with less than her customary reticence. He was seated in the drawing-room with her mother, and without waiting for him to straighten from his bow, she demanded eagerly,

'What news of the battle, Mr Frazer? If you have just ridden in from Transk, you must have passed Drummossie Moor.'

'I passed, yes, but not closely. It seemed only prudent to give the rebels a wide berth, lest I be taken for a spy.' He half-turned to her mother, and added, 'Nor would I have ventured forth this morning but to offer you and your family the protection of my home in case there is any disturbance in town.'

Mrs MacIntosh smiled at him placidly. 'How very thoughtful of you, my dear boy. But you must not put yourself in a taking for our sakes, for I am persuaded that we will be in no danger. Besides, Mr MacIntosh is not sufficiently recovered to undertake the drive in this dreadful weather. His cough still bothers him, you know, and Dr Andrews will not hear of his going out until it is quite gone.'

'In that case I must hope that my fears are without foundation,' Colin replied gravely. 'But, since Mr MacIntosh is still indisposed, perhaps it would be as well if I were to stay with you for a few hours. I met Laughlan on my way up, and I think he would be glad of a little reinforcement.'

'I feel sure my husband, too, would feel easier in his mind if he had your support,' Mrs MacIntosh beamed. 'And, I confess, it would be a comfort to me. But are you sure they will be all right at Transk?'

'My uncle and father are there,' Colin replied, 'and most of our servants have been with us for generations and can be relied upon not to run off at the first sign of looting. Not,' he added quickly, as both ladies showed signs of alarm, 'that I expect anything of the sort, but it is always wise to be prepared for any contingency. If you have not already done so, I would advise you to put all your valuables away in a safe place, since, if you are called upon to house any of the victorious army, it would be advisable to acquiesce.'

Isobel suspected that much of his consternation was assumed solely as an excuse to spend the day with her, but she thwarted him by showing him up to her father's room and leaving him there.

Late in the evening it was learned that although the Highlanders had been drawn up in battle formation across the moor since dawn, the Duke of Cumberland had not stirred from his camp at Nairn and, since it was his birthday that day, it seemed reasonable to suppose that his men would spend the evening in celebrating the event rather than in launching a night attack. Thus reassured, Colin had no excuse for prolonging his visit and took himself off, promising to return on the morrow should there be any cause for alarm.

In spite of this comforting news, Isobel spent a sleepless night and watched the dawn with heavy eyes. The wind was still beating in from the east bringing with it a blast of sleet that pattered on the window like a small animal trying to get in. The streets were deserted by all save those whose business was urgent, and over all hung that palpable tension, quivering in the air like a plucked harp-string. By mid-morning she could stand the strain of waiting no longer, and determined to slip out for a short ride before Colin's arrival made escape impossible.

It was unlikely that she would be missed for an hour or so, as her father normally stayed in his library most of the morning and Euphemia had enlisted Fiona's and Mrs MacIntosh's help in hiding away the best crystal. At first she had intended to take a servant with her, Laughlan being engaged with his tutor, but on reflection it seemed doubtful if any of the servants would accede to her request without making sure that she had her parents' permission to go out, so she decided to go alone. By informing Agnes that she had a headache and intended to lie down for an hour or so, she was able to prevent any awkward questions being asked should she be delayed, and as soon as she was left alone, she donned her warmest riding-habit, topping it with a hooded cloak to keep out the sleet, and let herself out into the boisterous wind.

The ostler at the livery stable where Stella was lodged gave her an odd look to see her unattended, but luckily he was either too polite or too uninterested to comment, and five minutes later she was clattering across the toll-bridge as fast as Stella's dancing hooves could take her. Until that moment she had not consciously decided to ride to Drummossie Moor, but it occurred to her in a flash that from the high ground some distance away from where she imagined the rebels to be camped, it would be possible to see whether a battle were imminent, so she turned Stella's head in that direction.

Mindful of Colin's remark of the previous day, she took a circuitous route in case she was seen, so that it was well after midday when she reached the moor. Skirting the precincts of Culloden House, from where she expected to be able to see the rebels in the distance, she breasted a slight rise and was astounded to perceive the two armies, government as well as rebel, manoeuvring for position not three hundred yards below her. Dismounting hastily, she drew Stella into the shelter of the wall, and stared down with frightened eyes.

To her left, the Duke of Cumberland's forces were moving forward, fixed bayonets glittering and colours flying, to the staccato rattle of drums. Facing them stood the rebels, motionless except for the ceaseless coming and going of aides-de-camp, the motley hues of their tartans darkened by the sleety hail that blew in their faces. In the centre of the front line she could see the yellow banner of her own clan, but the Atholl Brigade was not immediately apparent.

At last she located them, far away on the right wing— the last place where she would have thought to look for them, since that coveted position had been the hereditary right of the MacDonalds since the time of Robert the Bruce. One glance at the latter clan was sufficient to tell her that the exchange of positions had not been of their seeking. They were on the left wing, immediately below her, and the angry faces were clearly visible.

To Isobel, standing stiffly in the lee of the wall, it

seemed a typical piece of male bravado that the rebels should continue to stand patiently waiting until the redcoats were ready, instead of charging there and then while they were at a disadvantage. Most of Cumberland's regiments were up to the ankles in a bog, and the artillery horses were sinking and had to be unyoked, the soldiers slinging their carbines and dragging the gun-carriages to firmer ground. But although a tremor ran through the rebel ranks and a few derisive shouts rang out, they did not move.

A movement on a knoll behind the Highlanders attracted her attention, and she noticed a small party of gentlemen on horseback who had come, no doubt, from Inverness to witness the battle. Nor were they the only observers. At the far side of the field, within the Urchil enclosures, huddled a group of beggars, waiting like vultures to swoop down on the battlefield and strip the bodies of the slain.

Isobel was shivering uncontrollably. She did not wish to be a witness to the slaughter that she knew would follow, and she was well aware that her absence would be noted if she did not start for home right away, but the thought of Hugh Murray, facing his death among that dark-kilted corps at the furthest end of the front line, held her like a ball and chain. There might be nothing she could do to help him, and she did not even dare to emerge from her hiding-place so that he might see her if he looked that way, but nevertheless she stayed.

The Highlanders were moving now, not advancing, but rather trying to swing round so that the sleet was not driving full in their faces, but the redcoats, equally vigilant, contrived to counteract their movements. Presently a figure detached itself from the government ranks and, riding forward in a manner so coolly insolent as to

be a studied insult to the rebels, proceeded to reconnoitre. He was greeted by a skirl of piping and a loud
burst of Gaelic epithets, followed by a volley from the
Prince's puny two- and four-pounder guns, through the
smoke of which the rider was seen to beat a discreet, but
not hurried, retreat.

The feeble cannonade was sustained for several minutes, during which Isobel was forced to keep a firm hold
on Stella's head, but the faint rumble was drowned by a
thunderous roar as the Duke of Cumberland's cannon
opened fire. Volley after volley poured across the moor
from the mouths of the monstrous cannon that interspersed each regiment in the government front line, and
each time the smoke cleared to show gaps and, in places,
whole lanes blasted through the rebel ranks. Grapeshot
and cannon-balls ploughed into the motionless bat-
tallions, splattering the clansmen with the blood of their
comrades. Above the sound of the firing, Isobel could
hear the screams of wounded horses and the hoarse
cursing of the men nearest her. Ten . . . fifteen . . .
twenty minutes passed, and still the merciless fusillage
took its terrible toll, till she could hear herself sobbing,
her eyes pressed to Stella's quivering neck.

'Oh, *charge*, you fools! Why do you not *charge*?'

At last, inevitably, the rebel line broke. The Mac-
Intoshes, galled beyond endurance by the brutal
slaughter of their comrades, uttered a deep-throated cry
and hurled themselves forward into the gun-smoke,
followed by the MacLeans and the MacLaughlans on
their immediate left. Half-way across the intervening
space a vicious blast of fire from their enemy's centre and
right wing forced them to veer sharply to their right, full
in the path of the now charging Atholl Brigade, with
whom they mingled in such confusion that there was no
room to wield their broadswords. All the clans were

charging now, and the smoke-filled air was alive with the rattle of musketry and wild, half-animal yelling. Ignoring the hail of grapeshot that still thinned their ranks, blind to the sustained musket-fire of the three foremost government files, the rebels threw themselves across the heather, screaming the war-cries of their clans, brandishing their broadswords in a frenzy of hatred. Enveloped as they were in the smoke from the belching cannon, they could scarcely have seen their enemies until they were among them, but the firing was so incessant and accurate that pitifully few survived long enough to skewer themselves on the waiting hedge of bayonets.

Mercifully much of this carnage escaped Isobel's notice, as her eyes never left the Atholl Brigade who were now in possession of the two great guns between Barrell's and Munro's regiments and, at that distance, little could be seen with any clarity. Even at that, she was frightened as she had never been frightened before. Sweat trickled in an icy rivulet between her shoulder-blades and mingled with the tears and sleet on her face, but she clung resolutely to the terrified Stella's bridle and could not look away. The scene had taken on a nightmarish unreality. Shock and horror combined to deaden her perception, and the sharp edge of despair was blunted by the dogged hope that Hugh might, by a miracle, survive the conflict.

At last the rebels—those who could still stand—began to retreat over the mutilated bodies of their brothers, and the Duke of Cumberland's host formed up for the pursuit. The churned heather of the moor was strewn with dead and dying, and those who moved were summarily dealt with by the redcoats. Shielding her eyes from the slanting hail, Isobel stared across the plain to where the Atholl Brigade had fought. It seemed that the ground there was thick with bodies, no small proportion of them scarlet-coated. Among them might be Hugh Murray.

Without being aware that she had moved, she found herself skirting the field, keeping to the hill behind the now advancing government soldiers, and edging slowly and cautiously towards that ghastly pile of broken bodies. A little way ahead of her a ragged clansman darted across her path, blood spurting from the severed stump of his right arm, but he did not see her and, retching, she guided Stella towards the high wall of the Culwhiniac farm. This wall had been on the right of the Atholl men when they charged, but it had afforded them little protection from the fire of two hundred of their own countrymen, Campbells, stationed behind it, a fact borne out by the evidence of the massacred bodies piled in places three deep in its lee. Now Isobel saw, at close quarters, the hellish butchery that distance and gun-smoke had masked earlier, and the sight was one that haunted her for the rest of her life.

Forcing herself to scan the calm upturned faces, she went forward on foot, leading Stella and praying that Hugh might still be alive. At every few steps she was forced to halt until the waves of nausea and faintness that swept over her subsided, and it was while she was standing thus, with her forehead pressed to the wet stone of the Culwhiniac wall, that she heard her name called and, whirling round, saw Hugh. He was lying close to the wall, half-covered by the lifeless body of a burly redcoat. His face was so covered with blood as to be unrecognis-able, and had he not spoken, Isobel would almost certainly have passed him by.

'Hugh!' she gasped, running forward. 'Oh, my dear, you are wounded. But thank God you are still alive!' She heaved desperately at the corpse of the redcoat, and at length succeeded in pulling it aside. Hugh's jacket and kilt were saturated with blood. 'Can you sit a horse, do you think? We must be quick before the English find you. Here—Put your arm round my neck and I shall try to pull you up.'

He seemed dazed, and made no reply other than a muttered, 'Isobel . . . Isobel . . .' as she struggled to get him on his feet, but with her help he managed to bestride Stella behind the saddle. Trembling with shock and fatigue, Isobel scrambled up before him. He was swaying precariously, but she made him take a firm grip of her cloak, and drawing his free arm under her own, she held on to it with all her strength and gave Stella a kick that sent her springing into the woods.

At first she had no very clear idea of where she was going—anywhere away from the scene of inhuman violence behind her being preferable—but when the woods began to thin, she caught a glimpse of the turrets of Transk and an idea was born. If she could but reach Colin, or get a message to him, he would know where to hide Hugh. Probably he would still be in Inverness, but the servants knew her and would ride for him if she demanded it, so she turned south and began a stealthy descent to the big house. At times it seemed that Hugh would not be able to keep his seat long enough for them to reach safety, for he kept falling sideways and his face was as white as chalk. For the last hundred yards Isobel was forced to dismount and hold him in position, a feat which used up all but the last few ounces of her energy and left her aching and dizzy. The weight of her heavy cloak hampered her movements, and her stays were so tight that she could hardly breathe.

They entered Transk through the park gates, and kept to the cover of the trees until they approached the cobbled yard that fronted the stables. Here Isobel let

Hugh slip to the ground and made him comfortable in a small gap in the bushes.

'You must wait here for me,' she told him breathlessly. 'I shall be back for you as soon as I can, but I may be some time.'

He opened his eyes reluctantly and forced a smile. 'I . . . might have known . . . you would come . . . as usual.'

Isobel's eyes misted over, but she rose to her feet and led Stella towards the house. So absorbed was she with rearranging her cloak lest she present a suspicious appearance that she had taken several steps out of the trees before she looked up and saw the red-coated soldiers that seemingly filled the stable-yard.

She felt her knees give, and as a whirling blackness closed over her head, she heard voices shouting and footsteps hurrying towards her.

CHAPTER
TWELVE

THE ROOM in which Isobel opened her eyes was in pitch darkness, although a small grating high up on one wall showed a patch of dark blue sky, across which clouds drifted sluggishly. Near by there was an intermittent drip of water, and from the other side of the wall against which she lay came a shuffle of hooves and an occasional snort that told her she had not been carried far from where she had fainted. Getting rather unsteadily to her feet, she groped her way along the wall till she came to the door, but it was securely bolted on the other side and barely rattled in its frame when she shook the handle. The grating was too high for her to reach, so she returned to the bundle of straw on which she had been lying and sat down, suddenly too spiritless to do anything but weep.

That Hugh had been found was evident in the way she had been imprisoned, for otherwise she would have been taken for a visitor to the house or even a resident, and allowed to pass unmolested. As things had turned out, it would have been better to have left him on the battlefield, where he might have feigned death until he was strong enough to make good his escape. Instead of that he would now, of a certainty, be shot—if indeed such a fate had not already overtaken him.

You fool, Isobel told herself bitterly. You are so well able to look after yourself that you have brought about not only your own ruin but that of the man you tried to save. She tried to think of some way to save Hugh, but all her old self-confidence and resource seemed to have deserted her, and she did not dare to hope that it was not already too late. Even if he still lived, she realised with a pang of despondency, no reliance could be put on his powers of strategy. It was of no use waiting for him to make a move, as he would, without a doubt, be waiting for her to think of something.

It was impossible to calculate how long she had been unconscious as it had been almost dusk when she reached Transk, and although she could see that the sun had now set, it might have done so hours or minutes ago. Utterly despairing, she fell into a storm of weeping, and was so distracted that she heard nothing until a boot scraped on the cobbles just outside her door. Dashing a hand across her eyes, she cringed into her corner, and listened. Gently, almost soundlessly, she heard the key turn in the lock and then a slow, furtive rasp as the bolt was withdrawn. Wide-eyed, she watched the door swing inwards, and saw a tall figure stoop to pass beneath the low lintel.

'Are you there, Isobel?'

At the whisper, she was across the room like a deer, clinging to his arm and sobbing hysterically. 'Colin! Is it really you? Oh, thank God!'

He caught her shoulders in his two hands and held her away from him, steadily and reassuringly, as he said, 'You must be very quiet, Isobel. Follow me, and don't speak until I say you may.'

He grasped her arm and hustled her through the doorway, pausing to pull the door closed behind them and slide home the bolt. Loud voices echoed from the grooms' quarters at the far side of the yard, but Colin set off in the opposite direction, across the cobbles and down a steep embankment planted with fruit-bushes that caught at Isobel's cloak as she pushed her way through them. Striking a rough path, they turned off to the left, and in a few minutes she saw the river beneath them, the dark hump of a small bridge silhouetted against its steely gleam.

Colin hurried her towards this bridge, but instead of crossing it, he helped her down the bank and showed her where she might hide dry-shod under its steep arch. 'Now *stay* here,' he ordered, with what she considered to be unnecessary firmness, 'and do not move until I come back for you, no matter how long I am, and no matter *what* happens.'

'Wait, ' Isobel panted, a hand to the stitch in her side. 'Hugh Murray—Is he—Did they find him?'

'I am going for him now. Don't worry if I am a long time in returning.'

With that, he turned away and clambered up the bank, leaving her to contemplate the rushing water. Downstream lay the solid bulk of a turreted tower, only slightly darker than the moonless sky behind it. A glow of yellow candlelight illuminated one upper window, but no shapes moved in the room beyond and no sounds were carried on the wind that whipped her skirts about her legs and stirred the tresses of her tumbled hair. The silence of the night closed in round her, swallowing the gurgling of the river and the whining of the wind in its overpowering emptiness. She closed her eyes against it, but its loneliness was in her heart, and there was no one to turn to.

It seemed hours before Colin came back. Hearing the sound of hoofbeats, she had drawn back into the shadows, thinking it was someone else, when he slid down the bank in a miniature avalanche of pebbles and stretched out his hand to help her out of her refuge.

'Is he there?' she asked anxiously, not waiting to see for herself, and as he nodded, she scrambled up the bank impatiently. Two horses stood at the side of the bridge, her own Stella and the big chestnut she had ridden once before. Astride the latter sat Hugh, slumped over the pommel as though it took all his will-power to keep him there.

'Mr Murray!' She ran to him and laid a hand on his arm. 'Only hold out a little longer and we shall be safe away.'

He lifted his head and essayed a weak smile. 'Yes indeed, ma'am. I shall be quite recovered presently. If only I could shake off this infernal dizziness.'

Colin appeared at her shoulder, holding Stella's bridle. 'It is all right,' he said softly. 'Mr Murray is not as seriously wounded as he appears. Most of the blood is not his own.'

He helped her to mount, and then, springing up behind Hugh, led the way across the bridge at a brisk pace. A winding track led up into the hills, and they followed this for some miles before turning off across a stretch of barren hillside and skirting a raging torrent that fell a hundred feet to feed the swollen river. A little higher up, they came to the top of the pass, and from there the track descended so sharply that Colin was compelled to take hold of Stella's bridle and steady her for fear she would lose her footing. His own mount was as sure-footed as a garron for all its height, but Hugh was swaying drunkenly in the saddle and Isobel could hear Colin swearing under his breath as he strove to hold him steady.

She was not altogether surprised, therefore, when he halted abruptly and groaned, 'It seems Mr Murray is suffering from the effects of his head wound. I had hoped that we might be able to get further away from

Transk tonight, but we shall have to stop and let him rest for a few hours. There is a cave up there which may serve to shelter us.' He pointed up the precipitous boulder-strewn slope to his right, and looked at her quizzically. 'Do you think you can make it?'

Isobel was far from certain, but she nodded and followed him as he guided his mount off the path. They went up at an angle, stones rolling away from under the sliding hooves of their mounts to clatter down and down, further than she cared to look. She had her eyes on the ground when Colin called a halt and, looking up, could see no sign of the cave he had spoken of. Turning an enquiring gaze upon him, she found him watching her closely.

'Good,' he nodded, as if well satisfied. 'If *you* cannot see it, knowing it to be there, it may well escape notice in the daylight. I found it years ago when I used to run wild in these hills, but I never thought to put it to such practical use. See here.'

He had dismounted, leaving Hugh slumped over his horse's withers, and now pushed aside the branches of a stunted bush that grew against the rock, disclosing a dark aperture about the height of a man.

'Now, if you will hold these branches aside while I get Mr Murray inside, it will prevent any being broken and exposing the opening.'

He went to pull Hugh off his horse, lifting him in his arms with an ease that gave Isobel grounds to doubt the validity of the aspersions she had cast on his shoulders.

'Leave your horse where it is,' he grunted over his burden. 'I shall have to find some place to hide them.'

As she followed him into the cave, Isobel was unable to see anything of her surroundings because of the impenetrable darkness which fell like a blanket over her head, but she heard the scrape of a flint and, a moment later, a candle flickered into life. It illuminated a dry chamber about eight feet square, with a roof that was lost in the shadows. Wedging the candle into a crack in the rock wall, Colin rose from his knees and draped Hugh's plaid across the entrance, saying, 'Don't take this down while the candle is burning, as the light may be seen from a distance. And you had better take off that wet cloak. You will find two plaids in my pack, and also some bandages and a salve for Mr Murray's wounds.'

He went over to where Hugh was lying at the back of the cave and dropped on one knee beside him. 'There appears to be a ball in your shoulder, Mr Murray,' he said gently. 'But if you will allow Miss MacIntosh to bathe it, I shall take it out as soon as I have found some shelter for the horses.'

Hugh moistened his lips with the tip of his tongue and moved his head groggily. 'It does not pain me greatly,' he muttered. 'But my head . . . I feel so dreadfully dizzy.'

Colin nodded. 'A few hours' sleep will mend that. There is a slight wound on your head and quite a bit of bruising round it, but it is not deep.'

He straightened and crossed to the opening, ducking through it and letting the plaid swing to behind him, blotting out the darkness.

Isobel turned to the leathern pack which Colin had dropped on the floor. It was so tightly packed that she had difficulty in getting it open, and she was amazed to see what a variety of articles Colin had managed to cram inside it. Beside the two plaids, which took up most of the space, she found a small silver-mounted pistol with powder and shot, three candles, a razor, a small flask of brandy, a lump of cheese and, right at the bottom, a long strip of linen and a jar of salve. Carrying the last two, she sat down on the floor beside Hugh and prepared to bathe his wounds.

'You were very lucky to come off so lightly,' she told him, parting his hair to examine the cut on his scalp and finding it swollen but not deep. 'I never thought to see you alive again! Did the Prince know in advance that the Duke of Cumberland's army outnumbered his own by at least two to one?'

A faint tinge of colour came and went on his grey cheeks. 'He must have done,' he said haltingly, with closed eyes. 'It was sheer lunacy to fight today. The men were starving and worn out. They had been standing in battle-order all day yesterday from dawn till eleven at night. Then they marched almost to Nairn in the hope of attacking the redcoats while they slept. Even last night the men were so exhausted that it began to grow light before we were within three miles of Nairn. We had scarcely two hours' rest before word arrived that Cumberland was on the march. Most of us had nothing to eat since a chunk of bannock that was handed out to us yesterday.'

Realising from his heightened colour that her choice of a topic for conversation had not been a happy one, Isobel said soothingly, 'You must try not to upset yourself, Mr Murray. It is of not the slightest use to fret about something that is over and done with. Now, lie still while I take a look at your shoulder.'

His jacket was stiff with dried blood, but when she had eased it gingerly off his shoulder she was relieved to find that the wound beneath it was neither as large as she had expected nor bleeding profusely. While she was cleaning away what little blood there was, Colin returned, and stood for a moment just inside the doorway, shaking the raindrops from his wet hair. She smiled at him over her shoulder, but he affected not to notice and came to crouch at her elbow without looking at her.

'That's got the horses out of the way,' he said. 'Now let us see what can be done about this musket-ball.' He explored Hugh's shoulder with gentle fingers, and nodded. 'Yes, I thought so. The ball is still here, but, thank God, it must have been well-nigh spent before it hit you, because it is not deeply embedded.' Standing up, he stripped off his jacket and turned back the cuffs of his shirt.

'Will you move the candle a little closer, Miss Mac-Intosh, and then go and sit in that corner where you need not see what I am about to do.'

'I shall stay and help you . . .' Isobel was beginning, but he interrupted.

'On the contrary, you will do as you are told. The candle, if you please.'

Isobel placed the candle where he indicated, with such haste that it guttered, and then withdrew to the far side of the cavern, wondering if her ears were playing her tricks. Never, in all the years she had known him, had Colin used such a tone to her—or, indeed to anyone else in her hearing—and she was bitterly hurt that he should do so now. His whole attitude towards her had changed so completely in the last few hours that she was at a loss to account for it. He was angry with her, that much was obvious, but understandable, for her conduct in running away from home and allying herself with a rebel could not be expected to please him. He must have realised at once that she would henceforth be labelled as a traitor, and hunted like all other active Jacobites, which meant that his marrying her was out of the question, but why . . .?

Suddenly she realised what she had been too preoccupied to consider earlier, and the enormity of the thought made her gasp with dismay. Thanks to her own senseless meddling, she had managed to bring about Colin's downfall as well as her own. If he were to return to Transk now, after helping two rebel prisoners to escape, he would be arrested and thrown into jail to await a trial which could have only one outcome. He must have realised this from the outset, but, in all conscience, he had had no choice, and no wonder he was angry with her. Writhing with self-reproach, she glanced at the lean line of cheek that was all she could see of his averted face. I'm sorry, I'm sorry, she groaned inwardly, but the total inadequacy of the words was an added rebuke.

'Miss MacIntosh.'

He had straightened, and was wiping his hands on a bloodstained piece of cloth.

'If you wish to be of assistance, you may bind on this dressing while I support Mr Murray. Unfortunately, he has fainted, but the ball is out and the wound is not at all serious.' He raised his eyes to her anguished face, and added quickly, 'You need not, if you do not wish it. I only thought . . .'

Isobel drew a deep and painful breath. 'I am not squeamish,' she said, stepping over to kneel beside him. 'It is only that . . . I have just realised what a fool I have been . . . and I want to tell you that I am ashamed of myself.' She paused, gulping, determinedly blinking back the tears that blinded her. 'If you can forgive me for the ill-fortune I have brought upon you . . .'

He stopped her with a hand on her wrist, and she looked up to find him smiling gently. 'There is nothing to forgive, Miss MacIntosh. I beg you will not torture me with your tears. What I have done, I did of my own free will, and you are in no way to blame. If I was angry with you, it was only because of the danger in which you put yourself. But let us attend to Mr Murray, and then we can converse at ease.'

He raised Hugh's shoulders and held the pad in

position while she bound it on with trembling fingers, and then, having tucked a dry plaid about the limp body, motioned her to sit down with her back against the wall. He stretched himself out beside her.

A silence wrapped itself about them; that cold, desolate, silence that ate into Isobel's courage. To shatter it, she said quickly, 'What is to happen to us, Mr Frazer? When will it be safe for us to go back to Inverness?'

He looked at her and away again, hesitating.

'You do not seem to appreciate fully the seriousness of our position,' he said at last. 'No one who has had the slightest connection with the rebellion will be safe in Scotland for some time to come. It seems that the Duke of Cumberland intends to spare no pains to ensure that every last ember of revolt is stamped out. His soldiers— his *butchers*—were ordered today to give no quarter. After the battle, all those rebels who were too badly wounded to escape were killed where they lay. Inverness is seething with people only too willing to lay information against their friends in order to save their own skins. In my opinion, the only alternative to skulking in the heather is to take ship for France or the Low Countries.'

Isobel pressed a hand to the ache in her throat and steadied her voice with an effort, as she said, 'Yes, I see that now. Oh, what a Pandora's box I opened when I meddled in this business! My parents must be worried out of their wits.'

'At least they know I am with you,' Colin said soothingly. 'I took the opportunity to send them a message before I left Transk. But worried indeed they were when I saw them this morning. Your father and Laughlan and I rode miles in search of you, and it was only by a lucky chance that I saw Stella in the stables when I went home to see if you had been seen there. How came you to meet up with Mr Murray?'

Isobel gave him a brief *résumé* of the afternoon's events, and when she had finished, his face was so grim it frightened her.

'I suppose you realise you might easily have been shot or thrown into the Tollbooth for helping a rebel to escape?'

'Yes, but you have just done the same thing.'

'That is nothing to the point. From the little I saw of Culloden today, you were fortunate to escape with your life. Lord . . .' He passed a hand across his eyes and his teeth gleamed white in the semi-darkness. 'I never knew such a girl for being where she ought not to be.'

Isobel dropped her eyes from his, but returned meekly, 'I cannot entirely regret what I did, for if I had not, Mr Murray would have been murdered with the rest of the wounded.'

'There I am forced to agree with you,' Colin said with such fervour that she looked up at him curiously. 'If he had died . . .' He went on, querulously, 'Must you always be so independent? If you insist on helping lame dogs over stiles . . .' He broke off to peer at Hugh, who seemed to be coming round. 'Ah, that's better, Mr Murray. Do not try to sit up just yet, and you will feel more the thing presently.'

He rummaged in his satchel, and producing the flask of brandy, raised Hugh's head and allowed a few drops of the raw spirit to trickle between his lips. A little colour returned to Hugh's cheeks, and in a moment he looked up at Isobel, who was bending over him, and achieved a rueful smile.

'You must be . . . well inured to . . . the sight of blood by now, ma'am.'

'T'was but a small wound, I think,' Isobel assured him. 'But it appeared much worse than it was. The redcoat who was lying on top of you when I found you must have bled all over you. Does it feel more comfortable now?'

'Yes indeed.' His eyes swung to Colin, and he added, 'I am greatly indebted to you, sir. Without your assistance I would never have managed . . .'

'Pray do not speak of that,' Colin smiled, settling back against the wall. 'It was little enough I was able to do. But now I suggest we get some sleep, for we must be on our way as soon as it is light.'

'On our way to where?' Hugh asked. 'This district cannot be safe for us, and the roads leading south are sure to be patrolled.'

'Most certainly,' Colin agreed, 'and the longer we delay here the more dangerous it will become. Only by taking ship to France can . . .'

'France? Impossible!' Hugh interrupted, shaking his head. 'Do you suppose that Inverness harbour will not be infested with redcoats even now?'

Colin moved a hand negligently. 'On the contrary, I am quite convinced that it will be, but luckily that is not our only hope. One of my father's friends, who is a merchant in Inverness, is in the habit of supplementing his income with a little free-trading, and I happen to know that he is hoping to land a cargo at Tarbat Ness in a few days' time. Both the captain of the vessel and the agent at Tarbat Ness know me well, so I think it may be possible to secure passage for the return journey.'

'But Tarbat Ness is a long way from here,' Isobel said doubtfully. 'We may be arrested before we reach there. And what shall we do if we arrive too late?'

'There are risks involved, I know that,' Colin admitted. 'But, whatever we decide to do, we cannot avoid taking risks, and this way we at least have a chance of getting out of the country. However, if you have any other suggestions, I shall be glad to hear them.'

Isobel lapsed into a depressed silence, but Hugh raised himself on one elbow and stated positively,

'It appears that we have no choice but to make for Tarbat Ness, and that as soon as possible. The revolt is at an end, for the time being at least, but I shall never be able to go home to Dunkeld. All those who bore arms for the Prince will be marked men. But to leave Scotland altogether . . . I confess, the prospects all but unman me.'

'A change in one's environment is not always welcome, I know, but how often does it turn out to be as dreadful as one imagines it will be?' Colin pulled his satchel towards him and drew out the cheese which he began to cut into three pieces. 'It seems inherent in most of us to view the future with pessimism, does it not? When I was eight years old, my father decided that I was to be sent away to school at Dunfermline, and I still remember how violently I reacted to the proposal. I bullied my mother and pleaded with my father, but they would not relent. It seemed like the end of the world at the time, but my days at Dunfermline were among the happiest in my life to date, and when the time came to go on to college in Edinburgh I was not a bit eager to exchange my old friends and familiar tutors for the new experience of the capital. For all that, I enjoyed my college days and did not turn my back on them without regret.' He laughed lightly, and offered Isobel a piece of cheese on the point of his *sgian*, as he added, 'In future I am determined to reserve judgment until I am better acquainted with my situation.'

Isobel saw the point of this dissertation and felt a little cheered, but she refused the cheese on the grounds that she was not hungry.

'I dare say you are not,' Colin remarked without

moving. 'But, unless I am mistaken, you have eaten nothing since early this morning—or rather, yesterday morning, for it is now past midnight—therefore you will oblige me by eating this now. I cannot guarantee when our next meal will be, since we must henceforth live on what we can shoot, but you will sleep better if you eat first.'

Isobel's chin jutted mutinously, but rather than cause a scene in front of Hugh she took the cheese, and at the first bite discovered that she was starving. They ate in silence, wrapped in their own thoughts, and then Colin rose and strolled to the cave mouth, pulling aside the damp plaid to look out at the sky.

'The clouds seem to be lifting a little,' he reported. 'Let us get what sleep we can, and we shall be ready to set off early. There is a dry plaid here, Miss MacIntosh, and I shall roll up your cloak as a pillow for you.'

Isobel tucked the plaid round her, but sat up, hunched in her corner, too tired to sleep, too bitterly ashamed of herself to take comfort in being at last with Hugh. Colin gave her a long look as he bent to snuff the candle, but except for an expressionless 'Good night', made no remark. That he had not once upbraided her for causing his ruin was no balm to her conscience, and she fell asleep at last with a pain in her heart and a fold of the plaid across her mouth to stifle her sobs.

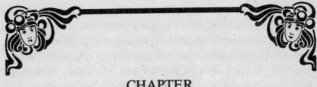

CHAPTER
THIRTEEN

THE DAY, when it dawned, was cold and starkly silver, barely penetrating the mist that hung low over the hills and drifted in lazy whorls through the cave mouth. Isobel woke reluctantly, irked by a peculiarly harrowing ebb and flow of sound that seemed to come from behind her. Upon investigation, she discovered this sound to emanate from Hugh who was still deeply and noisily asleep at the back of the cave. One arm was outflung from his plaid, and with his flushed cheeks and ruffled hair, he looked so young and vulnerable that she felt a warm rush of tenderness.

'Poor lamb,' she whispered to him. 'You need me more than ever now.'

Of Colin there was no sign, but supposing him to have gone to see to the horses, she was not unduly disturbed, and lay down again, drawing her coverings close against the chill of the morning air. Remembering the uncomfortable position in which she had fallen asleep, she was surprised to find herself so well rested, but this was explained in a minute when she found that she was wrapped, not only in the plaid, but in her own cloak and that under her cheek was Colin's jacket. Evidently he had done his best to make her comfortable while she slept. Uncertain whether to be grateful or embarrassed, she sat up and tried to smooth the creases out of her skirt, wishing that Agnes had not laced her stays so tightly the previous day. The coarse material was chafing her spine and waist, but she could not loosen them without assistance and could find relief only by holding herself very straight and taking shallow breaths. While she waited for Colin to come back, she folded his plaid and jacket and placed them neatly beside his satchel, but when this was done she became uneasy and decided to go and look for him.

The mist was lifting slightly, but it was still not light enough for her to see far and she hesitated outside the cave mouth, uncertain which way to turn. A faint splash of water decided her, and as she followed the sound, she heard singing, soft and eerie, interspersed with shuddering gasps. Intrigued, she crept closer, peering into the mist, but poised to turn and flee if it should not be Colin.

In a moment she came upon a rushing stream that leapt downhill with a hilarious babble of melted snow. On its bank lay four trout, neatly laid out side by side in order of size, and a few yards higher up a white shirt flapped idly from a jagged rock. Colin was crouched over the creaming torrent, stripped to the waist, slapping icy water on his face and chest. He was still singing, but broke off at every plunge to gasp with the shock, and the smooth muscles that sheathed his shoulder-blades twitched involuntarily. Mentally crediting her father with the five pounds he had wagered on the legitimacy of Colin's shoulders, she turned quickly on her heel, but he had seen her and called out,

'Good morning, Miss MacIntosh. Don't let me chase you away. I have finished now, so if you want to wash, the burn is all yours.'

When she looked round he was gathering up his shirt and razor, quite unperturbed, but he paused before picking up the four trout and beckoned her forward with an air of pride.

'Look, I have caught our breakfast!' He was grinning from ear to ear. 'Are they not nice fat ones? Could you eat a broon trootie, do you think?'

'Yes, indeed I could,' Isobel laughed, glad to notice that he appeared a trifle less ill-pleased with her this morning. 'I am quite famished. I didn't notice that you had a rod with you.'

'A rod?' He glanced up from his trophies and chuckled hugely. 'Lord, you don't need a rod to catch trout. Have you never heard of guddling? Laughlan is a past-master at the game. You must have him give you a few lessons.'

Isobel flinched slightly at the words, reflecting that she would probably never see her brother again, but noticing Colin's immediately contrite expression, she smiled gamely and asked, 'And what is guddling, pray? You must give me a few lessons yourself, since I may have need of the knowledge.'

'Easiest thing in the world, I assure you,' he told her, plainly relieved that she was disposed to be cheerful. 'It is based on the assumption that a trout likes to be tickled. First you find a fat, lazy trout like this one—the best place to look is close under the bank. Then you slide your hand under it, gently . . . gently, and begin to tickle it. Soon you have it so hypnotised that you can whisk it out on the bank before it knows what's happening.'

Isobel eyed him dubiously, uncertain whether he was teasing her, but he only stooped to scoop up his catch and added,

'Roasted over a bed of charcoal, there is not a dish in the world to touch it. So hurry up and wash, or there will be none left for you.'

He swung off down the hill, humming under his breath, his shirt over one shoulder, for all the world as if he were still lord of Dunarras and heir to Transk instead of a hunted man with all his worldly goods contained in one leathern pack. Watching him go, Isobel wondered, with a jolt of surprise, why she had thought the delightful twenty-three-year-old Colin gone for ever. He was still there, and not so very far beneath the surface of the older version.

The burn water was sparkling clear, and tangy with peat, but it was colder than she would have imagined possible. In seconds her hands were blue and aching, so she contented herself with rinsing her mouth and half-heartedly splashing her face before hurrying back to the cave and the faint but appealing aroma of cooking trout. She could hear Hugh's voice rumbling sleepily as she approached, and Colin saying as if in reply,

'Why should it? It has never done *me* any harm, I assure you. Borrow my razor, if you care to.'

He stopped speaking to smile at Isobel over his shoulder, and then returned his attention to the fire which he had built in a cleft on the rock face. Hugh was standing by the cave mouth yawning unrestrainedly, obviously still half asleep.

'Good morning, Mr Murray,' Isobel said, uncomfortably aware that her hair was damp and bedraggled and that her cheeks were still rosy from the sting of the icy water. 'You look very much better this morning. Did you sleep well?'

'Surprisingly well. I have spent many a less comfortable night in an inn.' He pulled forward a folded plaid for her to sit on, but she shook her head.

'Thank you, but if Mr Frazer will allow me, I would prefer to relieve him of his task. Do you trust me with your fine fish, Mr Frazer? I have never cooked trout over charcoal before, but I have no intention of letting you take charge of the kitchen.'

He yielded his place to her reluctantly, warning her

not to move the stones which he had set up before the dull glow to hide it, and began to pack everything that was not in use into his satchel so that they would be ready to set off as soon as they had eaten. Hugh helped him with more impatience than efficiency, complaining the while that they would do better to put as much distance as possible between Transk and themselves before they stopped to eat.

'Do you know which day the ship is due at Tarbat Ness?' he demanded of Colin, rolling a plaid into a tight ball. 'For all we know, it may be there tonight.'

'I think not,' Colin replied placidly. 'I cannot be entirely certain, of course, but I will confess myself much surprised if it puts in before Saturday night. That does not leave us a great deal of time, but unless we are very unlucky we should be able to get there first. One thing is certain—neither you nor Miss MacIntosh has had a decent meal for more than twenty-four hours, and if you are not to faint from hunger on the road you must eat before you leave.' He came to lean over Isobel, sniffing appreciatively, '*Certes*, they smell delicious, do they not, Murray? But, good God, how they have shrunk in the cooking!'

'That is not my fault,' Isobel defended herself, blushing. 'They always do so, I promise you. Here—I'll wager you will have no complaints about the taste.'

His eyes teased her as he accepted his one and precisely one-third fish, but there was no hint in them of anything other than friendliness, for which she was profoundly grateful. If he had stopped loving her, so much the better, since there would be no escaping from him at least until they reached France.

Isobel for one found no fault with her own cooking, making short work of her own share and licking her fingers clean of the last precious crumb, but Hugh swallowed his with one eye on the track, beating a restless tattoo with the toe of one dusty brogue. At last Colin cast him a baleful look, and went to bring the horses from the sheltered hollow where they had been tethered. He was back in a minute, leading his own bay and riding Stella, to whose back he had transferred his own saddle.

In answer to Isobel's lifted brows he dismounted and said casually, 'I hope you have no objection, ma'am, but I have taken the liberty of putting your saddle on my horse, since it seemed that your mare is less capable of carrying two riders for any great distance. Until Mr Murray's shoulder is a little better, I would suggest that he should ride Stella while I get up behind you on Magnus here.'

'Yes, of course,' Isobel acceded, not wholly convinced that his plan was prompted by logic rather than personal preference, but unwilling to make this evident.

He held her stirrup while she mounted, and having taken one last look about the cave to make sure that they had left no trace of their stay, he vaulted up behind her.

The treacherous slope was less awesome by daylight, but Isobel, unsure of her mount, was glad to reach the comparative safety of the path. Even here it was impossible to move with any degree of confidence, as the track sloped away sharply, twisting and turning, to end in a wooded valley a long way beneath them, but Hugh was too impatient for caution and led the way at a pace which caused Isobel to hold her breath in dismay. She found it impossible to keep up with him, but Colin, behind her, seemed quite content with their steady progress, tranquilly admiring the view and singing quietly to himself. It was the same tune as he had been singing as he washed, a Highland air that Isobel had known from childhood, and she found it increasingly irritating because he went off the tune at the end of each verse. At last she was driven to joining in, in order to correct him, stressing the faulty phrase till he altered it.

'Charming,' he complimented her as the song ended. 'I knew you would be forced to correct me if I continued to make a mess of it long enough. It is a trick that never fails.'

She turned round to glare at him, but finding him grinning provocatively, she burst out laughing. 'It was a shocking noise. I wonder Magnus did not throw us both.'

'Not him,' Colin assured her. 'He enjoys it. I am quite in the habit of singing to him when there is no one at hand to clap me into Bedlam. What shall we sing now? Do you know "Mally Lee"?'

'But someone will hear us, Mr Frazer. Sound carries so easily in these hills, and there may be redcoats about, early as it is.' She looked ahead to where Hugh had halted and was waiting for them to catch up. 'Besides, Mr Murray will think us maddish.'

'Perhaps he may join in,' he suggested with a chuckle. 'Who knows, he may be a tenor, which is just what we need.'

Isobel could visualise Hugh's reaction to any suggestion of this nature but forbore to laugh, suspecting that Colin was making fun of their companion's more serious nature. Instead, she said coolly, 'What we need more is another horse. Magnus is finding it hard to keep his balance, carrying both of us.'

Colin did not make any reply to this, but as they drew level with Hugh he said blithely, 'You are too quick for us, Mr Murray, but have patience, and we shall give you a run for your money when we reach level ground.'

Hugh did not appear to be greatly heartened by this assurance, but fell in behind them and continued at a more sober pace. Colin twisted round to see him and asked more seriously,

'I have been thinking about your brother, Mr Murray.

Was he with you at Culloden yesterday?'

Isobel's conscience smote her as she realised that she had not given a thought to Adam, and when Hugh did not answer at once, she felt her throat constrict with apprehension.

'No,' he said, after a moment. 'Adam was granted leave before the battle, as our home was occupied by Hessian troops and we wished to be sure that my aunt and cousins were safe. He did not return in time for the battle.'

This did not ring true in Isobel's ears, but she made no comment, reflecting that if Adam had had the sense to desert she thought none the less of him. Conversation languished as they negotiated a particularly hazardous stretch of path, and she found herself thinking morosely of the future. The loss of her home and family and friends was a bitter blow, and she did not relish the idea of arriving in France penniless and insecure, but the thought of leaving Scotland cut deepest of all. Never before had she realised how much she loved the land of her birth. Never before had the air seemed so keen and invigorating and the clear, rushing burns so inexpressibly dear. The hills held her to their bosoms, and the soft rain that was beginning to fall touched her face like a benediction. One day, she promised herself, I shall come home and die here, with the hills about me and only the curlews to cry over my grave.

'Look out!'

Colin's voice brought her back to the harsh present as he reached past her to snatch at the reins, jerking the horse's head round and guiding it swiftly behind a tall outcrop of rock. Before she could collect her senses, she was plucked out of her saddle with ungallant roughness and held, stuttering, against the wet boulders. Hugh was beside her with a hand over Stella's muzzle, his eyes narrowed as he peered down at the glen below.

'Bloody Campbells,' he whispered, and spat as though the words had a bad taste. 'Would to God I had my sword in my hand and half a dozen men of Atholl at my back.'

Isobel could see nothing from where she stood, and Colin's hand between her shoulder-blades held her immobile, but she breathed tremulously, 'What is happening? Have they seen us?'

Hugh glanced at her over his shoulder, and his eyes slid past her to Colin in a look which plainly meant, 'Watch her, she's going to pieces.' Aloud he said, 'No. They have their backs to us and are going the other way. If we stay till they are out of sight, we shall be quite safe.' He smiled at her rather tightly, and added, in a tone which she could not but deem patronising. 'You need not be nervous. They are on the other side of the glen.'

'I am not nervous,' Isobel informed him stiffly. 'At least, not now that I know we are not immediately to be taken prisoner. And, if I were, there would still be no likelihood of my losing my head. You should know that.'

Colin chuckled softly, bringing a flush to Hugh's cheeks. 'You perceive, my friend, that one does not belittle Miss MacIntosh's courage with impunity. Still, it is a comfort to know that we may rely upon her to look after us in an emergency.' He turned his amused eyes to Isobel. 'If you care to step over here, ma'am, you may catch a glimpse of the enemy before they are lost to view.'

He drew her in front of him, and raising her head cautiously above the rock, she made out a small party of kilted figures picking their way up the opposite hillside.

'Where can they have come from?' she wondered. 'Culloden is not in that direction, surely?'

'I suspect they have come from Kessock ferry,' Colin

hazarded. 'The Moray Firth is just on the other side of those hills, but we shall be forced to swing round in a wide arc to avoid meeting anyone. Doubtless that area will be well guarded in case any fugitives think to escape into Dornoch.'

Hugh swore under his breath. 'That ruins our chances, then,' he muttered glumly. 'If we cannot cross the Firth by Kessock ferry, we shall not be able to reach Tarbat Ness in under five days, for to go round by the head of the Firth will add miles to our journey.'

'There is an alternative,' Colin said quietly, scratching his bay's forehead with a long finger. 'An elderly couple who were once in my father's service live a mile or two to the west of the ferry. It may be that they can help us to get across.'

Hugh considered this briefly. 'But will not *all* the crossing-places be watched? It will be dangerous wherever we attempt to cross.'

'Probably,' Colin made no attempt to sweeten the pill, but his smile was as bland as ever. 'But the redcoats cannot be everywhere at once and I am persuaded that, given a night that is reasonably overcast, it should not be impossible to slip past them.'

Isobel eyed the lowering clouds above them, and shivered. Tonight would be perfect, but, oh God, if anything were to go wrong . . .! She opened her mouth to ask if there was no other way, but afraid that her voice would betray her consternation she shut it again and attempted to appear nonchalant, an effort which was wasted on her companions who were more interested in watching the retreating Campbells. When the last soldier had passed out of view, they waited for a few minutes to allow the patrol to get well away and then remounted and continued their descent.

The sun, although hidden by thick clouds, was now

high, but the presence of one or two small farms in the valley made caution imperative and they were unable to make up for lost time with a burst of speed. Within sight of the River Ness they stopped again, in the cover of a group of trees, while Colin went to reconnoitre the river bank.

Hugh sank down with his back against a fallen trunk, and closed his eyes. His face was grey with fatigue and the skin seemed stretched taut across the fine bones in his cheek and jaw. Isobel went to him and touched his shoulder with a compassionate palm. 'Does your wound still pain you, Mr Murray?' she asked, biting her lip with vexation. 'Oh dear, I wish I might do something to ease it.'

He shook his head and sighed, passing a hand across his eyes. 'My wound will heal, but it will take many years to mend the havoc that has been wrought in my life. A year ago I had wealth, family, the respect of friends— And now? Now I am alone, with nothing of any value to my name.'

'Oh, come, Mr Murray!' Isobel cried. 'You are not alone. Do you not have Mr Frazer and myself by you? And in France we shall meet with other exiles who, like ourselves, have been forced to leave our old lives behind. You may secure a commission in the French army or . . . or perhaps become a tutor or a fencing-instructor.'

He opened his eyes and smiled wanly. 'A fencing-instructor! Oh God! Better you had left me to die on Drummossie Moor.'

'Spare me such twaddle!' retorted Isobel with more than a suspicion of impatience. 'Who can say what the years hold in store for us—of joy, *or* of sorrow? Let us play the cards as they are dealt us, as I have heard my father say, and meanwhile keep our spirits up as best we can, for despondency will avail us nothing.'

Hugh's eyes travelled slowly over her face, wide-pupilled and absorbed. Gently he reached out and covered her hand with his own.

'My dear Miss MacIntosh,' he said, very softly. 'I am quite certain that, like a cat, you will fall on your feet whatever way you are tossed, but in France you will have need of a friend. I have known you only a few months, but already I feel . . .'

A sudden rustle of bushes behind him made him drop her hand as if it had suddenly become red-hot, and as Colin strode into the clearing, he jumped up, blushing every bit as violently as his chagrined companion.

'There is no one about,' Colin said briskly, 'so we must cross quickly while we have the opportunity to do so unobserved. Unfortunately, the river is pretty fast-flowing at present but there is a spot a little way up-stream where I think we should be able to ford it.'

He regarded Isobel's pink cheeks with unconcealed interest as he helped her to mount but as she answered his questioning look only with a malignant glare he shrugged and made no comment.

The river at this point was less than fifty paces wide, but it was swollen with the spring thaws, and when Isobel saw the place where they were expected to cross, her heart sank. Admittedly the level appeared to be slightly lower just there, but the current whipped the surface into a coffee-coloured foam that curled about the shoulders of several projecting rocks.

Colin dismounted and went to Magnus's head, wading calmly into the maelstrom that reached halfway up his thighs. Behind them, Stella struggled across gamely, her black nose held as high as she could get it, encouraged by a constant stream of blasphemies and endearments from her rider. When at last they gained the further bank,

Isobel felt that she was trembling every bit as much as the horses, but Colin would not permit another halt, as Inverness was no great distance away and he was afraid of being seen and questioned.

Keeping to the cover of the trees that clothed the river bank, they turned back downstream until a high hedge of hawthorn running off to their left offered partial concealment. This they followed for almost a mile, maintaining a sharp lookout for government patrols, and then broke cover and galloped across the springy turf to the choppy waters of the Moray Firth.

Close to the water's edge, in the angle of a rocky headland, squatted a small cottage roofed with turfs which were already sprouting a healthy crop of spring green. Here, at last, they drew rein, and Colin leapt down to hammer on the door, keeping a wary eye on the hill behind them.

The door immediately opened a few inches to disclose a brown monkey-like countenance framed by a frill of wispy grey hair. The wide pale blue eyes opened still wider in recognition.

'*Dhia!* Mac 'ic Eain! Is it yourself?'

'It is, Duncan. I need your help.' Colin stated tersely, wasting no time on trivialities.

'Trouble, is it?' Duncan's pale eyes took in Colin's companions as he pushed the door wider and gestured towards the opening. 'All I have is yours without the asking.'

'Is Morag there?' Colin hesitated. 'Miss MacIntosh will come in, but Mr Murray and I must get rid of the horses before they are seen. Do you know of someone who can keep them hidden from the redcoats?'

Duncan's face betrayed no hint of surprise as he nodded. '*Seadh gu dearbh!* Yes, indeed! Seumas Grant has room for them and will ask no questions. If the lady will be pleased to enter?'

Isobel relinquished her bridle into his gnarled fist and stepped through the low doorway into a dimness redolent of peat-fumes and damp earth. The interior of the bothy was fashioned along similar lines to countless others Isobel had seen, being in the shape of one long room divided into two by the chimneypiece in the centre, but it was much more comfortably plenished than most.

The packed-earth floor was covered with rugs of plaited straw and the firelight picked out the gleam of pewter among the wooden dishes on the shelves. An old woman was standing in the shadows, looking intently towards the door. Her gaze flicked past Isobel and came to rest on Colin, who was standing in the doorway.

'Blessed Lord!' she cried, and her plump hands fluttered out to him. 'Mac 'ic Eain! Will you not come in? Duncan must have taken leave of his senses to keep you standing in the rain!'

'Wheesht, woman,' Duncan rumbled, but Colin stepped past him and caught Morag's shoulders in his two hands, smiling down at her.

'Acquit him, Morag. It is my fault as usual. We have a little business to attend to, but we shall not be long about it, and then you may mother me as much as you please. Meanwhile, I want you to take care of Miss MacIntosh for me. She is very tired and has eaten scarcely anything since dawn.'

Morag's hand went to her breast as her sharp eyes flicked from Isobel's soaking habit to Hugh's unshaven face, just visible behind Colin. 'Oh, Mary Mother! There is trouble here! What has come to you, *mo chridhe*?'

'Nothing for you to be worrying about,' Colin grinned, giving her a little shake. 'You shall hear the whole story when I get back.'

She stood at the doorway watching him as he rode away, and then turned with a start and bobbed an awkward curtsy to her guest. 'Indeed, it is a poor foolish old woman you will be thinking me, ma'am, and you with a long road at your back, I don't doubt, and needing something hot inside you. Come you here and sit at the fire, while I make something to put a little warmth into you.'

Isobel gratefully took the seat that was offered, and smiled ruefully at her hostess. 'I hope we have not endangered you by coming here,' she said unhappily. 'I think you should know that Mr Murray was "out" with the Prince, and Mr Frazer and I were both seen helping him to escape. It is to be hoped that you are not visited by any redcoats tonight.'

Morag folded her arms across her chest. 'The redcoats have never yet been to my door!' she said militantly. 'And if they come tonight, we shall know what to do about it. No one will lay a hand on Mac 'ic Eain while Duncan and I are alive to stop it. There are ways of dealing with redcoats.' She snuggled a pan of milk into the red peats and nodded grimly to herself. 'It is not the first time I have helped Mac 'ic Eain out of hot water, nor will it be the last, unless he mends his ways. He knows that Duncan and I always look on him as our own son.'

Isobel leaned her chin on her hand and watched her hostess as she began to whisk up the milk into a creamy foam. 'You must have known him for a long time,' she remarked, stifling a yawn. 'You were in service to his father, were you not?'

'Nigh on forty years,' Morag stated proudly, 'and with no wish to be anywhere else on top of this earth. If Duncan had not been so fond of the boy, we would have been there yet. I was in the kitchen then, and he was groom to the old laird. My, the stables they kept at

Transk is those days . . . before the 'Fifteen, I mean. But everything is changed now. Ay, weel. But they will be as good as ever in a few years, if all goes well . . . and if Mac 'ic Eain is allowed to inherit after this ploy . . .'

Isobel winced, knowing well that this was now impossible, but said hurriedly, 'What did you mean when you said that you would still be at Transk if Duncan had not been so fond of Mr Frazer?'

Morag handed her a wooden porringer of the foaming milk, and smiled absently. 'Och, the lad was a wild one when he was young, and he was never away from the stables. Duncan thought more of him than of our own two, and could never refuse him anything. One day the laird got himself a new horse, and nothing would suit the young master but he would get a ride of it. A great black devil, it was, with eyes like Satan himself and a temper to match, so the laird told Duncan not to let the boy near it. But in the end the young master made Duncan let him bestride it, and it threw him against the stone trough.'

'How dreadful,' Isobel shuddered. 'It was a miracle that he was not killed. Was that when he broke his ribs?'

Morag seemed to be lost in thought, her eyes unseeing on a worm that had dropped out of the roof turfs and was wriggling obscenely on the warm floor in front of the fire. 'Two ribs,' she nodded. 'And he did not recover his senses for two days. I could never blame the laird for sending us away.' Rousing herself, she smiled cheerfully and said, 'Och, but the laddie never blamed Duncan for it, and now he makes sure that we are as well off here at Kessock as we would have been at Transk.'

She bustled about with a big iron cooking-pot, keeping up a constant flow of reminiscences about her early days at Transk, until Isobel begged her assistance in loosening her corsets. No sooner had this been accomplished than a step sounded at the doorway, and

Morag ran to open the door for the three men.

'Yes, they are safe and snug,' Colin replied to Isobel's unspoken question. 'Your Stella will be well looked after, rest assured, but it seems that we must go the rest of the way on foot. Duncan tells me there is no boat available which will carry horses, but we have borrowed one that will take the four of us.'

'Four?' Isobel asked, surprised. 'Is Duncan coming with us, then?'

Hugh had sat down beside her and was beginning to pull off his brogues, but he turned amused eyes on her and shook his head. 'Someone must bring back the boat,' he reminded her, and sniffed appreciatively. 'That stew smells most appetising. I had not realised how hungry I have become.'

Morag lifted the pot from the fire, eyeing him with strong approval. 'Hunger is the best sauce,' she said comfortably. 'Draw in your chair, sir, and as soon as you have eaten we will have that jacket off you and see what makes one of your shoulders bigger than the other.'

Colin gave a hoot of laughter. 'Do you ever miss anything, Morag? No hawk ever had eyes like yours, I swear it. But Mr Murray's shoulder has already been attended to and has stopped paining him. When we have eaten, it will be necessary for us to get some sleep, for we are to be ready to leave the hour before dawn. That is the time the redcoats are least watchful.' He regarded her disapproving countenance for a second, and then added, 'Am I still to tell you the tale of my troubles, or have you managed, in your usual way, to worm it out of Miss MacIntosh?'

'Devil a thing I would ever know if I were to wait to hear it from you,' Morag told him, trying to frown. 'Glad I am that I am no longer servant to your father, and so able to tell you what I think of your daft ploys.'

CHAPTER
FOURTEEN

THE WIND across the Moray Firth sliced the white caps
off the waves and splattered the three waiting figures
with blown spume. The night sky was still heavily overcast, but behind the rolling clouds was a three-quarter
moon that could illuminate the whole beach if given the
opportunity. A mile or two to the east lay Kessock ferry
and the party of government soldiers who had kept
watch for nearly two days. Duncan had spent the evening observing the redcoats and reported that they were
not over-zealous in the performance of their duty, pre-
ferring the shelter of a near-by cottage to the buffeting of
the April wind. Waiting now for him to row the boat
round from where he had hidden it in a tiny bay, Isobel
found that fear had left her. All night she had lain on her
pallet, unable to sleep for the thought of this crossing,
and yet, now that it was at hand, she did not even
tremble. Hugh, at her shoulder, could not be still, but
kept drumming his fingers on the handle of his dirk and
even Colin could not keep his eyes from the direction of
Kessock.

'What in heaven's name can be delaying Duncan?'
Hugh muttered irritably. 'Can he have run into trouble?'

At that second the muffled creak of oars heralded
the approach of the boat, and without waiting for it
to beach, Colin swung round to lift Isobel in his arms,
and waded through the shallows to dump her

unceremoniously in the prow.

'Don't waste any time, Duncan,' he whispered, one hand half-dragging Hugh over the gunwale. 'The clouds are beginning to break up over in the north, and we may not have as much time as we had calculated.'

Looking over her shoulder, Isobel could see this to be true. Through a sizeable rift in the clouds two stars were clearly visible in a square of dark blue that widened as she watched. The moon, for all she knew, could be close to that rift or on the other side of the sky.

Soundlessly, and with infinite slowness, the cobble pulled away from the shore and moved out into the black waters. A wave, higher than the rest, smacked over the prow and drenched Isobel from the waist down, forcing an anguished yelp from between her clenched teeth. Colin and Duncan bent and straightened in unison, and the oars rose and fell with the softest of creaks in the padded rowlocks.

Beyond their straining backs Isobel could see Hugh twisting round in his seat, his fine hair fluttering in the wind like a trapped bird. How slowly the shore retreated! It seemed at first that they were making no progress at all, and then, quite abruptly, the shadowy outlines of houses that had been visible a moment ago were swallowed by the darkness and, turning, she saw the hills of the Black Isle outlined against a now considerable patch of clear sky . . . And at that moment, the moon slid forth from behind the clouds; inexorable, pitiless and as impartial as Death itself. They could watch the brilliant beams sweeping across the water towards them until their craft was clearly pinpointed on a path of molten silver. Colin swore roundly.

'Get down in the bottom of the boat, Miss MacIntosh,' he ordered over his shoulder. 'We may not have been spotted yet, and even if we have, I imagine we are out of musket-range, but there's no sense in taking chances. You, too, Mr Murray. Quickly!'

Isobel crouched, not altogether unwillingly, in the three or four inches of bilgewater that was swilling about her boots, and stayed there in spite of the occasional wave that broke over her head to complete her sousing. From this position she could see nothing, but there was no sound of firing, and in a very short space of time Colin bade her resume her seat as they were now well out of danger.

Minutes later they pulled into a small cove, and Duncan, leaping into the water, dragged the boat up on to the pebbles and made it fast to a projecting spur of rock. Since she was now as wet as if she had been completely submerged, Isobel did not wait for assistance but stepped into the shallow weed-wreathed eddies and made her own way ashore. The beach sloped upwards to a ridge of sand and coarse grass that ran inland for fifty yards or so before giving way to a line of bushes and stunted wind-bent trees. Towards this shelter they hurried, stiff-shouldered against the chill wind, and there halted while Colin turned to Duncan and gripped his hand between both his own.

'Thank you, my good friend,' he said deeply. 'God grant that no harm come to you through this night's work. You must leave us here now. No . . .' he added as Duncan began to argue. 'You have done more than enough, and I will not have you endangered more than is necessary. Go home now before the dawn breaks and let Morag know that we are safe across the Firth.'

Duncan's wrinkled face was wooden with disapproval. 'It is sorry you'll be when you see the road before you,' he muttered, shaking his head. 'And Morag will have a skelp waiting for my ear if I let you go alone.'

'What would she say if you never came home at all?' Colin grinned. 'It would be *my* ear that would ring if anything happened to you. Now we must be on our way before we freeze in our wet clothes or are seen by some inquisitive tacksman. Goodbye, Duncan. Take care that you are not seen.'

Duncan hesitated a moment longer, and then nodded. 'Just whatever you say yourself, Mac 'ic Eain.' He sketched a bow that included them all, and then retraced his steps to the shingle, reluctance in every line of his thin body.

Without waiting to watch him push out the boat, Colin turned to Isobel, and took her arm. 'You are shivering, Miss MacIntosh,' he said shortly. 'Pray swing your arms as you walk, and you will soon warm up. We must move briskly in any case, for it will soon be dawn, and before it is light we must find a shelter where we can dry our clothes. In this sodden state we shall attract enough attention to be remembered, if there are redcoats on our trail.'

'Do you fear that we were seen when the moon came out?' Hugh asked worriedly. 'If we were, it seems odd that we were not fired upon.'

Colin shrugged non-committally. 'They may have judged us to be out of range, but I think it more likely that we were unobserved. However that may be, we are not sure that this area is completely free of Loudon's troops, so it would be wise to be as circumspect as possible. If we were not so pressed for time I would advocate keeping under cover by day and travelling only after dark, but if we are to reach Tarbat Ness tomorrow night we must keep going. Are you much fatigued, ma'am?' he asked Isobel, who was having considerable difficulty in keeping up with him. 'I pray you, persevere a little longer. We shall soon find a place of refuge where we can rest awhile.'

To Isobel it seemed as if her feet had been replaced by two lumps of lead which swung outwards with every step, seemingly of their own volition, at the end of her trembling legs. But the brisk pace warded off the chill, and had it not been for the thick 'haar' or sea-mist which came rolling in off the Firth just as dawn broke she would have been reasonably warm. As the haar thickened, they were forced to slow their pace in order to see where they were placing their feet, as the ground they were crossing was strewn with rocks and large boulders that materialised out of the haze. All sounds seemed muffled by the white blanket, the rush and swish of the tide fading abruptly into an eerie silence in which their footsteps sounded like tuck of drum.

With her eyes on the ground, Isobel was the last to see the ruined house that loomed suddenly before them. Most of the roof had been ripped off by the gales that blasted this coast in spring and autumn, but the walls were sturdily built and would stand for generations against any blast. The few rafters that still remained were fire-blackened, as were the door-posts and window-frames, and heather flourished to the very hearthstone.

Hugh uttered a wordless croon of delight. 'It is an ill wind that blows nobody any good, is it not?' he remarked. 'I'll wager the owner of this fine house would think it odd that three folk who never knew him would bless the day his house burned down.'

'Indeed, it is ideal for our purpose,' Colin agreed, laughing. He stepped across the threshold and looked about him. 'That room in the corner still has a roof over it, and will be quite snug once we get a fire going. Luckily we have a fine supply of wood here, and the mist to hide the smoke, so we shall be able to dry off our clothes in no time.'

The little room at the end of the house was cold and windowless, but there was only a small hole in the roof. The floor, although littered with dead bracken and fallen leaves, was comparatively dry. Colin dropped the pack he had been carrying over one shoulder, and opening it, drew out two plaids. Handing one to Isobel, he bade her go elsewhere and exchange it for her clothes, and with a slight blush, she took it without a murmur.

Changing in the draughty ruin was a daunting experience, but the plaid proved an adequate covering and was even warmer than her cloak, which had not been completely dry since she left Church Street. How long ago that seemed, she thought, unpinning her wet hair and combing it as best she could with her fingers. Only two days had passed, but it felt more like two years. It would have been odd, somehow, to peep in at the window of her home and find things exactly as they had been: her embroidery still half-finished, Fiona's last posy still fresh on her dressing-table, the kitchen cat still rearing the same set of kittens.

Isobel sighed wistfully as she thought of the company and entertainments she would never more enjoy, but paused with her mouth open in amazement as she realised, suddenly, that she was deluding herself. The comfortable, unexciting round of parties, tea-drinking and gossiping appealed to her even less from the unlovely viewpoint of this draughty ruin than it had done when she was last in the capital. Uncomfortable she might be, apprehensive she certainly was, but at least she felt herself to be more alive than she had ever been before. The complete emptiness of the Edinburgh way of life was now anathema to her. The overweening haughtiness of the matrons, the empty-headed affectations of the misses, the foppishness of the young men and the pedantry of their fathers set her teeth on edge.

She leaned an elbow on what had once been a window-sill and stared out into the slowly drifting mist, and it came to her, with unmistakable certainty, that she would refuse to return to that way of life should the opportunity to do so ever arise. There would be no such opportunity, of course—she accepted that fact. Just as Hugh had thrown away the scabbard when he had drawn his sword for the Prince, so there would be no turning back for either Colin or Isobel. Redcoats had long memories, and there would be redcoats in Scotland for many years to come. What life would be like in a strange country, amid strange people who spoke a tongue that she understood imperfectly, no one could foretell, but Hugh would be there. Colin, too, would be a comfort, for all his faults, and perhaps . . .

'Miss MacIntosh, are you all right?'

Hugh's voice brought her back to the present with a jolt. She gathered up her discarded clothing and went back to the little room. Colin had already lit a fire under the hole in the roof while Hugh, wrapped about with the other plaid, was arranging a makeshift trestle on which to dry their clothes. Having draped his own apparel over this together with Isobel's, and a large proportion of Colin's, he looked at it doubtfully.

'Are yours all here, Miss MacIntosh? What about your boots? Give them here, and you may drape a fold of your plaid about your feet to keep them warm.'

'But that would mean I must sit here until they are dry,' she demurred. 'I would be better employed in collecting some more wood for the fire.'

'No, I shall do that,' Colin decided, rising and pushing his bundle of twigs closer to her. 'Do you sit at the fire, and pile on this kindling gradually as it begins to catch. Not too quickly, or you will smother the flame.'

At another time Isobel might have retorted that she was quite able to kindle a fire without step-by-step instruction, but somehow it hardly seemed worth while any more. Colin had quite naturally assumed leadership of the party, and although Isobel had never been wont to follow wherever she was led it was something of a relief, in this predicament, to leave the decisions to someone else.

Colin went out of the room, and presently sounds of creaking and snapping issued from where he was making short work of the charred rafters. After a moment's silence, Hugh lifted his eyes from the boot which he was holding to the tiny blaze and met Isobel's across the smoke. Inexplicably, her heart gave a sudden lurch and she felt her cheeks burn, but he only said, sombrely,

'We shall never reach Tarbat Ness by nightfall tomorrow at this rate. It must be all of twenty-five miles from here, and we have still to get across the Cromarty Firth, which will be dangerous—if not impossible. Also we shall have to make a detour round Fortrose and Rosemarkie, which will add a few miles to our journey.'

'We have not made very good time up till now,' Isobel admitted. 'But that was because we had to be careful not to be seen by government troops. In this area there are fewer farms, and probably fewer redcoats, too, so we are bound to move faster.'

Hugh turned the small boot over in his hands, smoothing the soft leather with his thumbs. His face had lost much of its pallor, but it was still pinched and drawn with cold, and the reddish stubble that shadowed his jaw made him look hollow-cheeked. 'There was a time,' he said with an impotent lift of one shoulder, 'when I could have walked twenty-five miles in one day without considering it worth the mention. But these last few days with the Prince, we did not have the making of a decent meal between us, and I feel as if I have not slept for a week. Nor will I sleep sound until I set eyes on the coast of France. If only there were a less hazardous way to get there.'

Isobel was beginning to suspect that her store of sympathy was not inexhaustible, but as Colin entered the room at that moment, she only lifted her chin and said with perfect truth, 'I have ceased to worry about the possibility of being apprehended. One cannot always be in the fidgets, so one must simply leave the matter in the lap of the gods.'

Colin crouched beside her, dropping an armful of sooty wood to the floor. 'Our Miss MacIntosh is a woman of unsuspected character, is she not?' he said to Hugh, and turned to her with his familiar, half-teasing, half-tender grin. 'You never fail to surprise me, ma'am. I am lost in admiration.'

She was inordinately pleased with this tribute, and returned his smile with one of warm benevolence. 'Oh moonshine!' she said, absent-mindedly removing a smuge of soot from his chin with her fingers. 'I am persuaded there is nothing to worry about. You have contrived to bring us this far without endangering us, and I'm sure your ingenuity will not fail us now. If anything should . . .'

A quick movement from Hugh caught her eye, and she turned to find him staring at her with an expression that made her flush guiltily. Clearly he had seen her touch Colin's face, and was putting two and two together to make five. His face was a study of conjecture and surprise, and it was evident that no explanation other than the obvious one seemed to have occurred to him.

But *was* there another explanation? Isobel dropped her eyes to look at her hand, as though it were not attached to her body but possessed a life of its own. Had she really only wanted to remove the soot from his chin? Or had she acted instinctively, knowing in advance the small *frisson* of pleasure she would derive from the contact?

Colin broke the silence by getting to his feet. 'Since we are likely to be here for some time,' he said matter-of-factly, 'we may as well have something to eat. If we do so now, it will save us having to stop later on.'

Isobel was glad of the distraction, not only because it gave Hugh's thoughts a different turn, at least for the moment, but because it gave her an excuse to postpone thinking about her own motives. She was aware that she was very close to exhaustion, both mentally and physically, and if her actions under such conditions were—she searched for a word—uncharacteristic, it was surely not surprising. Time enough to probe deeper when they arrived in France.

Morag had given them a generous parcel of provisions, and they were able to make a hearty breakfast on toasted bannocks, cheese and hot milk. By the time they had finished, the haar was beginning to clear, so they hurriedly extinguished their fire, and donning their half-dried clothes, resumed their tramp.

The break in the clouds which had so nearly proved their undoing earlier had now widened to show a large expanse of blue sky. The wind had dropped, and the distant waters of the Firth lapped the deserted shore with scarcely a ripple.

Colin set a brisk pace across the moors, and Isobel, at first, found the going not too arduous. But all too soon the uneven terrain began to take toll of her tired muscles, and she was not sorry when Colin took her arm and tucked it firmly through his. Hugh might think what he chose, but it was half the battle to have Colin's arm to lean on. If she were not to collapse, she would have to muster all her strength.

She would have bitten out her tongue rather than ask for a respite, but in no time her boots had begun to chafe her heels, and she found the soles to be no protection against the pebbles that bruised her feet at every step. Even later, when they turned inland to avoid Rosemarkie, there was no reprieve, since here the calf-high heather cloaked a surface that was corrugated with humps and furrows that could twist the ankle agonisingly if one was not constantly alert. Several times Colin would have called a halt, but Hugh was in a fever of impatience, and Isobel had made up her mind that if they arrived at Tarbat too late, it would not be her fault.

Apart from a few brief pauses to take their bearings or to drink from a tempting burn, they did not stop till the sun was past the meridian, when Colin spotted a thick copse of rowans and alders and insisted that this was the ideal place to rest. Isobel dropped exhausted on the turf, and ate the food that was put into her hand without being completely aware of what she was doing, but Colin, for all it was he who had been so set on stopping, ate his share standing, while he discussed with Hugh their chances of getting across the Cromarty Firth before dusk.

Isobel listened with half an ear, bemusedly watching Hugh's quick, nervous gestures as he talked, and was lost in thought when Colin said,

'Miss MacIntosh, I think you were limping a little while ago. You had better let me have a look at your feet.'

She sat up quickly, scarlet with mortification. 'No— No indeed they are not! I mean, thank you, but I would rather not. There is nothing you can do.'

'Come, now,' he said, smiling. 'Are you not being rather foolish? We still have a long way to go, and you will never stay the pace if your feet are blistered.'

'No,' Isobel repeated loudly through clenched teeth. 'I beg you will leave me alone. I will do excellently as I am, and I promise you I will not hold you back.'

Colin returned her black look with interest. 'But I insist,' he said, quietly determined. 'Now are you going to remove your boots and stockings, or must I do it for you?'

He took one purposeful step towards her, but Hugh, flushing hotly, caught at his sleeve. 'Really, sir!' he protested. 'Is this necessary? If Miss MacIntosh does not wish it . . .'

'. . . she is being very irrational,' Colin finished for him. 'Do *you* imagine that she will be able to keep going in that condition? Look at those boots.' He swung round and indicated her flimsy footwear with a scornful gesture. 'They were never intended to withstand such hard wear. She would be as comfortable without them. We shall leave you alone for a few minutes, ma'am,' he added to Isobel, grasping Hugh's arm and beginning to lead him away. 'Do you give a shout when you are ready.'

Stiff with impotent rage, Isobel watched them retreat, but realising that Colin was quite capable of carrying out his threat, she quickly stripped off her stockings and tucked her skirt tightly round her ankles. At her call, Hugh and Colin reappeared carrying tufts of sheep's wool which they had evidently found caught in the bushes. Hugh was still rather flushed, as though he had continued to oppose the therapy, but he was considerate enough of her modesty to remain at a distance as Colin knelt at her feet.

As always, she was strongly affected by Colin's nearness. Although his manner was as cool and impersonal as a doctor's, it could not mask the essential maleness that surrounded him and reached out to her like a fire. The very air between them seemed to shift and shimmer with the force of their interaction. Even his rough hands on her skin made her foot appear, by contrast, so tiny and smooth that they were both aware of it. She heard his breath catch in his throat and knew that, despite his coolness towards her, his feelings had not changed.

His head was still bent over her foot, but she could see that his face had drained of colour. His eyelashes made black semi-circles on his cheeks, and a muscle ridged momentarily at the corner of his mouth. Then slowly, almost unwillingly, his head came up and his eyes caught at hers with such an expression of tender pleading that her heart began to pound painfully.

For the first time in their relationship she met that gaze without evasion, but then, abruptly, it was over, and she was left trembling.

Hugh was speaking from the edge of the trees, but his words meant nothing to Isobel, and even Colin's rather husky reply caused scarcely a ripple on the surface of her consciousness. All her mind was still centred on those few seconds of total rapport. She felt vaguely that it was important to analyse her feelings, but she was too over-whelmed by the experience to think calmly. It had never occurred to her that such intense communication with another human being was possible, and yet it seemed that she had always sensed that potential in Colin. Whereas he rejoiced in the closeness, Isobel was by no means sure that she wanted to yield herself so totally. To give her whole being into the hands of someone else was too dangerous to contemplate, but Colin would accept nothing less.

She watched him covertly as he dressed her heels with the salve he had brought for Hugh's shoulder, but when he raised his head she was careful not to meet his eyes.

This thing required some thought, and the time for that was not yet.

Hugh and Colin were now discussing plans for procuring a boat to carry them the remaining few miles of their journey, but she could not bring herself to take any part in the discussion, and merely nodded her thanks when Colin helped her ease her boots on over the dressings.

He had padded the soles with the wool, so she had little difficulty in keeping up when they started off once more, but it was a relief when, about four in the afternoon, they sighted a small boat sailing aimlessly close inshore. Throwing caution to the wind, Hugh sprinted down to the water's edge and hailed the solitary mariner with a loud halloo. Colin and Isobel, keeping out of sight, watched the boat pull into the shore and waited while Hugh conversed inaudibly with its occupant. In a few minutes he turned and ran back to them, glowing with success.

'He's a simple old soul,' he chuckled. 'He says he will carry us across the Firth, but no further, as the currents are tricky. But, once we are on board, he will have no choice but to do as we tell him.'

'Oh, no!' Isobel burst out agitatedly. 'You mustn't! *Please* do not threaten that poor old man! I would by far prefer to walk than to be party to such brutality. *Please* let us just go across the Firth with him, and walk the rest of the way. We still have plenty of time.'

'I am not advocating brutality,' Hugh rounded on her in wide-eyed innocence. 'I assure you that we need do no more than hint that we might kick a hole in his boat . . .'

'I agree with you there,' Colin put in, much to Isobel's dismay. 'It would not take much to intimidate him, but I am inclined to believe that nothing would be gained by it in the long run. Of a certainty the whole neighbourhood would be aware of our crime by nightfall, which is what we least desire. This leaves us two alternatives—either to dirk him and take his boat, or to let him ferry us across the Firth. And since Miss MacIntosh appears to be about to faint at the mere mention of the first, I vote for the second.'

Isobel seconding this proposal in a faint voice, Hugh allowed himself to be out-voted and led the way back to the beach. The patient old man had drawn his leaky craft on to the shingle, and was passing the time in baling out some of the water with which it was awash. He showed not the slightest curiosity as to the identity or destination of his passengers, but Colin told him such a moving story about Isobel's grandmother being taken ill in Tain that he eventually agreed to carry them a little further than he had initially intended, and set them ashore less than two miles from Tarbat Ness.

This unexpected stroke of luck put new heart into the fugitives. Darkness was falling as they started out on the last stage of their journey, but all signs of fatigue seemed to have been left behind in the boat. A subdued sense of exhilaration took hold of Isobel, making her step light with the satisfaction of a job well done. To have won so far towards their goal in so short a time was no mean feat—surely their luck could not fail them now? The long miles slipped away, almost unnoticed, and conversation dwindled into a confident silence as a wisp of smoke in the distance indicated the end of the road.

Isobel was just about to attract Hugh's attention to this, when Colin gripped her arm and brought her to a sudden halt. Too startled to speak, she followed his pointing finger, and saw at once what he had noticed.

Not more than fifty yards ahead of them, in the shadow of a half-tumbled wall, stood a motionless figure, and the faint moonlight played on the pale facings of a soldier's coat.

CHAPTER
FIFTEEN

FOR A LONG minute no one moved. The stillness was so intense that Isobel could hear the dry grasses stirring in the wind, and the beating of her heart rose to a deafening THUD . . . THUD. The soldier's face was turned away from them towards the beach, but had he looked round he must have seen them clearly outlined against the frost-silvered hillside.

Dragging her eyes away lest he should feel her gaze upon him, Isobel turned to Colin and saw him motion silently towards a ridge of gorse-bushes a few feet to their left. With agonising slowness, and testing each step before they took it, they edged towards this cover and crouched there for a second, touching each other in their need for reassurance. Both Hugh and Colin were grim-mouthed, with shining beads of sweat on their brows, and Isobel smiled suddenly as she realised that her own face wore the self-same expression. They stared at her, horrified, and gripping her arms, they drew her along the line of bushes till a dip of the ground hid them from the redcoat.

'Do you feel all right?' Colin whispered anxiously, bending to examine her face, but she jerked her arm away from his grasp and snapped with blazing eyes,

'Can I not smile if I want to? You should have seen your own face.'

He threw up an arm to guard his head and laughed

softly. '*Touché!*' He turned to Hugh, and spoke in an undertone, his eyes raking the dark decline they had just descended. 'From here on we must go very carefully. Where there is one redcoat, there are likely to be others, and we could too easily blunder into one as we almost did just now.'

'What are they doing here? That's what worries me,' Hugh breathed. 'Can it be possible that they are looking for us? That old fool in the boat . . .'

'I doubt it. But nevertheless we shall keep out of their way. Sandy MacCormack's house is up there on the hill, and you can be sure that he will know the whole story. But we must be careful in case he has redcoats billeted on him. I will go on a little way ahead, while you and Miss MacIntosh follow at a safe distance.'

Colin moved off silently into the shadows, making good use of every scrap of cover, and Hugh drew Isobel's hand through his arm and led her after him, whispering,

'Only a few more minutes, ma'am, and then we shall be safe.'

Isobel smiled at him, keeping her doubts to herself, and struggling against a sudden overpowering lethargy, bent to the slope. At the top, Colin was waiting for them.

'There it is,' he said quietly, pointing to a substantial stone building among the trees. 'Wait here until I beckon you. If anything goes wrong, try to get down to the beach. There are plenty of caves there where you can hide until the redcoats have gone.'

This casual warning struck fear into Isobel's heart. The prospect of continuing the flight without Colin's guidance and protection was terrifying. Indeed her hand flew out to catch at his sleeve, but he had already started towards the house, and her fingers closed on empty air.

'Oh, God!' she whispered, more panic-stricken now than she had been throughout this entire adventure.

Suddenly she knew that a necessary part of her courage, all along, had been the certain knowledge of Colin's support. From the moment she had found Hugh on Drummossie Moor, she had known that Colin was there to turn to. Even the prospect of exile in France had failed to daunt her completely only because Colin would be with them, taking charge, making the decisions. If anything were to go wrong now . . .

He was moving silently through the trees, inching cautiously towards a window where a thin band of light showed under the shutter. Without breathing, her shoulders aching with cold and tension, she watched him peer through the crack and heard faintly the quick rap of his knuckles on the wood. In a second the window opened an inch, there was a whispered conversation, and then Colin turned and urgently waved them forward. With knees that threatened to give way at every step, she was propelled across the grass and through a hastily-opened door into a warm, stone-flagged kitchen.

Sandy MacCormack was a stunted giant of a man. His wide, powerful shoulders and heavy arms were supported by a pair of bowed legs that seemed to buckle under the weight, but he bowed over Isobel's hand with all the grace of a courtier, and apologised for the absence of his good lady who was, he explained, already abed. After setting cold meat and cheese and bannocks on the table, he produced two dusty bottles of brandy and stood with his back to the fire, watching them eat.

'The redcoats will not bother you here,' he assured them, spitting into the fire with more scorn than accuracy. 'They have been clattering about on the cliffs like a herd of bullocks for two hours, but we are expected to notice nothing. It's deaf they'll be thinking us, as well as blind, but there is little they are doing that we don't know about. Like bairns they are, and couldn't catch a wasp in a honey-pot far less a wily free-trader like Sandy MacCormack.' He unlocked a small wooden chest and began to spoon tea into a handsome copper tea-kettle. 'The exciseman, forbye, snooping around, sly as you like, and thinking himself invisible.'

Hugh laid down his knife and swung round in his chair. 'The exciseman, did you say? So that is what brings them here. Do they suspect that you are about to land a cargo?'

'Ay. They have had their eyes on us for months, but they have never been able to catch us red-handed. Nor will they tonight, for now that we know they are in the vicinity we shall just signal the *Molly* not to put in.'

His three guests exchanged anguished glances.

'You don't seem to understand our position, Sandy,' Colin said evenly. 'It is essential that the ship put in. Even if it is too risky to land a cargo, they must take us off. Martin McColl is my friend. I know he would bring his ship in, if we could only distract the soldiers for long enough to make it reasonably safe for him.'

Sandy shook his head firmly. 'I am your friend also, Mr Frazer, but I will not risk men's lives. While the redcoats are within a mile of this place, I cannot take the responsibility of signalling the *Molly* to put in. I can keep you and your friends safely hidden till the next time the *Molly* is due, but . . .'

A faint moan of anguish escaped Isobel. Already the tension of the past few days was beginning to tell on her: to remain in fear of capture every second of every day for weeks or possibly months to come would be more than she could stand.

Colin rose from his seat and went to grip Sandy's shoulder. 'I would not dream of asking you to risk any man's life for my sake,' he said tightly. 'But if I can get the redcoats away, will you bring the boat in for long enough to pick us up?'

'How would you get them away?' Sandy hedged, frowning unencouragingly.

'I don't know. I'll think of something. It shouldn't be too difficult to decoy them away if they are as gullible as you say they are, and I give you my word not to incriminate any of your people.'

Sandy studied his face, and then turned to look at Hugh and Isobel, who were watching him hopefully. Finally he drew a long breath, and pulling up a chair to the table, sat down heavily.

'Very well,' he said. 'But I must be sure that the soldiers are well away, and you must all be ready to go on board without any waste of time. Remember that. There must be no delay while the *Molly* is standing to.' He shot Colin a sharp look from beneath his bushy brows, and nodded again. 'Just so. Now, how do you propose to decoy the redcoats away?'

Colin sat down beside him, pushing aside empty platters to make room for his folded arms. 'There are one or two things you will have to tell me before I can begin to make a plan. First, when is the *Molly* expected?'

Sandy glanced at his repeating watch. 'In about five or six hours. She wasn't expected till tomorrow, but she is already standing off, out of sight, and high tide will be at half-past three.'

Isobel felt a wave of alarm sweep over her. If it had not been for that darling old man with the boat, they would have been too late after all!

'Good,' Colin was saying calmly. 'Can you signal her to put in elsewhere?'

'Yes, we have a prearranged code of signals, but the nearest suitable place is Helmsdale, which is at least half a day's ride from here . . . longer without a ferry.'

'I see.' Colin gnawed his lip thoughtfully, drawing on

the table with the point of his knife. 'Have you any idea how many redcoats there are in the district?'

'A platoon, maybe. Most of them think themselves hidden in a cave on the beach.'

Colin lapsed into a ruminative silence, which Hugh interrupted at length by saying impatiently,

'I must confess myself quite unable to perceive where the difficulty lies. Can we not just tell them that the ship is to put in at Helmsdale instead?'

'By all means,' Colin agreed with faint irony. 'Which of us do you nominate to bell the cat? And can you think of any reason why they should believe us?'

Another long silence ensued, during which Isobel battled against a strong desire to go to sleep. The liberal dash of brandy with which Sandy had insisted on lacing her tea had gone straight to her head, and she had great difficulty in keeping her eyes open.

'One thing is certain,' Colin said at last. 'If they could be made to believe that the Young Pretender is skulking near by, it's a fair bet that they would consider a party of smugglers very poor game. A reward of thirty thousand pounds calls with a louder voice than Duty. But how can we implant the idea in their heads?'

'They would not believe me if I were to tell them,' Sandy remarked. 'I am pretty sure the exciseman does not suspect me of being involved with the free-traders—in fact I'll wager I'm the only one he really trusts—but if I presented myself with a story like that, he might just smell a rat.'

'Besides,' Hugh pointed out, 'they would then know that their presence here was no secret. Couldn't some-one dress up as the Prince and show himself at a distance?'

Colin and Sandy considered this hopefully.

'Patrick Chisholm has red hair,' the latter offered. 'At

a distance he might be taken for the Prince.'

'Unless the redcoats were thinking along these lines, they would simply take him for what he is—a red-haired man,' Colin answered, shaking his head. 'Whereas if they were *expecting* to see the Prince, every red-haired man would resemble him. The problem is, how to make them suspect that Charles is in the district.'

Isobel roused herself with an effort, and without really thinking what she was saying, suggested in a slurred voice, 'If *you* told them, they would *have* to believe Frazer of Transk.'

Hugh looked at her scathingly. 'You forget, Miss MacIntosh, that Frazer of Transk is now no more than a felon, wanted for treason.'

Colin stopped him with a hand on his shoulder. 'Just a minute—I believe this might be the answer. They might not yet know that I am wanted for treason, and if they thought me to be newly-arrived at Tarbat Ness and unaware of the situation, they would have no reason to disbelieve me. I could give some innocuous excuse to account for my presence here, and say that I had heard a rumour of the Prince's landing here tonight. Then, if Sandy can signal the *Molly* to stand off till the next tide, which will be in daylight, we can lead the soldiers a merry dance over the hills till she picks us up.'

He turned to Sandy for approval, but the agent shook his head doubtfully.

'It might work,' he allowed, 'if it were not for one thing. The soldiers will not allow you to come to this house in case word leaks out of their presence here.'

'Not *allow* me?' Colin barked, and his nostrils narrowed in an expression of haughty disdain. 'Not allow a Frazer of Transk? On the contrary, Sandy, I'll wager that they will be only too glad to accept my word not to betray their position, rather than risk being reported for inconveniencing a friend of Lord President Forbes. I can be quite autocratic when I choose, as Miss MacIntosh will no doubt confirm.'

He sent Isobel a brief grin, but she was too sleepy to notice. 'My arrival can wait until morning, however,' he added. 'There is a chance that the redcoats will go away when they see that there has been no attempt to land a cargo tonight. They will hardly expect you to be mad enough to make the attempt in broad daylight.'

Sandy filled his glass morosely, watching the play of candlelight on the amber liquid. 'It is possible, of course, but I wouldn't bank on it. Another thing I am not happy about is Patrick Chisholm. He knows the hills well enough, but his wind is not as good as your plan would call for it to be. With a platoon after him, our man will need to be fast on his feet.'

'Then I will do that part myself,' Colin replied airily. 'It is not necessary to have red hair. Any other outstanding feature would do as well. If I tell the redcoats that the Prince was said to be disguised as a woman, for instance, every tall woman will attract their attention, so I can rig myself in female garb and draw them away for a mile or two before doubling back in time to board the *Molly*.'

'It sounds very dangerous to me,' Isobel quavered unhappily. 'Cannot someone else do it? What shall we do if you are arrested?'

Colin took this rhetorical question literally. 'If anything happens to me, keep Hugh hidden at all costs, and get him off as soon as the coast is clear. You will be safe enough in the meantime, because I shall tell the redcoats that you have been staying with your uncle and aunt, Mr and Mrs MacCormack, for the past month, and that I am come to escort you home to Inverness, now that the fighting is over. Sandy, can you arrange for your friends to corroborate this story?'

Listening to them as they went over and over their plan, examining it for faults, buffing off the rough edges, Isobel was gripped with foreboding. It was too audacious, it left too much to chance. What if the redcoats had already learnt of Colin's crime? What if he was unable to outrun them on the hills? What if the soldiers returned before the *Molly* could pick up her passengers? There were too many 'ifs', but if she were to point them out, she knew she would not be heeded, so she lay back in her chair and closed her eyes in an attempt to blot out the sensation of impending disaster. In a moment, she felt a touch on her arm and started up to find Sandy bending over her.

'You need not sleep here, ma'am,' he smiled gently. 'If you will come with me, I shall show you where you can be more comfortable.'

She followed him out of the room, leaving Hugh and Colin steaming in front of the fire, and presently found herself in a small room containing a miscellany of occasional chairs, three tables, a japanned cupboard, a washstand and a small bed. No sooner had she been left alone than she dropped her damp clothes in a heap on the floor and, crawling between the blankets, was immediately asleep.

It seemed to be only a very short while before she opened her eyes to find the room flooded with sunlight. She sat up quickly, groaning as a sharp pain gripped her tired muscles, and stared at the place where she had left her clothes. They were gone. At once she was convinced that Hugh and Colin had gone off without her, but before she could decide what to do about it, there was a discreet tap at the door and it opened to admit a small, freckled girl of about twelve, carrying a tray.

'Good morning, miss,' she dimpled, blushing. 'I have

your breakfast here. Your clothes are not ready yet, but my mother will bring them to you in a few minutes.'

Tucking the blankets under her bare arms, Isobel received the tray on her knees, and said with considerable relief, 'I wondered where they had gone. You must be Mr MacCormack's daughter, for you are very like him. Do you know if Mr Frazer is still in the house?'

Miss MacCormack shook her brown curls. 'He rode out an hour since, and my father and Mr Murray are waiting for him to come back at any minute.'

'Then I must hurry up.' Isobel began to bolt her porridge incontinently. 'I want to be there when he gets back. Do you think my clothes will be nearly dry yet?'

The damsel took herself off to find out, and just as Isobel finished disposing of the last slice of cold mutton, Mrs MacCormack herself arrived with the freshly-pressed garments over her arm. She was much younger than Isobel had expected her to be, and must have topped her husband by at least three inches, but she had no complaints to make about her life in such a remote spot and helped Isobel into her well-cut habit and lace-trimmed petticoats without a trace of envy. This done, they repaired to the kitchen where they found Hugh and Sandy pacing the floor in ill-concealed anxiety.

'What is it?' Isobel felt the blood drain from her cheeks, while an inner voice reminded her, 'I told you so.' 'Should he have been back before now?'

Hugh dragged his eyes away from the window for a second to smile at her, and say unconvincingly, 'No, no. There is nothing to worry about. He will be here soon.'

'Mad idea,' Sandy put in irritably. 'I wish I had never signalled the *Molly* to stand off till the next tide. The young fool will get us all hanged.'

'What nonsense,' his wife told him, drawing Isobel to a seat at the fire. 'There is no need to put yourself in a taking yet awhile. Mr Frazer has been gone little more than an hour, and he will not wish to appear in too much of a hurry. Do you come away from the window, Mr Murray. He will not come any sooner for your watching, and it will not do for you to be seen here.'

Hugh half-turned and then halted, his eyes on the path that ran along the cliff-top. '*It's him!*'

Isobel was at his shoulder in an instant, and picked out a solitary horseman making his way across the heather, apparently lost in contemplation of the sun-tipped hills. Without waiting for him to come any nearer, she ran out of the open door and met him at the edge of the trees.

To her surprise, he swung himself off his horse and put his arms about her, laying his cheek against her hair.

'I trust you will forgive me,' he whispered, his lips brushing her ear. 'But I told the redcoats that we were betrothed, so in case they can see us, it will not do to be too formal, especially since I have not seen you for a month.'

Isobel was totally unprepared for the explosion of emotion that was ignited by his touch. Every vein in her body seemed be afire, and the sensation spread through her to her fingertips. But as her hands slid up to clasp his shoulders, she was rudely jerked backwards, and turned to find Sandy gripping her shoulder.

'Best not to stay in the open too long,' he said grimly, hurrying them back to where his wife and Hugh hovered in the doorway.

Isobel's knees were trembling under her, and she moved into the kitchen as though she were sleepwalking, only half-aware of the voices of the others as they clustered round Colin, demanding to know how things had gone.

'Perfectly!' Colin laughed, evidently enjoying himself hugely. 'Just as we planned! I made sure they saw me well in advance, so that there were three or four of them waiting to intercept me before I came within sight of the house. "By Jove!" says I, before they could say a word. "The militia in this district could show these fools in Inverness how to do a job! Egad, the Young Pretender landed here only last night, and you are on the spot already. Well done." I could see that they did not quite know how to take this, but after a moment, the captain said, "Er . . . Yes, sir. Would you mind telling us how you come to be aware that the Young Pretender has landed here?" So I said, "Why, the whole coast is aware of it, but they are a pack of damned Jacobites hereabouts, and will not report it. They say he is got up in a woman's skirt and cloak, but one may spot him a mile away by his stride." They thought this over for a little while and then the captain—who was a dashed decent fellow, really, I hated doing it to him—the captain said he was very sorry, but he would have to detain me for a few hours, as they did not wish the inhabitants of Tarbat Ness to be aware of their position. Upon which, I turned nasty as we had rehearsed, and they eventually agreed to let me pass, on condition I swore not to warn you. Which, of course, I would not dream of doing.'

He leaned against the fireplace and grinned complacently, as Hugh and Sandy rubbed their hands with satisfaction.

Isobel could not take her eyes from him. It was as if she had never seen him before, so suddenly, wonderfully, *terrifyingly* necessary to her had he become. She wanted him to hold her in his arms again more than anything else on earth, to feel the strong touch of his hands on her arms, and to hear him say, as he had once said, that he loved her. For all these months that she had known him, she had never suspected that if anything happened to him she would be inconsolable, but that morning she had had a glimpse of what life would be like without him, and it had been an experience she had no wish to repeat.

He slid her a smiling glance along his shoulder, and a warm surge of love welled up inside her, bringing a flush to her cheeks and drowning out the jubilant voices of Sandy and Hugh in the singing of her heart. Soon they would be safe in France, and then . . . She sat upright, abruptly snapping back to the present as she saw Mrs MacCormack producing a bright red skirt and a long cloak of black wool.

'These are ideal, ma'am,' Colin was saying, measuring the skirt against him. 'A little on the short side, perhaps, but that is all to the good. The main thing is that they be clearly visible against the grass and heather. I regret that I shall be unable to return them to you, since I must jettison them before I begin to double back.'

'Must you do this?' Isobel pleaded, twisting her hands. 'I have the most dreadful premonition that something is going to go wrong.'

'Nonsense, Miss MacIntosh,' Hugh said heartily. 'What you take to be a premonition is nothing more than the merest irritation of the nerves. In two hours from now, we shall be safely aboard the *Molly*.'

'Two hours?' Colin repeated, rolling the cloak and skirt into a tight ball and thrusting them under his jacket. 'Then it is time I set off. I shall be back here at half-past nine exactly, but if there is any danger, do not hold the ship for me, do you understand?' He turned and gripped Sandy's arm. 'Remember that, Sandy. Don't take any chances for me.'

Walking over to the door, he opened it a crack, and having scanned the cliffs for a second, said softly, 'Right, then. I shall see you on the beach,' and stepped out.

He had not looked at Isobel. He was unaware that he held her heart in his hands, a circumstance which she was to regret bitterly before the day was much older.

CHAPTER
SIXTEEN

A SMOTHERING SILENCE fell over the kitchen as the latch clicked behind Colin. For a while, Mrs MacCormack tried to disperse it by keeping up a flow of small-talk, but soon ran out of material and found herself drawn to the window like the other three. The stretch of heather atop the cliffs was deserted, and the untenanted appearance of the nearer cottages implied that their occupants were keeping the sabbath holy. In all the wide expanse of heather and sea nothing moved but the gulls, and even the mighty pounding of the breakers on the cliffs seemed hushed by the atmosphere of waiting.

Keeping one eye on his watch, Sandy pointed out the spot where the redcoat sentinel was hidden, and after a breathless wait of half an hour, they saw a thin figure break cover and sprint down to the beach as though it had seen a ghost.

'So far, so good,' Sandy breathed, mopping his moist brow. 'If we could see the hills from here, it would be less wearing, but at least we know that Mr Frazer has been spotted and, apparently, taken for the Young Pretender. It now remains to be seen whether the look-out's superior officer is equally gullible.'

No one answered him. Isobel's teeth were clamped together painfully, and her knees were trembling so much that she could hardly stand. Colin, she prayed silently, Oh my love, my love, be careful.

Then, suddenly, a group of uniformed figures appeared at the top of the narrow path that led down to the beach, and stood staring and gesticulating up at the hills. Peeping round the shutters, Isobel watched as they spread out and disappeared inland at a run, never taking their eyes from their quarry.

Hugh expelled his breath in a long sigh of relief. 'I can hardly believe it,' he laughed, in a tone several keys higher than his normal, and moved away from the window. 'They reacted just as we hoped they would. Now it's up to Colin—and the skipper of the *Molly*. What time is it, Sandy?'

'Almost half-past eight. The *Molly* is not likely to show herself for at least three-quarters of an hour, so you have plenty of time to get your things together. Miss MacIntosh, I am going to give you a glass of brandy, and I want you to drink every drop, because it is very evident that you are going to faint otherwise. Now come and sit over here.'

He put a glass in her hand and stood over her until it was emptied, but for all his outward assurance she could see his hand shaking. The fiery spirit steadied her, however, and she was able to watch Hugh packing the satchel with a fair assumption of calm, wondering under what conditions it would next be unpacked.

The minutes dragged by like hours, until Sandy whispered from the window where he had been keeping watch, 'Here she comes. Stay here until I signal her that all is well.'

He ran outside, and his place was taken by Hugh and Isobel, who gazed out with mixed feelings at the small merchant ship which had just come into view, her white sails sparkling against the green waters of the Firth.

'I say,' Hugh muttered in consternation, 'she is not as big as I had expected. I wonder how many guns she carries? There are still too many of the Elector's ships patrolling off the east coast to make the crossing a pleasant one.'

'I dare say the captain will be able to hide us well enough, even if he is boarded,' Isobel answered, trying to breathe although her ribs seemed to be enclosed in steel stays. The brandy was making her feel sick and light-headed, and her throat was pulsing with apprehension. Was Colin on the beach? 'Look! She is turning in.'

The door flew open, and Sandy strode in, saying curtly, 'Quickly, now. We must get down to the beach. There is not a moment to lose.'

He shouldered the satchel, and barely allowing her time to embrace Mrs MacCormack, hustled Isobel out of the house and across the heather to the cliff path. From the top of the path it was possible to see the narrow fringe of rocky shingle, and here they paused momentarily to look for Colin. Both the shore and hills behind lay void and silent in the sunlight. Isobel's eyes began to widen with panic, but Sandy took her arm in a rough grip, and said crisply,

'There is time yet. Did you think he would have time to be here before us and stand picking his teeth till the *Molly* had dropped anchor? Come on.'

They scrambled down the path at a dangerous rate, and stopped under the cliffs while Sandy ran across the beach to where he had concealed his boat in a small cove. While he dragged it out, they waited, breathless and cold, their eyes flicking from the now motionless ship to the empty cliff path. From that point, it was impossible to see anything except the pounding waves that threw themselves upon the rocks with a roar that echoed against the cliffs, and Isobel covered her face with her hands, praying that, when she took them away,

Colin would be there before her. But when she looked up, at Hugh's touch on her shoulder, all she could see was Sandy's boat at the water's edge.

'No!' she cried helplessly, as he pulled her forward. 'We *must* wait for Colin. He cannot be far away! Please . . . please wait!'

Sandy left his boat and came to grip her other arm. 'You know we cannot wait,' he said angrily. 'If we waste time now, the redcoats will be back.'

They had reached the shallows, and she was twisting in their grasp, trying to see the cliff path. 'Just a few minutes . . .' she begged, tears blinding her. 'For God's sake! Just a few minutes . . .'

Ignoring her, Sandy stooped to pick her up, but she wrenched her arm away from Hugh's grasp and darted away from them. At a safe distance she paused, and looked back at their shocked faces. Drawing a deep breath, she called,

'I'm sorry . . . I'm *terribly* sorry, Hugh. You must go alone. I cannot go without Colin.'

'You're mad,' he shouted above the roar of the waves. 'He may be dead, or taken prisoner. What will you do if he does not come back for you?'

He started to run towards her, but Sandy's muscular arm caught him and swung him round as Isobel prepared to take flight.

'If you are going,' she heard the agent thunder. 'Get into that bloody boat!'

Hugh hesitated, looking up at the cliffs, and then turned abruptly and scrambled into the boat.

Immediately, Isobel made a dash for the cliff path and began to run up it as quickly as she could. Exactly where she was going, or what she was going to do, she was not sure, but she was dimly conscious that every step took her closer to Colin . . . alive or dead. Oh God . . . dear

God . . . don't let him die . . . without saying goodbye to me . . . without knowing that I love him . . . don't let him die . . . Great sobs racked her body, and her breathing was so laboured that it seemed to tear lumps out of her raw lungs with every gasp, but she kept going until she was almost at the top. She did not hear the rattle of stones above her head until it was too late.

Someone was descending the path in a series of suicidal leaps, and before she could cry out, a large body catapulted round a bend and cannoned into her, sending her spinning against a buttress of jagged rock.

'*Isobel!*' Colin's voice shouted in anguished tones. 'What are you doing here? Look, the *Molly* is pulling away already. Why are you not on board? Where is Mr Murray?'

She opened her eyes and stared at him, hardly daring to believe that he was really there.

'Mr Murray?' she said foolishly. 'He . . . He has gone . . . on the *Molly*. I . . . Don't be angry with me . . . I . . .' Her head dropped on her breast and she began to weep again, tears rolling down her cheeks and off her chin. 'I thought you were dead, Colin, or . . . or taken . . . I couldn't . . . I *couldn't* go without you.' Hiccupping uncontrollably, she added, with what her mother would have termed a revolting lack of modesty, 'Oh, Colin . . . Colin, I love you so very much . . . I . . .'

Rudely interrupting this impassioned speech, he snatched her into his arms, holding her very tightly and burying his face into her hair. 'Isobel, my dearest on earth,' he said unsteadily, 'don't cry like that. There is nothing to be afraid of now.' He caught her chin between thumb and forefinger and tilted back her head. 'Hush, now. Can you not see I am waiting to kiss you?'

His lips lingered on her brow, her lashes, her wet cheeks with a tenderness that had her swaying in his arms even before their lips met, and when he at last raised his head she fell against him, weak and shaken.

'Don't let me go,' she whispered unnecessarily. 'If you take your arms from me now, I shall die of loneliness.' His arms tightened imperceptibly, but he made no reply other than a muffled groan as he laid his lips to the soft hollow behind her ear. It was the sound of footsteps approaching from the beach below that recalled them to an awareness of their surroundings.

'Sandy,' Colin whispered irritably. 'We do not want to speak to him now. Come this way, I have a lot to tell you.'

Hand in hand, they ran up the last few yards of path and turned in the opposite direction to that of the house, halting in a hollow in the rocks which hid them effectively on all sides. Here they could sit comfortably, shielded from the wind and away from the deafening pounding of the breakers.

For a long time there was very little conversation, but at last Isobel pulled away and said, 'Colin, darling . . . if you have things to tell me, you must tell me now. Sandy and his wife will be worried about us, and it's not fair to keep them on tenterhooks.'

'Very well,' he sighed, ungallantly refusing to slacken his embrace. 'But you must allow me to continue holding you in my arms, otherwise I shall not have the courage to tell you.'

'The courage?' Isobel smiled, rubbing her cheek against his chin. 'Do you expect me to be very angry with you, then?'

'I hope not, but one can never tell with women. Perhaps I deserve that you should be, for I have caused you a great deal of needless grief. But indeed, if I could have spared you, I would gladly have done so.'

Isobel tried to sit up, the better to see his face, but

finding herself immobilised, she was forced to content herself with saying, 'Whatever you have done, I shall forgive, if only you will tell me quickly.'

'Then I shall certainly do so,' Colin replied in a gratified tone, proving the truth of this statement by falling abruptly silent. At last Isobel gave him a tiny shake, and he said in a rush, 'It was not entirely my fault, of course. I want you to believe that, for if your father had not put the idea in my head, I would never have thought of it.'

Seeing him about to lapse into thought again, Isobel prompted quickly, 'What did my father say?'

'Well, two things, really. The first was when I asked his permission to address you, last September. He thought, and so did I, that if we could be alone together occasionally, we might have a chance to become better acquainted and you might overcome your dislike of a man who did not really exist. I managed to talk him into turning a blind eye now and then, but you were so much on the defensive that I gained nothing by it.' He broke off to nibble the tip of her nose in reprisal, before continuing, 'Then, the day of the battle, I lost patience with you completely. It was such a silly thing to do . . . Well, there is no point in going over that again. Your father was even angrier than I was, and he kept saying, over and over again, that you would have to be taught a lesson this time or you would keep on doing such brainless things all your life—With which I was in perfect agreement.'

'Yes, but . . .' Isobel broke in, anxiously.

'There was another reason, too,' he went on. 'I thought you might be beginning to form an attachment for Hugh Murray, and I was certain that he was not the man for you, so I decided to give you an opportunity to become better acquainted with *him*. Thank God he was not killed in the battle, for if he had been, you would have been in love with his memory for years, and whatever you say to the contrary, you need someone to look after you, not a man who will take all you have to give and then turn to someone else.'

'Very well,' Isobel mumbled, glad that her face was hidden in his jacket. 'Now that I have heard your excuses, do you mean to confess your crime before I burst with curiosity?'

'Be patient, beloved. I am screwing up my courage.' He gazed thoughtfully over her head as though choosing his words carefully. 'When I saw Stella in the stables on the day of the battle, I naturally expected to find you inside the house, but of course no one had seen you. The redcoats had only just got there, and my people were in a taking, thinking they meant to burn the place down. So I went round to the stables, and found they had made the place a sort of base, while they rounded up stragglers from the field. It was then I learned that they had already taken two prisoners, whom I had no difficulty in recognising from their description—a golden-haired young lady and a half-dead rebel. Evidently,' he added in a dry tone, 'the young lady had, scarcely an hour since, been apprehended in the *very act* of helping the rebel to escape.'

His manner invited comment, but receiving none, he continued, 'Luckily, the officer in charge was a friend of ours—Captain Ogilvie, who had so nearly caught Hugh Murray once before. He was very much in charity with me because I had, as promised, given a very good report of him to his superior officer, so he allowed himself to be persuaded to join me in a glass or two of brandy. Now we come to the clever bit.'

He paused tantalisingly, but Isobel was too engrossed to speak.

'When I had got him installed in the library with his feet on the hearth and a glass of well-doctored brandy in his fist, I excused myself on some pretext, and went in search of the soldier who had been detailed to keep an eye on Hugh. Here I was not so lucky, and it cost me fifty guineas and an excellent horse to persuade the guard to report his prisoner dead.'

Isobel sat up suddenly, bumping her head on Colin's chin. 'Dead? What on earth do you . . .?'

'If you will stop interrupting . . .?' returned her beloved crisply. 'As I was saying, I then went back to the library and found Captain Ogilvie in an advanced stage of intoxication, just as I had hoped. A few minutes later, the guard came in and played his part to perfection, whereupon I suggested that the corpse should be taken out and buried in the west wood, and Ogilvie agreed. Of course, I had arranged that Murray should not be buried, but only hidden until I had leisure to get him away.'

Here he ducked his head to see Isobel's face, in evident expectation of a word of praise for his ingenuity, but she could only gaze at him with such an expression of awed admiration that he was forced to kiss her before resuming his story.

'Up to that time,' he said, apologetically, 'I had not managed to think of a plan for freeing you, but Captain Ogilvie, bless his heart, was by then so drunk that he suggested a hand of cards, which gave me an idea. I kept plying him with brandy and letting him win every game until he was as affectionate as a muddy dog. Soon he loved me like a brother and wanted me to visit him at his home and meet his dear old mother and his two ravishing sisters. Then I suggested a hand for the key to your prison. Yes, darling, I know it seems rather optimistic, but, you see, he assumed that I meant only to . . . visit you. You must remember the degrading situation in which we had made his acquaintance, and realise that he had formed no very flattering opinion of my morals. Furthermore, he was certain that he was on a winning streak, and was quite appalled when he lost.'

Isobel received this information with a gulp.

'Naturally, when I returned the key to him when I went back for Hugh, and he discovered that I had set you free, he was not at all pleased. However, I managed to convince him that I believed that was why he had given me the key, and he was so befuddled that he could not remember *what* we had agreed. When I pointed out to him the awful consequences of letting it be known that he had gambled away one of the Duke of Cumberland's prisoners, he was only too glad to let the matter drop without alerting his men to search for you.'

Isobel wriggled free of his embrace and sat back, anxiously scanning his face. She was dimly aware that he had just told her something of shattering importance . . . something unbelievably wonderful . . . But her mind refused to grasp the import of his words. For a long time she was so stupefied that she could do no more than stare at him.

'Forgive me,' she said at last, and it astounded her to hear her own voice sounding so steady in spite of the way her heart was thudding. 'I am not sure that I perfectly understand. The only person who knows that you helped me to escape is Captain Ogilvie—that is so, is it not?— and he will not dare to admit it. That must also mean that he will be at pains to conceal the fact that I was ever his prisoner, else he might have to explain why he let me go. And Hugh . . . no one knows that he was not really dead when he was taken out to be buried in the wood—except the guard, who also would not dare to tell. Then surely there is no case against you?' She watched him nod, and with an odd sensation of dizziness, stammered. 'You mean I have not robbed you of your inheritance? You are not implicated? You need not go away to France?'

'None of those terrible things.' He kissed away the tears that had gathered on her lashes and rocked her gently in his arms. 'Are you very angry with me, my heart's darling? It was torture to me to see you so unhappy about it, but I wanted you to choose between Hugh Murray and myself; to tell you that I could still offer you wealth and position would have been to take an unfair advantage.'

'But, Colin . . .' A hundred thoughts were jostling for precedence in her brain: jubilation struggling with an awful dread. Colin was free to return to Transk, but she herself would be in danger as long as the reprisals were continued. Too many English soldiers would be able to recognise her, and Inverness would be full of redcoats for a long time.

Drawing her cloak about her, she sat up and attempted a smile. 'I cannot be angry with you, Colin,' she said steadily. 'My foolishness might well have caused even more trouble than you allowed me to believe, and I deserved to be taught a lesson. But it was unfair of you to make me choose between Hugh and yourself, because . . . because I have chosen you, and . . . and I cannot allow you to marry me.'

'Isobel, my love,' Colin said earnestly, repossessing himself of both her hands, 'I intend to marry you without delay—with or without your permission.'

'No. I must never see you again.' The voice sounded so cool and detached that it seemed to Isobel that someone else was voicing her thoughts. A strange calmness had taken hold of her. It was as though her whole mind and body were encased in a solid block of ice, which numbed her aching heart and the pain of her reasoning. 'You are free to return to Transk, Colin—for which I will thank God on my knees for the rest of my life—but it is otherwise for me. If I am seen and recognised by any of the soldiers who found me with you, then you too will suffer. Yes, you will, Colin . . . and I refuse to bring you fear and persecution as my dowry. No . . . do not try to dissuade me. I am resolved to take leave of Scotland . . . and of you . . . as soon as I may. Would that I were aboard the *Molly*, for then I would be already on my way to France . . . and you . . .'

'And I,' interposed Colin forcibly, 'would be already on my way to Helmsdale, where Sandy could have signalled the *Molly* to pick me up.' He smiled at her, but gravely, and gave his head a little reproving shake. 'Did you think I would have let you escape me, Isobel? And you with my heart in your two hands? Not now—or ever. I will have you as my wife, in my home—and neither Cumberland nor his butchers shall gainsay me.'

'Colin, please do not . . .'

'Hush. Listen to me. Captain Ogilvie and his regiment will not remain at Transk for long. They may not even remain in Scotland, for King George has other uses for his soldiers. By the time we return from our honeymoon—which will certainly be a long one, since I want to take you to Venice—the hue and cry will be dying down. At the worst we may be constrained to live quietly at Dunarras for a while, but I am persuaded you would not find that insupportable.'

Isobel's eyes searched his face. 'Could it really be so, Colin? I will not take any risks with your future. You must be certain that you can keep me safely.'

'I shall keep you safely, my heart's darling! Never doubt it,' he murmured passionately, drawing her into the circle of his arms. 'Nor will I be parted from you, for as much as a single day, as long as we live. Each night I shall fall asleep with my arms about you, and shall wake each day to see your head on the pillow beside me. *Nothing* can part us, Isobel. We are one entity— indivisible—you must always have known it . . .'

'Oh, my love . . . my love . . . I know it now,' Isobel whispered, dissolving gladly into the whirlwind tenderness of his kiss.

Mills & Boon
COMPETITION

How would you like a year's supply of Mills & Boon Romances
ABSOLUTELY FREE?

Well, you can win them!

All you have to do is complete the word puzzle below and send it into us by 31st August 1985. The first five correct entries picked out of the bag after that date will each win a year's supply of Mills & Boon Romances (Ten books every month— worth over £100!). What could be easier?

```
M R E T T E L T W I N M
B I T T E R O O R E H A
N C L H A Y V N E E R R
O I G L R S E E E S O R
S T U O S E S S I K D I
O O H Q F A E R T A O A
R X M T E C N S Y N A G
E E N R N L U D A C I E
A F F A I R R R M B R P E
L O M E T E O A L O G W
M O E H A W I S H A O E
R L N M D E S I R E S N
```

Mills and Boon	Letter	Envy	Hug
Harlequin	Love	Rage	Men
Romance	Rose	Exotic	Hero
Tears	Wish	Girls	Heart
Bitter	Hope	Vow	Win
Daydream	Trust	Woman	Desires
Affair	Kisses	Eros	Realm
Marriage	Fool	Woe	

**PLEASE TURN
OVER FOR
DETAILS
ON HOW
TO ENTER** ➡

How to enter

All the words listed overleaf, below the word puzzle, are hidden in the grid. You can find them by reading the letters forwards, backwards, up or down, or diagonally. When you find a word, circle it, or put a line through it. After you have found all the words, the left-over letters will spell a secret message that you can read from left to right, from the top of the puzzle through to the bottom.

Don't forget to fill in your name and address in the space provided and pop this page in an envelope (you don't need a stamp) and post it today. Hurry — competition ends 31st August 1985.

Mills & Boon Competition, FREEPOST, P.O. Box 236, Croydon, Surrey CR9 9EL.

Secret message ——————————————————

Name ——————————————————

Address ——————————————————

—————————————————————

—————————————————————

——————————————— Postcode ———————

COMP 1